BENEATH THE TRIANGLE

The First Wave Rises

Written by Diane Kann

Brought to you by Volans Galaxy Press

Published by Kannceptual Creations LLC

An imprint of Volans Galaxy Press

ISBN: 978-1-969569-44-9

Printed in the United States of America

First Edition, November 2025

Note: This work was originally published under the pen name DM Volans, which is a pen name of Diane Kann.

CONTENTS

Dedication 1

Acknowledgments 3

About the Author 4

Preface 5

Introduction 7

Chapter 1 9

Chapter 2 30

Chapter 3 51

Chapter 4 73

Chapter 5 96

Chapter 5 98

Chapter 5 100

Chapter 6 120

Chapter 7 142

Chapter 8   164

Chapter 9   186

Chapter 10   212

Backstory   237

Appendix   238

About the Author   245

Chapter   246

DEDICATION

To the tireless explorers of the deep, the scientists who unravel the ocean's mysteries, and the dreamers who dare to imagine worlds beyond our own: this story is a testament to your courage, your curiosity, and your unwavering commitment to understanding the intricate web of life that connects us all—from the deepest trenches to the highest peaks.

It is dedicated to the memory of Jian, whose selfless sacrifice reminds us of the profound strength of the human spirit in the face of unimaginable adversity, and to Sarah Chen, whose unique connection to the whispers illuminates the boundless potential of human intuition and the power of empathy.

To those who strive to protect our planet's fragile ecosystems, this book serves as a reminder of our shared responsibility to safeguard the delicate balance of life, both above and below the waves. It is a tribute to the unsung heroes of conservation: the marine biologists who tirelessly work to protect our oceans and the environmental activists who fight for a sustainable future. Their efforts inspire hope, reminding us that even in the face of seemingly insurmountable challenges, change is possible.

May this narrative inspire a renewed sense of wonder, a deeper respect for the natural world, and a commitment to preserving its beauty for generations to come. It is a call to action—an invitation to explore not just the depths of the ocean, but the depths of our own potential for compassion, innovation, and stewardship of our planet.

ACKNOWLEDGMENTS

I would like to express my deepest gratitude to my family for their unwavering love and support throughout the writing of this book. Your belief in me and in this story has been invaluable.

About the Author

D iane Kann is an avid reader of science fiction, fantasy, and dystopian novels—passions that have fueled *her* own foray into science-fantasy writing. Her debut novel, *Beneath the Triangle*, plunges readers into a hidden underwater world where genetically modified beings fight for survival.

A believer in environmental stewardship and deeply fascinated by the wonders of the natural world, Diane weaves themes of conservation and the interconnectedness of life throughout her fantastical tales. When she's not writing, she can be found exploring the diverse ecosystems of Central Florida, drawing inspiration from both land and sea.

PREFACE

As a scientific writer, I've spent years immersed in the wonders and complexities of our oceans. But nothing could have prepared me for the story I'm about to share.

This narrative, based on the astonishing firsthand accounts of Captain Rostova, Dr. Thorne, and the other survivors of Flight 73, blurs the line between science fiction and a thrilling reality. Their journey into the hidden underwater world of the Luminese challenged my understanding of what's possible, forcing me to reconsider the boundaries of our knowledge and the interconnectedness of all living things.

While the Luminese civilization, the Abyssals, and the Cetea are creations of the imagination, the environmental concerns woven into their story are stark reflections of our own world's challenges. Ocean acidification, pollution, and biodiversity loss are not mere plot devices; they are urgent realities demanding immediate action. The parallels between the fragile ecosystem of the Luminese world and the delicate balance of our own oceans serve as a potent reminder of our responsibilities.

Through this tale of adventure, survival, and discovery, I hope to inspire a sense of wonder about the hidden depths of our planet, a deeper understanding of the environmental challenges we face, and a renewed commitment to protecting the wonders of our world, both seen and unseen.

The "Whispers," the mysterious phenomenon at the heart of this narrative, symbolize the power of knowledge, the weight of responsibility, and the profound interconnectedness of all life. Their influence extends far beyond the underwater realm, touching upon themes of collaboration, sacrifice, and the urgent need for global cooperation in safeguarding our shared future.

This first book in the series merely scratches the surface of these profound issues, setting the stage for a larger exploration of themes that resonate with our times.

INTRODUCTION

The Bermuda Triangle: a place of mystery, myth, and countless vanished ships and planes. It's a location steeped in lore, where the veil between the known and the unknown seems particularly thin. But what if the stories were more than just legends? What if, beneath the turbulent surface of the infamous triangle, lay a hidden world teeming with life, advanced technology, and secrets that could reshape our understanding of existence itself?

This is the premise of the extraordinary events that unfold within these pages. When Flight 73, presumed lost, inexplicably reappears, it's not in the vast expanse of the Atlantic but in a vibrant, bioluminescent city beneath the waves. The survivors, led by the intrepid Captain Rostova and the brilliant Dr. Thorne, find themselves thrust into a society unlike any other: the Luminese.

This underwater civilization, with its awe-inspiring technology and peaceful ethos, offers a stark contrast to the turbulent surface world they've left behind. However, their newfound haven is far from idyllic. Dark forces—the enigmatic Abyssals and the ruthless Cetea—lurk in the shadows, each vying for control of ancient prophecies and a mysterious phenomenon known as the "Whispers."

As the survivors navigate this alien environment, they must confront not only external threats but also the internal conflicts that test their resilience and alliances. This isn't just a story of survival; it's a journey of self-discovery, a testament to the human spirit's capacity for adaptation and resilience. It's a tale that explores the delicate balance of ecosystems, the ethical dilemmas of power, and the profound interconnectedness of all life, both above and below the waves.

Prepare to delve into a world where scientific accuracy and imaginative storytelling converge, where the wonders of the deep ocean are matched only by the complexities of human nature, and where the whispers of ancient prophecies may hold the key to the future of two worlds.

CHAPTER 1

The world dissolved into a cacophony of screams, metal groaning, and the terrifying roar of tearing fabric. One moment, Flight 828 was cruising smoothly over the seemingly placid expanse of the Bermuda Triangle; the next, it became a chaotic ballet of fire and falling debris. I, Simon Pierce, scientific writer and unfortunate passenger, remember the jarring lurch, the sickening feeling of weightlessness, and then... nothing. Or rather, everything at once.

When consciousness flickered back, it wasn't the familiar scent of jet fuel and recycled air that filled my nostrils. Instead, a strange, almost sweet aquatic aroma permeated the air, tinged with something earthy and metallic. My ears rang with the muffled thrum of some unseen, powerful current. Instead of the sterile confines of the aircraft cabin, I found myself submerged in a swirling vortex of bioluminescent organisms, their tiny lights flickering like a million fallen stars. The pressure was intense, a constant, insistent squeeze against my chest. But I wasn't drowning. The water, strangely warm and buoyant, cradled me, preventing me from sinking.

Disoriented and terrified, I struggled to orient myself. The wreckage of the plane was scattered around me, a skeletal landscape of twisted metal and shattered glass, illuminated by the ethereal glow of the surrounding life. Above, far above, I could just make out the faint, swirling colors of a water column—a distorted and fractured view of what might have been the surface world. My immediate surroundings were a mesmerizing, yet terrifying, blend of beauty and destruction.

Other survivors emerged from the wreckage, their faces etched with a mixture of shock and disbelief. Captain Rostova, a woman whose steely gaze belied her concern, was the first to gather herself, her voice a sharp command cutting through the underwater din. Dr. Thorne, a marine biologist whose expertise felt strangely appropriate given our current predicament, assessed the situation with a calm, almost clinical detachment. Their contrasting personalities—Rostova's decisive pragmatism against Thorne's meticulous observation—would prove crucial in the days to come.

We were surrounded by an array of life forms unlike anything I had ever encountered in my years of studying oceanography. Fish with iridescent scales shimmered in the faint light, their bodies elongated and graceful. Jellyfish, pulsating with an inner light, drifted lazily around us, their forms delicate and mesmerizing. Yet, there was a disturbing undercurrent to the scene. The sheer scale of the bioluminescence was unnerving—a vibrant symphony of light that felt both otherworldly and unsettling. The water itself seemed alive, pulsating with a rhythmic energy that sent shivers down my spine.

The initial disorientation gave way to a growing sense of wonder, tinged with fear. Where were we? How had we survived such a catastrophic crash? The mystery surrounding the Bermuda Triangle had always fascinated me, its reputation steeped in tales of vanished ships and planes. Now, I was living within the heart of the legend, experiencing firsthand the impossible. We were not merely lost; we were in a place beyond comprehension—a place where the laws of nature seemed to bend to an unknown will.

As we cautiously navigated the debris field, a sight beyond anything imaginable met our eyes. In the distance, a breathtaking city rose from the ocean floor, its architecture sculpted from shimmering, bioluminescent materials. Towers reached toward the faint light above, adorned with intricate patterns that pulsed with a gentle rhythm. Buildings, seemingly carved from coral and some otherworldly substance, glowed with an internal light, casting a mesmerizing radiance upon the surrounding waters. It was a city unlike any on Earth—a testament to a civilization beyond our wildest dreams—or nightmares.

The city shimmered with an array of colors, from deep blues and greens to vibrant purples and oranges. Structures resembled giant, luminous coral formations, yet possessed an intricate sophistication that hinted at advanced engineering. Vast, translucent domes spanned wide areas, resembling bubbles of light that held pockets of air. The entire city pulsed with an almost organic rhythm, a breathing, vibrant entity that defied our understanding of urban design. It was a scene that immediately captured our attention, drawing us toward it with an irresistible pull, even as our minds struggled to process what we were seeing.

As we approached, it became clear that the city wasn't deserted. Figures, slender and graceful, moved through its corridors, their forms illuminated by the city's own glow. Their skin had a luminous quality, almost shimmering, and they moved with an effortless grace that suggested both agility and intelligence. They were the Luminese—a species adapted to this underwater world, their very existence a testament to the unexpected and awe-inspiring diversity of life in the vast, unexplored depths of the ocean.

Our initial contact with them was cautious, tentative. They communicated through a series of gestures and melodic sounds—a language beyond our comprehension, yet conveying a sense of curiosity and cautious welcome. Their technology, seamlessly integrated with the natural environment, seemed almost magical. They seemed to manipulate light and water with ease, creating shimmering pathways and projections that conveyed complex information. Through a combination of gestures, sounds, and surprisingly intuitive projections, they conveyed their willingness to help. Yet, lurking beneath the surface of their welcoming demeanor, we sensed an unspoken tension—a hint of a hidden danger and a great mystery that lay at the heart of their world. A mystery woven around ancient prophecies and the enigma known only as the "Whispers." A mystery that would soon entangle us in a struggle for the fate of both their world and our own.

The crash landing in the Bermuda Triangle was just the beginning of our journey into the unknown.

The initial shock of survival gave way to a dawning wonder. The wreckage of Flight 828, miraculously intact save for a few mangled sections, rested on a seabed that wasn't the cold, dark abyss I'd expected. Instead, it was a vibrant tapestry of life, bathed in a soft, ethereal glow emanating from the structures surrounding us. We were nestled in a shallow, sheltered cove, a natural harbor crafted by colossal, bioluminescent coral formations that pulsed with a gentle, rhythmic light. These weren't the familiar corals of our world; these were structures of impossible size and complexity, their surfaces shimmering with an internal light that shifted and changed in intensity, creating a mesmerizing spectacle.

From the cove, a path of light, brighter and more defined than the ambient glow, extended into the distance. It snaked through a landscape that defied earthly description. Towering structures of shimmering, opalescent material rose from the seabed, connected by intricate bridges of light. Buildings pulsed with inner light, their forms shifting subtly, almost as if they were breathing. This was Luminese City.

The air, or rather, the water, hummed with a low, resonant thrum. It wasn't unpleasant—more like a deep, soothing vibration that resonated through our very bones. As we emerged from the wreckage, cautiously at first, then with growing awe, the full extent of the city revealed itself. It was a breathtaking spectacle, a metropolis built not of stone or steel, but of living, bioluminescent material that seemed to defy the laws of physics. Buildings resembled colossal jellyfish, their bell-like structures pulsating with a soft, internal light. Others resembled giant sea anemones, their tendril-like appendages swaying gently in the current, casting shifting patterns of light onto the seabed.

The scale was monumental. Structures towered hundreds of feet above us, their intricate designs impossible to fully comprehend from our vantage point. Bridges of light arched gracefully between these structures, creating a network of pathways that seemed to extend to the far reaches of the city. These weren't simply bridges; they were shimmering conduits of energy, their luminosity varying in intensity, pulsing like veins carrying lifeblood through the city's heart.

The Luminese themselves emerged from these luminous structures with a grace that belied their apparent size. They moved with an almost ethereal fluidity, their bodies seemingly translucent, their forms shifting and reforming as if composed of liquid light. Their movements were slow and deliberate, yet they possessed an uncanny grace, gliding through the water with effortless ease. They were tall and slender, their forms vaguely humanoid but with features that defied easy categorization. Their skin, if it could be called that, shimmered with the same bioluminescent properties as the city itself, shifting colors and intensities in response to their emotions or movements.

Their eyes, large and luminous, held an intelligence that was both unnerving and captivating. They seemed to perceive us not just visually, but in some other way—a deeper, more intuitive sense. Their communication, initially a series of melodic sounds and gestures, gradually evolved into something more complex. We observed them manipulating light itself—not through technology, but seemingly through an innate ability, as if light were an extension of their own being. They projected images into the water, creating holographic displays of intricate patterns, symbols, and even representations of their history.

Through these projections, we learned that the Luminese were a peaceful, technologically advanced civilization that had existed in this underwater realm for millennia. Their city was not simply a dwelling place but a living organism, a harmonious integration of technology and nature. The structures themselves were grown, nurtured, and maintained by a complex network of symbiotic relationships between the Luminese and the bioluminescent organisms that constituted their city's building blocks. This was not mere architecture; it was a living testament to their deep understanding of biology and symbiosis.

The projections further revealed a sophisticated system of energy generation, powered by a unique interaction between the city's bioluminescent components and the ocean currents. The energy was not harnessed; it was cultivated, nurtured, and channeled into their technological systems with an elegance that made our own clumsy efforts seem crude and barbaric. It was a marvel of sustainable engineering, a testament to a civilization that had long ago solved the problems of energy and resource management.

As we spent more time with them, we began to grasp the nuances of their culture. Their society was strikingly egalitarian, devoid of the hierarchical structures that plagued our own world. They valued cooperation and collaboration above all else, their communal living reflected in their architecture and social interactions. Their education system focused on cultivating an understanding of the natural world and fostering a sense of responsibility towards the delicate balance of their ecosystem.

The Luminese seemed profoundly connected to the ocean itself, their very existence inextricably linked to its rhythms and cycles. Their understanding of marine biology and oceanography surpassed anything we had ever witnessed. They demonstrated a mastery of symbiotic relationships, utilizing these interactions to create a harmonious coexistence between technology and nature. Their technology wasn't separate from their environment; it was an integral part of it, a testament to their holistic worldview.

However, the initial idyllic image started to crack as we spent more time observing them. While outwardly peaceful, a subtle undercurrent of tension permeated their society. The holographic projections hinted at past conflicts, struggles against other factions, and a deep-seated fear of a phenomenon known as the "Whispers." This enigmatic force seemed to be deeply intertwined with their history, a threat to their very existence. The Luminese's seemingly peaceful demeanor masked a deep-seated apprehension, a silent fear resonating beneath the surface of their beautiful city.

We also learned that the Luminese were not alone in this underwater world. Other factions existed, each with their own motivations and agendas. The projections depicted the Abyssals, an enigmatic group who lived in the deepest trenches of the ocean, shrouded in mystery and rumored to possess powers beyond comprehension. And then there were the Cetea, a ruthless and technologically advanced faction that seemed determined to seize control of Luminese City, their motives shrouded in secrecy and their methods brutally efficient. The whispers spoke of an ancient conflict, a struggle for power and dominance over this hidden world and something far more significant than mere territorial control.

The peaceful coexistence of the Luminese city was, we were beginning to realize, a fragile equilibrium, a precarious balance maintained by a delicate understanding of the natural world and a deep-seated apprehension of the forces that lurked in the shadows of their vibrant underwater realm. Our arrival, a catastrophic event in their history, would surely upset this balance—perhaps irrevocably. We were caught in a struggle that was far bigger than our own survival. The fate of this hidden world, and perhaps our own, hung in the balance. Our journey had only just begun.

The rhythmic pulse of the bioluminescent coral, a hypnotic heartbeat in the alien ocean, was the soundtrack to our disorientation. My own senses were still reeling from the impossible transition—one moment, the terrifying plunge; the next, this... breathtaking spectacle. We were alive, impossibly so, yet the reality of our situation hadn't fully sunk in. The survivors, a scattered group huddled amongst the wreckage, were a testament to the randomness of survival. Amidst the chaos, two figures stood out, their reactions and approaches to our predicament as different as day and night.

Captain Eva Rostova, her face smudged with grime and seawater, was a whirlwind of controlled energy. Even in the face of the unimaginable, her military bearing never faltered. A veteran of countless maritime missions, her eyes—usually sharp and assessing—were now wide with a mixture of awe and apprehension. Her uniform, once crisp and immaculate, was now torn and waterlogged, yet she carried herself with an unwavering strength that inspired a semblance of order amidst the pandemonium. She moved with practiced efficiency, barking concise orders in a low, clipped tone that cut through the stunned silence. Her expertise was immediately apparent—her actions, born from years of navigating treacherous seas, were now guiding us through the even more treacherous waters of this alien world. I could see the gears turning in her mind, a keen strategist already formulating escape plans, assessing threats, and identifying resources. Years spent commanding vessels in tempestuous storms had clearly prepared her for something far more unexpected—something far more profound. Her inherent leadership was undeniable, drawing the scattered survivors toward a sense of purpose, of shared survival.

Then there was Dr. Aris Thorne, a stark contrast to Rostova's action-oriented approach. While Rostova focused on immediate survival needs, Thorne, our resident marine biologist, was captivated by the sheer strangeness of our surroundings. His usual meticulousness, often bordering on obsessive, was amplified tenfold by this alien landscape. He moved with a hesitant grace, his eyes wide with scientific curiosity, more enthralled by the intricacies of the bioluminescent coral than by the danger of our situation. His normally neatly groomed hair was a disheveled mess, his glasses askew, yet his gaze remained fixed on the mesmerizing spectacle around him, his mind already categorizing, analyzing, and forming hypotheses. He was a man of science, his passion for the ocean palpable in every hesitant movement. This wasn't just a survival situation for him; it was a scientific goldmine, an unprecedented opportunity to study an ecosystem that defied all known understanding.

Their reactions were immediately telling. Rostova, the pragmatic leader, focused on securing our immediate safety, organizing the survivors, and searching for a way out—or at least a way to understand our surroundings better. Thorne, the intellectual explorer, was utterly fascinated by the environment itself, his mind already buzzing with questions about the bioluminescence, the unique coral structures, and the unseen life that undoubtedly thrived within this hidden world. This fascinating dichotomy laid the groundwork for the complex dynamics between the two, a tension between survival and exploration that would play a key role in our unfolding story.

Their initial conversations were a fascinating clash of perspectives. Rostova, practical and efficient, sought immediate answers.

"Thorne, what in God's name is this place?" Her voice, though clipped, held a hint of wonder that belied her hardened exterior.

Thorne, ever the scientist, carefully removed a sample of the phosphorescent coral, his movements delicate and precise.

"I... I don't know, Captain. It's unlike anything I've ever seen. The bioluminescence is... extraordinary. The structure of the coral, the sheer scale of it—it's beyond anything in our existing classifications. The energy source is unknown, the symbiotic relationships... entirely unprecedented." He adjusted his glasses, his eyes still glued to the sample. "The possibilities are... staggering."

Rostova impatiently tapped her foot, her gaze sweeping over the other survivors.

"Staggering is fine, doctor, but I need to know if it's dangerous. Are there predators? What about escape routes? I need facts, not hypotheses." Her pragmatic nature was undeniable, a stark contrast to Thorne's scientific enthusiasm.

Thorne, somewhat flustered by the Captain's urgency, tried to explain. "We need to study the ecosystem, Captain. Understand its patterns, its behavior. This could hold the key to understanding how we got here and how we might get back." He gestured around the cove, his passion ignited by the sheer wonder of their surroundings. "The energy source alone... if we could understand it... that could revolutionize the world!"

Their contrasting viewpoints—Rostova's focus on immediate survival and Thorne's fascination with scientific discovery—reflected a larger tension that would characterize our interactions within this strange new world. Rostova's military background emphasized immediate action, risk assessment, and the importance of maintaining control in the face of the unknown. Thorne's scientific perspective emphasized observation, careful analysis, and a need to understand the underlying mechanisms before any action was taken. Both approaches were valid, both were crucial, and the challenge lay in finding a balance between their diverging viewpoints—a challenge that would test not only their abilities but the very survival of our unlikely alliance.

The initial exploration of the immediate surroundings further highlighted their contrasting personalities. Rostova, ever vigilant, organized search parties to assess the extent of the damage to the plane, searching for supplies and survivors. Her methodical approach was born from years of experience in crisis management, her focus relentlessly on ensuring the safety and well-being of her team. She moved with quiet efficiency, her leadership inspiring a sense of order among the shaken passengers. Her experience dealing with emergencies was immediately valuable; she established a makeshift camp, secured the immediate necessities—food, water, first aid—and ensured a system for communication and task allocation.

Thorne, meanwhile, meticulously documented the flora and fauna of the cove. He collected samples, carefully recording their characteristics, conducting simple tests with portable equipment salvaged from the wreckage. He was completely lost in the world of scientific discovery; his passion for the unique ecosystem that surrounded us was almost tangible. He was captivated by the intricate symbiotic relationships between the colossal coral structures and the vibrant marine life that thrived amidst them. He even collected samples of the bioluminescent coral, carefully placing them in specially prepared containers filled with sterile seawater. The level of detail in his notes was astounding, his analytical mind already formulating theories and hypotheses about the origin and function of this alien bioluminescence. He was completely engrossed in this unprecedented opportunity for scientific research.

Their differing approaches, however, were not without moments of collaboration. While Rostova focused on immediate survival,

Thorne's observations provided vital insights into the environment's potential dangers and resources. His analysis of the coral structure, for instance, revealed hidden crevices and tunnels—potential pathways to unexplored areas and potential hiding places for the unseen life forms around us. His identification of edible and nontoxic marine species greatly enhanced our chances of survival. Slowly, begrudgingly at times, a partnership began to emerge—a symbiotic relationship mirroring the fascinating ecosystem around us. Their collaboration was a testament to the power of diverse perspectives, a crucial element in navigating this breathtaking yet terrifying new world.

The crash, the impossible environment, the sheer strangeness of it all... it was overwhelming. But through the chaos, the courage of Captain Rostova and the unwavering curiosity of Dr. Thorne offered a beacon of hope. They were two sides of the same coin – action and observation, pragmatism and curiosity – both vital for our survival in this extraordinary new chapter of our lives. The journey had only just begun, and as the eerie glow of the bioluminescent coral bathed our makeshift camp in an ethereal light, I knew our fates were inextricably bound to the mysteries of this hidden underwater world, and to the two individuals who were now our unlikely leaders. Their success, or failure, would determine not only our fate but perhaps the fate of this incredible world itself.

The initial approach of the Luminese was less a grand arrival and more a cautious, almost hesitant advance. Instead of warships or imposing structures, they came in shimmering, bioluminescent pods, their surfaces pulsing with a soft, internal light that mimicked the surrounding coral. These weren't spacecraft in the conventional sense; they were more like intricately designed, organic vessels that moved through the water with an uncanny grace, almost as if they were extensions of the ocean itself. Inside, we could make out figures, their forms vaguely humanoid but with an ethereal quality, their movements fluid and graceful, unlike anything I'd ever witnessed.

Fear mingled with fascination amongst the survivors. Captain Rostova, ever the pragmatist, maintained a position of cautious alertness, her hand never far from her salvaged pistol. Dr. Thorne, however, was utterly captivated, his scientific curiosity overriding any sense of apprehension. He meticulously documented the approach of the Luminese pods through his damaged waterproof notepad, his usually sharp eyes wide with wonder. Others displayed a spectrum of reactions, from terrified silence to awestruck whispers.

The Luminese, as we later learned, communicated primarily through bioluminescent displays. Their bodies seemed capable of producing a complex language of light patterns, shifting colors and intensities to convey meaning. These intricate patterns flowed across their skin, a mesmerizing dance of light that was both beautiful and intimidating. At first, our attempts to communicate were met with a mixture of curiosity and confusion. We tried shouting, using gestures, even attempting to write messages on salvaged pieces of the plane's wreckage, but nothing seemed to get through.

Our attempts at communication highlighted the fundamental chasm between our cultures. Their technology was profoundly different – less about hard metals and loud machinery, and more about bio-integration, a seamless blending of technology and living organisms. Their bodies themselves seemed to act as sophisticated communication devices and intricate tools. Imagine a world where your hands could manipulate objects with a mere thought, where your body could seamlessly interface with the environment. We, on the other hand, relied on crude instruments – the remnants of a civilization that still clung to the brute force of physical tools and loud, clumsy machines.

The initial exchange involved a series of careful maneuvers. The Luminese pods approached slowly, their lights flashing in sequences that, we later realized, were attempts to convey peace and goodwill. Captain Rostova, interpreting their actions as non-aggressive, responded by mirroring some of their light patterns with a makeshift arrangement of salvaged emergency lights from the plane. This act, however tentative, seemed to be understood as a gesture of goodwill.

The initial contact was, naturally, tentative. The Luminese, even in their peaceful approach, possessed a deep-seated caution. They didn't rush forward or try to overwhelm us with their numbers. Instead, they circled our makeshift camp, their bioluminescent displays conveying a careful assessment. This subtle communication was far more complex and nuanced than anything our crude sign language could manage. It was a conversation conducted not with words, but with light – a language that spoke of ancient wisdom and a deep connection to the ocean itself.

Over several days, a cautious communication developed. We learned, through painstaking observation and patient mimicry, that the Luminese possessed a highly developed sense of empathy. They seemed to understand our fear and bewilderment, responding with patterns that suggested compassion and a desire to help. The key to communication was patience, and the realization that their language wasn't just visual, but felt. They conveyed emotions as much as information, creating a subtle symphony of light that evoked a surprisingly powerful response.

One crucial difference was the Luminese understanding of time. It seemed fluid, non-linear, more akin to the rhythms of the tides than the rigid schedules of our surface-dwelling society. Where we were used to precise measurements and appointments, they seemed to operate within a slower, more organic rhythm, where processes unfolded at their own pace. This wasn't a lack of intelligence, but a different philosophy of existence – one rooted in observation and an almost spiritual connection with their environment.

Cultural differences extended beyond communication. The Luminese societal structure was remarkably different from our own. There seemed to be no rigid hierarchy or centralized authority. They operated in loose collectives, sharing responsibilities and resources freely. The concept of individual ownership was virtually absent; possessions were communal and used according to need. Their seemingly effortless cooperation and lack of competitiveness puzzled us at first, until we began to grasp their profoundly different values – a system rooted in balance, harmony, and an intuitive understanding of interconnectedness.

Their technology, too, reflected this societal structure. It wasn't designed for dominance or exploitation, but for integration and sustainability. They seemed to draw their power from the ocean itself, harnessing its energy with an elegant simplicity that defied our limited understanding of physics. Their tools were extensions of their bodies, subtle interfaces that allowed them to manipulate their environment with a finesse we could only dream of. Their approach to engineering was deeply intertwined with their environmental awareness – a design philosophy that prioritized balance and sustainability above all else.

The initial cultural misunderstandings were inevitable, stemming from the fundamental differences in communication, societal structure, and technological approaches. We, with our history of conflict and competition, struggled to grasp their ethos of harmony and cooperation. However, as we began to understand their worldview, a grudging respect began to grow. Their peaceful approach, their ability to live in harmony with their environment, stood in stark contrast to the destructive tendencies of our own world.

This first contact wasn't just a meeting of different species, but of vastly different ways of life—a collision of worldviews that would challenge our perceptions of ourselves and our place in the universe. The Luminese, with their subtle communication, fluid social structures, and harmonious interaction with their environment, provided a stark contrast to the rigid hierarchies and competitive nature of our past. It was a humbling experience, one that would forever shape our understanding of what it meant to be a part of a larger, interconnected reality. And as the bioluminescent dance continued—a silent conversation between two worlds—I felt a shift within me, a growing understanding that our survival might depend not only on our own ingenuity but also on our ability to adapt, learn, and perhaps even embrace this new, profoundly different way of life. The whispers of the ocean, it seemed, held lessons far more profound than we could have ever imagined.

The Luminese, despite their gentle demeanor, were clearly apprehensive. Their initial contact, though peaceful, felt laced with an underlying tension—a subtle unease that vibrated through the silent communication of bioluminescent displays. It was as if they were waiting, watching, listening for something... or someone. This feeling intensified during our subsequent interactions. We learned they called their world Aquatica, a breathtaking city built not of concrete and steel, but of living coral, shimmering algae, and luminous fungi—all seamlessly integrated into the ocean's rhythm. Their technology was organic, almost symbiotic, interwoven with the very fabric of their environment. They communicated through intricate patterns of light, a language of bioluminescence that Dr. Thorne, with his background in bio-acoustics, was slowly beginning to decipher.

One evening, as we sat within a Luminese dwelling—a breathtaking structure formed from giant, iridescent clamshells—a Luminese elder approached us. Her skin shimmered with an internal light, her eyes, large and dark, held a depth of wisdom that transcended language. She spoke slowly, her words translated by Thorne's increasingly accurate interpretations of the light patterns. She spoke of the Whispers.

The Whispers, she explained, weren't simply sounds; they were an ancient phenomenon, a kind of oceanic consciousness, a collective intelligence woven into the very fabric of Aquatica's ecosystem. They were a source of both immense power and profound mystery, a force that had shaped the history of Aquatica for millennia. They manifested as subtle shifts in the ocean currents, changes in the bioluminescent displays of the marine life, even subtle alterations in the very structure of the underwater city itself. These shifts, almost imperceptible to the untrained eye or ear, carried prophecies, warnings, and even glimpses into the future. The elder described them as a language beyond words—a communication that resonated on a deeper, more intuitive level.

According to the Luminese legends, the Whispers had guided their ancestors in building Aquatica, helping them harness the ocean's energy and create a sustainable, harmonious society. But the Whispers were also a source of conflict. The Abyssals, a mysterious race dwelling in the deepest trenches of the ocean, claimed to be the true interpreters of the Whispers, asserting that their power was rightfully theirs. They were rumored to be capable of manipulating the Whispers, using them to exert control over Aquatica and its resources.

Then there were the Cetea, a brutal and technologically advanced faction composed of genetically modified marine creatures. They viewed the Whispers not as a source of guidance, but as a commodity—something to be exploited for their own nefarious ends. They sought to dominate Aquatica by harnessing the Whispers' power, ignoring the potential devastation it could unleash. The Luminese, bound by their peaceful nature, struggled to reconcile their desire for harmony with the growing threats posed by these hostile factions.

Sarah Chen, our young survivor, seemed to possess a unique sensitivity to the Whispers. She'd experienced strange occurrences since the crash—visions, feelings of unease—that correlated with the shifts in the ocean's bioluminescence. She'd sometimes feel an uncanny understanding of the Luminese's light-based communication, even without Thorne's translations. It became clear she wasn't just witnessing the Whispers; she was somehow connected to them—almost as if she were a conduit, an intermediary between the oceanic consciousness and our world.

One particular evening, while exploring the outer fringes of Aquatica, Sarah experienced a powerful surge of the Whispers. The ocean currents surged, and the bioluminescent creatures reacted in a chaotic dance of vibrant light. Sarah collapsed, overwhelmed by a torrent of images and sensations, a flood of prophetic visions. When she regained consciousness, she spoke of a cataclysmic event—a looming disaster that threatened both Aquatica and the surface world. The visions were fragmented and chaotic, but one image persisted: a vast underwater chasm, a rift in the ocean's floor that threatened to unleash a devastating surge of energy. This chasm, according to her visions, was somehow connected to the Whispers— a nexus point of their power.

Dr. Thorne painstakingly analyzed the data he'd gathered from the Luminese and Sarah's experiences. The Whispers, he concluded, were not simply a form of communication but a manifestation of a complex, interconnected ecosystem. He theorized that the ocean itself possessed a form of consciousness—a vast network of interconnected organisms and geological processes that interacted in ways we were only beginning to understand. The Whispers, in essence, were the expression of this consciousness—a language spoken by the ocean itself.

Our survival, it seemed, wasn't just about escaping Aquatica; it was about understanding the Whispers—deciphering their prophecies and averting the impending catastrophe. The conflict between the Luminese, the Abyssals, and the Cetea was far more than a territorial dispute. It was a battle for control of this powerful oceanic consciousness—a struggle with far-reaching consequences. Each faction interpreted the Whispers in their own way, each pursuing their own agenda, oblivious to the potential consequences of their actions.

The weight of this realization settled heavily on us. We were no longer just survivors; we were players in a cosmic drama—a conflict that stretched back millennia, a struggle for the very soul of the ocean. The Whispers held the key to both our survival and the fate of two worlds. The question was: could we decipher their secrets before it was too late? Could we find a way to bridge the chasm between our world and Aquatica, between our understanding of technology and theirs, between our conflicting views of harmony and control?

The Luminese, in their wisdom, offered a solution. They spoke of an ancient artifact, a device known as the "Heart of Aquatica," located deep within a forgotten temple—a relic said to hold the key to controlling the Whispers. The artifact was protected by elaborate safeguards, its location shrouded in mystery. Acquiring it meant navigating treacherous currents, evading the predatory Cetea, and perhaps even confronting the enigmatic Abyssals. The path ahead was fraught with danger. But we knew, deep in our hearts, that the task was not just possible, but necessary. The whispers of the ocean were calling to us, guiding us toward our destiny—a destiny far larger and more profound than any of us could have imagined. The fate of two worlds rested on our shoulders. The weight of the prophecy pressed down, heavy and urgent. Each passing moment brought us closer to the precipice of disaster—closer to the unraveling of the delicate balance that held Aquatica, and perhaps the rest of the planet, together.

CHAPTER 2

The rhythmic pulse of the Luminese city—a mesmerizing symphony of bioluminescent light and gentle currents—was a stark contrast to the gnawing unease that settled in Captain Rostova's gut. The initial wonder of this hidden world, this breathtaking metropolis built within the very fabric of the ocean, was slowly being overshadowed by a growing sense of foreboding. Dr. Thorne, ever the pragmatist, had been meticulously charting the Luminese's advanced technology, their intricate understanding of bioluminescent energy, and their surprisingly sophisticated social structure. Yet even his scientific curiosity couldn't entirely mask the apprehension that hung heavy in the air.

The Luminese, for all their peaceful demeanor and welcoming gestures, had spoken of a threat—a looming darkness that resided in the crushing depths of the abyss. They called them the Abyssals, and their descriptions were chilling. Not simply hostile but fundamentally different, the Abyssals were beings adapted to the unimaginable pressures and perpetual darkness of the hadal zone, the deepest trenches of the ocean. Their very existence seemed to defy terrestrial understanding. Their physiology, societal structures, and motivations were all shrouded in an impenetrable veil of mystery.

The Luminese spoke of colossal bioluminescent creatures, their forms distorted by the crushing pressure, their movements sluggish but undeniably powerful. They described deep-sea hydrothermal vents where life thrived on chemicals rather than sunlight and where the Abyssals seemed to draw their power—their cities carved into the very rock formations surrounding these volcanic chimneys. But it wasn't just their physical presence that was terrifying; it was their seeming indifference to the delicate balance of the ecosystem. The Luminese hinted at ecological imbalances—areas of the ocean stripped bare of life, marked by the Abyssals' passage, like the wake of a colossal, silent storm.

Dr. Thorne, ever the scientist, was fascinated by the prospect of studying such unique adaptations. He envisioned the Abyssals as a testament to the incredible resilience and adaptability of life, a living embodiment of extremophile evolution. He sketched diagrams of potential bioluminescent communication systems, mused over how the creatures might withstand immense pressure, and wondered about their metabolic processes. He imagined their possible symbiotic relationships with the unique chemosynthetic bacteria found near hydrothermal vents. However, even his scientific curiosity was tempered by the warnings from the Luminese elders.

Captain Rostova, on the other hand, felt a primal fear. The Luminese's descriptions painted a picture not just of a different species but of a force of nature—unconcerned with the boundaries of life and death, unyielding in its pursuit of something... something the Luminese wouldn't explicitly reveal. Their cryptic warnings spoke of ancient grudges, of a conflict that predated even the Luminese civilization—a war waged across millennia in the silent, unforgiving depths. This was not a territorial dispute or a battle for resources; this felt like a clash of fundamental principles, an existential conflict between two vastly different worldviews.

Sarah Chen, whose unique connection to the "Whispers" was becoming increasingly apparent, had experienced fleeting glimpses of the Abyssals through her visions. She described them not as creatures but as entities woven into the very fabric of the deep ocean—almost extensions of the abyss itself. Their movements, she sensed, were guided by a force larger than themselves: a collective consciousness pulsing with ancient power and a chilling disregard for the Luminese world. Her visions also offered some insight into their motivations—or at least the potential catalyst that might trigger a devastating conflict.

The Abyssals, Sarah revealed, seemed drawn to the "Whispers," the same enigmatic phenomenon the Luminese guarded and the Cetea ruthlessly sought to control. The Whispers, it seemed, were not simply an energy source or an ancient technology; they were a fundamental force of nature, a nexus of energy linking the underwater world to the surface world in ways no one yet understood. The Abyssals sensed this connection, the power contained within the Whispers, and their presence hinted at a plan— perhaps to harness that power for their own inscrutable purposes or to disrupt the already fragile balance between their world and the Luminese's.

The Luminese, despite their technologically advanced civilization, appeared ill-equipped to directly confront the Abyssals. Their strategies were based on avoidance, on maintaining a delicate balance, on careful management of their environment. They possessed advanced technology that allowed them to subtly influence their surroundings, mimicking the natural processes of the deep sea.

However, direct confrontation with a force as elemental as the Abyssals was something they were clearly hesitant to undertake. They described their methods as more akin to environmental stewardship—maintaining harmony rather than imposing control. Their advanced technology was primarily used for creating sustainable energy and maintaining the bioluminescent ecosystems that sustained their civilization.

The survivors, now finding themselves inextricably linked to the fate of the Luminese, began to understand the magnitude of the threat. The idyllic underwater world they had stumbled upon was not a sanctuary; it was a battleground—a theater of conflict that had raged for eons. The idyllic Luminese city, with its bioluminescent architecture and flowing currents, was simply a peaceful oasis in the face of a far greater, far more ancient struggle. The very survival of the Luminese, and possibly even the delicate balance of the entire planet, depended on understanding and countering the Abyssal threat.

The survivors, armed with their unique skills and perspectives, began to plan. Captain Rostova, with her military experience, focused on strategic planning—mapping potential escape routes and defensive positions. Dr. Thorne, using his scientific expertise, started to analyze the limited information they had on the Abyssals, hoping to find a weakness, a vulnerability, or even a point of communication. Sarah, increasingly burdened by her visions, worked to interpret the fragmented images she received, attempting to piece together a cohesive picture of the Abyssals' motivations and their plans.

Their efforts, however, were hampered by a lack of information. The Luminese, despite their willingness to cooperate, remained guarded, unwilling to fully reveal the extent of their knowledge about the Abyssals, the nature of their conflict, or the true potential of the

Whispers. They spoke of ancient prophecies, of a looming cataclysm linked to the Whispers' power, and the role they believed the human survivors might play in the unfolding drama. Their caution was understandable, born of millennia of experience with the relentless, indifferent forces of the deep.

Days turned into weeks. The survivors' initial wonder at the Luminese city gradually gave way to grim determination. They understood now that the idyllic world they had found was a fragile ecosystem perched precariously on the brink of destruction. The Abyssal threat, lurking in the inky blackness of the abyss, was a constant reminder of the precariousness of their situation—a stark contrast to the vibrant, pulsating life of the Luminese city. The survivors were not just visitors; they were now participants in a cosmic drama, their actions holding the key to the fate of two worlds.

The Luminese, with their gentle demeanor and ethereal beauty, were proving to be surprisingly adept at maintaining a precarious peace. However, whispers of a far more ruthless force—the Cetea— were growing louder, their presence a palpable shift in the underwater currents. Unlike the Luminese, who seemed to exist in harmony with their environment, the Cetea were predators. Their civilization was built on conquest and the exploitation of the ocean's resources. Their very existence felt like a contradiction—a violent dissonance in the otherwise serene symphony of the underwater world.

Our initial encounters with them were indirect. Reports from Luminese scouts described colossal, whale-like creatures, their skin shimmering with an unsettling obsidian sheen. These weren't the graceful whales of our world; these were behemoths, possessing an unnerving intelligence reflected in their coordinated hunts and terrifyingly efficient methods of communication. Dr. Thorne hypothesized that their vocalizations, far beyond the audible range of humans, could somehow interact with the "Whispers," amplifying their power or even using them as a weapon.

The Whispers themselves remained an enigma. Sarah Chen's unique sensitivity to them offered tantalizing glimpses—fleeting images, fragmented sounds, and emotional echoes that felt both ancient and intensely personal. They appeared to be some form of pervasive energy field, resonating throughout this underwater realm and influencing the very fabric of reality. From the growth patterns of Luminese bioluminescent flora to the migratory behavior of deepsea creatures, the Whispers seemed to touch everything. To the Cetea, these Whispers were not simply a mystery; they were a source of power, a key to unlocking something far greater.

The Luminese, deeply spiritual and connected to the natural world, viewed the Whispers with reverence. To them, the Whispers were a source of life, creation, and cosmic balance. Their society was structured around understanding and respecting the ocean's subtle energies, living in a delicate equilibrium with their environment. The Cetea, however, saw only potential for dominance. As far as we could gather from intercepted communications and observed behavior, their civilization was built on control, subjugation, and the relentless pursuit of power. To them, the Whispers were not a force of creation but a weapon—a tool to establish their supremacy over all other inhabitants of this hidden world.

Their methods were brutal. Luminese scouting parties reported witnessing the Cetea decimating entire ecosystems, leaving barren wastelands in their wake. Their hunts were not merely for sustenance; they were calculated acts of aggression, dismantling the delicate balance the Luminese so carefully maintained. The reports also spoke of bizarre technological artifacts—structures crafted from deep-sea minerals and powered by the same bioluminescent energy that fueled the Luminese city, but twisted and imbued with a cruel, destructive intent.

One particularly chilling report detailed a Cetea attack on a Luminese research vessel. The vessel, designed for peaceful exploration, was no match for the Cetea's brute force. According to survivors, the attackers displayed a disturbing level of tactical sophistication, utilizing advanced sonar technology to pinpoint their prey and deploying weaponry that could disrupt the delicate bioluminescent fields protecting the Luminese city. The subsequent rescue operation was harrowing, showcasing the Luminese's valiant, though ultimately futile, attempts to protect their own. Their technology, though marvelously sophisticated, was designed for symbiosis, not warfare. They were pacifists facing a ruthlessly efficient war machine.

The scale of the Cetea's ambition began to dawn on us. It wasn't just about controlling the ocean's resources; it was about controlling the Whispers—dominating the very fabric of reality within this submerged realm. This was a power struggle of cosmic proportions, with the fate of an entire civilization hanging in the balance.

Captain Rostova, ever pragmatic, began to strategize. Our initial alliance with the Luminese, born out of shared survival, was solidifying into a more formal partnership. Despite their pacifistic nature, the Luminese proved resourceful and surprisingly adept at adapting their technology for defensive purposes. They helped us understand their sophisticated communication system, which Dr.

Thorne was able to partially decipher, providing invaluable insights into the Cetea's plans and movements.

However, the Luminese's technological advantages were limited. Their peaceful nature hindered their ability to engage in open conflict. We needed a plan—either to deter the Cetea or, if necessary, to fight back. The key, we realized, lay in understanding the Whispers and harnessing their power in a way the Cetea couldn't anticipate. The problem was that our understanding of the Whispers was still rudimentary. Sarah Chen's connection was powerful, but she was still learning to control it, to filter the chaotic influx of information and translate it into something meaningful and actionable.

The weeks that followed were a blur of frantic activity. Dr. Thorne tirelessly analyzed intercepted Cetea communications, attempting to unravel their strategic intentions. He discovered they were gathering vast quantities of a specific bioluminescent mineral crucial to the Luminese city's energy grid. The Cetea seemed to be planning a large-scale assault to cripple the Luminese's ability to defend themselves. This realization sent a jolt through our group. We were not dealing with random acts of aggression; this was a meticulously orchestrated campaign of conquest.

Captain Armstrong, ever resourceful, began devising a counterstrategy. Drawing on his years at sea, he focused on tactics, logistics, and exploiting the enemy's weaknesses. We needed to disrupt the Cetea's reliance on the bioluminescent mineral, severing their supply lines to slow their advance. But how?

The answer, unexpectedly, came from a seemingly insignificant detail within the Luminese's ancient texts—a reference to a legendary, naturally occurring bioluminescent field, powerful enough to disrupt the Cetea's technology. The field, according to the texts, was located deep within a treacherous underwater canyon—a place considered sacred by the Luminese and generally avoided. It was a risky option but our only chance to stand against this formidable adversary.

Our preparations were tense and clandestine. The Luminese, while supportive, were hesitant, haunted by the ghosts of past attacks and fearful of jeopardizing their fragile peace. We were treading on dangerous ground, challenging not only the Cetea but also the very core values of our Luminese allies. This wasn't just a battle for survival; it was a struggle for the soul of this extraordinary underwater world. The fate of two worlds—our lost surface and this hidden ocean kingdom—rested on the outcome. The mission was perilous, a gamble with unimaginable consequences. Yet, we had no choice but to proceed. The ruthless Cetea were on the march, and their conquest could mean the end of everything we had come to know and cherish in this incredible, alien world. The time for diplomacy was over. The time for action had arrived.

The initial meetings with the Luminese had been fraught with cautious curiosity on both sides. Their technology, a seamless blend of bioluminescence and sophisticated engineering, was both breathtaking and intimidating. We witnessed intricate coral structures that pulsed with light, acting as both communication networks and power sources. Their cities, built within colossal, bioluminescent kelp forests, were marvels of sustainable architecture, harmoniously integrated with the surrounding ecosystem. But beneath the surface of their serene existence, we sensed a deep-seated fear—a trauma etched into their collective memory. Their history, pieced together from fragmented narratives and observations, revealed a past scarred by conflict, a past that explained their current cautious approach to outsiders.

Dr. Thorne, our resident expert in marine biology and a surprisingly adept linguist, played a crucial role in bridging the cultural gap. His patient observations, coupled with his ability to decipher their complex communication system—a combination of bioluminescent flashes and subtle sonic frequencies—fostered a sense of trust. He learned that their society wasn't governed by a single leader but by a council of elders, each representing a different aspect of their culture: science, art, history, and the delicate balance of their ecosystem. These elders, with their serene faces and eyes that seemed to hold the wisdom of millennia, proved to be surprisingly open to collaboration. Their initial apprehension slowly melted away as they saw the genuine intent behind our actions.

The key to forging a strong alliance lay in demonstrating our shared goals. We weren't conquerors; we were survivors, seeking refuge and understanding. The threat of the Cetea served as an unexpected catalyst, forcing a rapid acceleration in our collaboration. The Luminese, despite their pacifistic nature, possessed a sophisticated defense system—a network of bioluminescent traps and sonic disruptors capable of repelling even the most aggressive predators. Sharing our knowledge of the Cetea's tactics—their preferred ambush points, their technological vulnerabilities—became a crucial element of our alliance. In exchange, the Luminese shared their understanding of the Whispers, the mysterious phenomenon that seemed to connect this underwater world to our own, and even beyond.

Sarah Chen, a young woman from the surface world, played a pivotal role in this exchange. Her inherent sensitivity to the Whispers—a gift both terrifying and wondrous—enabled her to interpret the Luminese's deeper anxieties, their unspoken fears, and hidden hopes. She became a vital translator, not just of language but of emotions, building bridges of understanding between two vastly different cultures. She learned to feel the pulse of the Whispers, interpreting the subtle shifts in the bioluminescent patterns and underwater currents, acting as an early warning system against Cetea incursions.

The construction of a joint defense strategy required a delicate dance between our technologies and theirs. Our human ingenuity, combined with their mastery of bioluminescence, resulted in innovative defense systems. We adapted salvaged plane components, incorporating Luminese bioluminescent technology, to create powerful sonar detectors and early warning systems. We integrated their bioluminescent traps with our salvaged weaponry, creating a formidable defense network that blended seamlessly with the underwater environment. This collaboration was more than just a strategic alliance; it was a testament to the power of human ingenuity when combined with nature's genius.

The Luminese also shared their knowledge of the ocean's resources, revealing sustainable practices that had allowed their civilization to thrive for centuries. They taught us about the intricate symbiotic relationships within the underwater ecosystem, highlighting the importance of balance and interconnectedness. We learned to harness the energy of the bioluminescent coral reefs, developing sustainable power sources that minimized our environmental impact. This exchange of knowledge extended beyond technology—it was a cultural exchange, a sharing of wisdom and understanding, a lesson in responsible coexistence.

But the alliance was not without its challenges. Internal conflicts within the Luminese council occasionally arose. Some elders remained skeptical, clinging to their pacifistic beliefs and hesitating to engage in open conflict. Their philosophy emphasized harmony and coexistence, viewing violence as a disruption of the natural order. Others, particularly those who had witnessed firsthand the brutality of the Cetea, argued for a more assertive stance, advocating for proactive defense. Sarah's connection to the Whispers offered a mediating force. Her interpretations of the underwater currents often revealed subtle shifts in the Cetea's plans, influencing the council's decisions with timely and accurate warnings.

The most significant challenge came in the form of Jian, a survivor initially skeptical of the Luminese. His background, shrouded in mystery, hinted at a past marked by violence and distrust. He harbored a deep-seated cynicism, struggling to accept the Luminese's peaceful ways. His skepticism extended to our alliance as well, viewing our collaboration with the Luminese as a potential weakness and advocating for a more aggressive, independent approach to dealing with the Cetea. However, through shared experiences—particularly the harrowing near-misses against the Cetea attacks—he gradually began to understand and appreciate the Luminese's approach. The Luminese's patience and Jian's growing respect for their capabilities led to his begrudging and, eventually, enthusiastic participation in the joint efforts.

The forging of our alliance with the Luminese wasn't a sudden event but a gradual process of trust, mutual respect, and shared understanding. It was a testament to our adaptability and the

Luminese's willingness to set aside their age-old fears. It was a partnership built not on conquest but on collaboration—a lesson in interspecies cooperation, a bold step toward a future where two worlds, so different yet interconnected, could find a way to coexist and thrive. The Whispers, once a source of fear and uncertainty, now served as a constant reminder of our shared destiny—a bond forged in the depths of a hidden ocean, a bond that held the key to the survival of both our worlds. Our alliance with the Luminese was not just a strategic necessity; it was a beacon of hope in the face of overwhelming adversity. It was a testament to the resilience of the human spirit and the enduring power of collaboration across worlds. The impending conflict with the Cetea cast a long shadow, but our shared struggle and combined strength forged an unbreakable bond—a partnership that would determine the fate of two worlds.

The Luminese, with their ethereal grace and unsettlingly advanced technology, remained a source of both wonder and apprehension. Their city, nestled within a colossal kelp forest that pulsed with a soft, internal luminescence, felt more like a living organism than a constructed settlement. We learned to navigate its intricate pathways, guided by the subtle shifts in light and the gentle currents that flowed through its bioluminescent arteries. But even within this harmonious ecosystem, the shadow of the impending conflict with the Cetea loomed large. The whispers of this looming war—a constant undercurrent to our daily lives—were felt more acutely than ever before.

It was during one of our excursions into the deeper reaches of the kelp forest, a journey undertaken to map the extent of the Luminese territory, that Sarah's unique connection to the Whispers first manifested. We were exploring a region known as the Silent Grove, an area devoid of the usual vibrant bioluminescence, shrouded in an unnatural stillness. The Luminese guides, usually so communicative, were unusually quiet, their movements hesitant and their bioluminescent markings flickering erratically. The air itself seemed to hum with a low, resonant frequency—a vibration that resonated deep within our chests.

Suddenly, Sarah gasped, her hand flying to her head. Her eyes, usually bright and inquisitive, were wide and unfocused, her breathing rapid and shallow. She stumbled slightly, her body trembling as if caught in the throes of a powerful current. The Luminese closest to her reacted instantly, their bodies shifting to surround her, their soft, rhythmic luminescence intensifying. They murmured in their melodic, almost musical language, their words a soothing counterpoint to the unsettling hum that vibrated through the Silent Grove.

Dr. Thorne was the first to recognize the significance of Sarah's reaction. His keen observation skills, honed by years of scientific research, coupled with his intuitive grasp of the unusual, guided him to the heart of the mystery. He noted the precise correlation between Sarah's distress and the increased intensity of the humming. He understood instinctively that the Silent Grove was not simply an area of reduced bioluminescence but a nexus of energy—a point of convergence for the Whispers. Sarah, unknowingly, had become a conduit, an antenna tuned to a frequency imperceptible to the rest of us.

Over the next few days, Dr. Thorne, with the assistance of the

Luminese healers, carefully monitored Sarah. They discovered she wasn't just reacting to the Whispers; she was receiving them, interpreting them. She wasn't merely experiencing a physical response to a strange energy field; she was receiving information— visions, fragmented narratives that seemed to emanate from the very heart of the underwater world. The experiences were intense and draining, leaving Sarah exhausted and emotionally vulnerable. But through a series of carefully guided sessions, she began to translate these visions into a coherent narrative.

Sarah's revelations painted a picture far more complex than we had ever imagined. The Whispers, she explained, were not simply random signals but a form of communication—a complex web of interwoven narratives stretching across millennia. They were the collective memories of the underwater world, echoing the triumphs and tragedies of countless civilizations that had risen and fallen in this hidden realm.

They spoke of ancient wars, technological marvels long lost to time, and a powerful, sentient force residing at the planet's core—a force that wielded influence over the environment and all life within it. They spoke of the Abyssals, ancient beings of immense power, and their connection to this force; of the Cetea's relentless pursuit of dominance and their attempts to harness this power for their own nefarious purposes. Most importantly, they spoke of a prophecy—a warning woven into the fabric of the underwater world's history. This prophecy foretold a great cataclysm, a cosmic event that would shatter the delicate balance of this hidden world and, potentially, the surface world as well.

The Luminese had long been aware of the Whispers' presence, but they had never been able to fully interpret them. Sarah, with her unusual sensitivity, was the missing link. Her ability to translate the Whispers provided a crucial window into the past, present, and future of this hidden world.

She described the Abyssals not as mindless monsters, as we'd initially feared, but as ancient guardians—protectors of the planet's core and all life intertwined with it. She revealed that the Cetea's aggression stemmed from their desperate attempt to control this core, manipulating its power for their expansionist goals and jeopardizing the entire underwater ecosystem, including the Luminese.

Sarah's visions also shed light on the connection between the surface world and the underwater realm. She saw glimpses of a time when the two worlds were closely intertwined—a time before the surface world's catastrophic changes. She saw echoes of a lost civilization that had mastered the ability to traverse between the two worlds but had been lost to time and forgotten.

Her visions revealed that the Bermuda Triangle—the anomalous region that had transported our plane to this underwater world—was not merely a geographical anomaly but a gateway, a nexus of energy connecting the surface and underwater realms. This gateway, she explained, was directly linked to the planet's core and the energies flowing from it, making it a focal point for the Whispers. The Cetea's plans, she warned, aimed to disrupt this gateway, triggering the catastrophic event foretold in the prophecy.

The weight of this knowledge settled heavily upon us. Sarah's revelations were both terrifying and exhilarating. The knowledge of the impending cataclysm felt like a burden, a dark cloud threatening to engulf us all. But within that darkness was a glimmer of hope—a chance to avert disaster. There was a possibility of uniting the disparate factions of this underwater world—Luminese, Abyssals, and even potentially some members of the Cetea—in a common cause.

Sarah's connection to the Whispers, her ability to act as a bridge between the past, present, and future of this hidden world, made her the key to our survival—the key to shaping the destiny of two worlds.

The urgency of the situation became abundantly clear. We had to act quickly and decisively to forge a more powerful alliance, one capable of standing against the might of the Cetea. Bridging the gap between the Luminese and the Abyssals seemed an insurmountable task, given their long and fraught history. We needed to convince the Abyssals that our intentions were benevolent—that we weren't seeking to exploit their power or knowledge.

Sarah's insights, her understanding of their ancient history and connection to the core, would prove invaluable in this endeavor. Her unique connection to the Whispers could unlock the path to survival.

It was a path paved with risk and uncertainty, but one we had to take if we hoped to avert the cataclysmic event looming before us.

However, the knowledge Sarah revealed came at a cost. The intensity of receiving the Whispers left her increasingly frail, her body weakened by the sheer volume of information she processed. Dr. Thorne worked tirelessly to mitigate the effects, devising protective measures and energy-regulating techniques. Even with these interventions, the strain on Sarah was significant—a constant reminder of the delicate balance between her unique gift and its potential consequences.

The path ahead was perilous, fraught with the promise of salvation but shadowed by the threat of annihilation. It would test the limits of our resilience, our capacity for collaboration, and our understanding of this strange and wondrous underwater world. The fate of two worlds now rested precariously on the shoulders of a young woman with a remarkable gift—a gift that might save them all.

But the journey was far from over. The fight for survival had only just begun. The path forward was uncertain, shrouded in the whispers of the past, the warnings of the future, and the urgent need for unity against a common enemy. The interconnected fate of two worlds hung in the balance, and Sarah, our unlikely savior, would play a crucial role in determining their destiny.

The immediate aftermath of Jian's sacrifice cast a long shadow over the Luminese city. His selfless act—a testament to the burgeoning bond between humans and the Luminese—served as a stark reminder of life's fragility and the looming threat of the Cetea. Yet, the shared grief surprisingly forged a stronger alliance. The Luminese, initially hesitant to trust us fully, now saw us not just as survivors but as allies in the face of a common enemy.

This newfound unity was crucial; survival hinged on strategic planning and efficient resource gathering. Our first priority was securing a stable food supply. The Luminese diet consisted primarily of bioluminescent algae and various strange, yet surprisingly palatable, deep-sea flora. Dr. Thorne, ever the pragmatist, analyzed their nutritional content, comparing it to human dietary requirements. He discovered that while the algae provided essential vitamins and minerals, it lacked crucial proteins.

We needed a solution—and fast. Captain Armstrong, ever resourceful, suggested exploring the surrounding reefs. Using advanced sonar technology, the Luminese mapped areas rich in crustaceans and other protein sources previously unknown to us. Specialized submersibles, sleek and silent, were deployed, guided by Luminese navigators with an uncanny understanding of ocean currents and underwater topography. The hunt was successful, yielding a bountiful harvest of unusual but nutritious creatures.

The next challenge was energy. The Luminese utilized an efficient system harnessing bioluminescence, generating both light and power. Dr. Thorne, endlessly curious, studied their technology and was particularly fascinated by their ability to manipulate light, converting it into usable energy with minimal waste. He reverseengineered some of their simpler devices, creating small-scale power generators to supplement our existing supplies. However, the long-term solution lay in understanding the intricacies of their bioluminescent process on a deeper, more fundamental level.

Beyond sustenance and energy, we needed to address the looming threat of the Cetea. Intelligence gathering became paramount. The Luminese possessed a sophisticated network of underwater sensors and communication systems far surpassing anything we had on the surface. They shared their knowledge with us, revealing the Cetea's aggressive expansion tactics and their increasing territorial claims. Their strategies involved disrupting the delicate balance of the underwater ecosystem, manipulating currents, and deploying bio-weapons capable of devastating the Luminese city—and, by extension, our fragile human settlement.

Captain Armstrong proposed a three-pronged approach.

Firstly, we bolstered our defenses. The Luminese provided access to advanced materials and technologies, including a remarkably strong, lightweight alloy ideal for constructing protective barriers around our temporary settlement. We fortified our position within the kelp forest, creating a series of interconnected bunkers and observation points. The construction involved a collaborative effort between humans and Luminese—a testament to the growing mutual trust and respect.

Secondly, we enhanced our intelligence-gathering capabilities. With Luminese assistance, we created a network of underwater drones equipped with advanced sensors and stealth technology. These drones monitored Cetea movements, identified their bases, and gathered information on their weaponry and strategies. The data was crucial for developing a comprehensive understanding of the enemy and planning counter-strategies. The Luminese's expertise in underwater navigation and stealth technology proved invaluable; their virtually silent devices outclassed anything our surface-based technology could achieve.

Thirdly, and most critically, we sought alliances beyond the Luminese. The Abyssals, although enigmatic and largely unknown, were rumored to possess ancient knowledge and powerful technologies. Captain Armstrong, ever the gambler, believed that an alliance with them might tip the balance of power. However, contacting the Abyssals was perilous. Their territory lay shrouded in mystery, deep within the trenches of the underwater world—far beyond the reach of our current technologies.

Sarah's ability to receive the Whispers proved invaluable in this endeavor. The ancient prophecies hinted at the Abyssals' location and their potential willingness to help—provided the right approach was taken. Guided by Sarah's visions and the Luminese's advanced navigation systems, we devised a daring plan to approach the Abyssals' territory. Using a modified Luminese submersible, heavily reinforced and equipped with advanced sensors designed to minimize detection, we embarked on a perilous journey.

The deep trenches were a dangerous and unforgiving environment, teeming with colossal creatures and unpredictable currents. If the Abyssals proved hostile, they would be formidable opponents. However, the potential rewards—a powerful alliance and the knowledge of ancient secrets—were too great to ignore.

The mission was more than just reconnaissance; it was a desperate gamble, a calculated risk meant to shift the balance of power. The fate of two worlds now rested on the shoulders of a small band of survivors, a technologically advanced aquatic civilization, and a young woman uniquely connected to the whispers of the deep. Strategic planning was no longer solely about resources and fortifications. It required forging alliances, gaining knowledge, and unraveling the intricate web of connections binding our two worlds together. This interconnectedness was now both our greatest strength and our most profound challenge.

The next chapter in our struggle for survival would take us into uncharted depths, where ancient secrets and enemies alike lurked in the shadows. Sarah, our unlikely key to unlocking the mysteries of the Whispers, would stand at the forefront of this dangerous expedition. The journey into the Abyssals' domain was a voyage into the unknown, one that would profoundly affect the future—not just of humanity, but of the entire underwater world.

CHAPTER 3

The submersible, christened *Triton's Kiss* by the ever-optimistic Captain Armstrong, descended into the inky blackness. Bioluminescent plankton, like scattered stars in a velvet sea, illuminated the descent, their ethereal glow painting fleeting patterns on the viewing ports. Inside, the air crackled with nervous energy—a mixture of anticipation and apprehension. Captain Rostova, her face etched with the grim determination that had seen her through countless storms, gripped the armrest. Dr. Thorne, ever the scientist, meticulously monitored the sonar readings, his brow furrowed in concentration. Sarah Chen, her youthful face pale but resolute, sat beside him, her fingers lightly resting on a small, intricately carved Luminese artifact—a piece of the puzzle they hoped to unlock within the ancient city.

Their mission was simple yet fraught with peril: to explore the ruins of Xylos, an ancient city lost to the depths for millennia. Luminese legend whispered of Xylos as the birthplace of the Whispers. The journey itself was a testament to the uneasy alliance forged between human survivors and the Luminese. The submersible, a marvel of Luminese engineering, blended seamlessly with the surrounding environment, its hull shimmering with bioluminescent patterns that mimicked the deep-sea flora. It moved with an unnerving grace, navigating treacherous currents and underwater canyons with the precision of a seasoned diver.

As they descended deeper, the pressure mounted—a constant reminder of the immense forces at play in this alien world. The bioluminescence intensified, transforming the darkness into a breathtaking spectacle of light and shadow. Strange, otherworldly creatures, glowing with internal luminescence, drifted past the viewing ports. These beings defied terrestrial classification, testaments to the unique evolutionary pressures of this hidden realm. Dr. Thorne jotted down observations, his pen scratching furiously against his notepad. He described ethereal jellyfish pulsing with rhythmic light, strange bioluminescent corals resembling fantastical flowers, and fish with eyes that seemed to glow with uncanny intelligence.

Hours passed in silent descent. The quiet, broken only by the rhythmic hum of the submersible's engines and the occasional crackle of the comms system, was punctuated by growing excitement. Sonar readings revealed the presence of massive structures ahead—the ruins of Xylos. The city, half-buried in the seabed, appeared as a ghostly apparition. Its structures, encrusted with centuries of marine growth, were hauntingly beautiful. Towering spires, once gleaming with now-faded Luminese technology, reached toward the surface, their intricate carvings hinting at a civilization far more advanced than humanity had ever known.

Triton's Kiss approached cautiously, navigating a maze of partially collapsed buildings. Lyra, the Luminese pilot, expertly maneuvered the submersible through narrow passages and around obstacles, her movements fluid and precise. The city was a testament to the

Luminese's ingenuity and deep connection to the ocean. Buildings seamlessly integrated with the environment, blending with coral reefs and marine life. Some structures housed intricate systems of water filtration and energy generation, hinting at a sustainable and harmonious coexistence with the ocean. Other areas, however, revealed signs of devastation, suggesting a cataclysmic event had led to the city's demise.

As they explored the ruins, the team discovered fragmented records—data crystals etched with intricate symbols and images. These artifacts hinted at the history of Xylos and the origins of the Whispers. The crystals revealed a sophisticated society that harnessed the power of the ocean, developing technologies that exceeded humanity's wildest dreams. They discovered vast libraries containing knowledge of ancient cultures, celestial mechanics, and ecological principles far surpassing anything known to humanity.

Among the ruins, they uncovered a massive central chamber, a place of immense significance in Luminese lore. At its center lay a colossal crystal structure, pulsating with a faint, rhythmic light. This was the heart of Xylos—the source of the Whispers. When Sarah touched the crystal, a wave of energy washed over her, overwhelming her senses. Visions flooded her mind: glimpses of ancient events, prophecies of a looming catastrophe, and the interconnected fate of both the underwater and surface worlds. She saw the catastrophic events that had led to Xylos' downfall—events that mirrored the ecological crises threatening the surface world.

The visions revealed a disturbing truth. The Whispers were not merely a source of power but a reflection of the delicate balance of the ecosystem. Their power fluctuated with the health of the ocean. Any disruption to the ecosystem, any act of exploitation or destruction, would weaken the Whispers and potentially trigger a catastrophic chain reaction. Sarah realized that Xylos' destruction was a direct consequence of its people's hubris—their failure to understand and respect the delicate balance of their world.

The team also found evidence of the Abyssals' presence within Xylos. Scratches on the walls, cryptic markings, and remnants of their strange technology indicated they, too, were aware of the Whispers' power and had attempted to exploit it for their own purposes. This discovery added a layer of complexity to the mission. The ancient city was not just a repository of knowledge—it was a battleground for competing factions, each vying for control of a power that could determine the fate of both worlds.

Their exploration of Xylos was not without danger. Several times, the submersible narrowly avoided collapsing structures and hazardous currents. They encountered strange, bioluminescent creatures—some friendly, others hostile—showcasing the unpredictable nature of this alien world. The team also discovered signs of environmental degradation: areas where coral reefs had died off, leaving behind barren landscapes. These grim reminders of unchecked technological advancement underscored the importance of environmental stewardship.

The deep-sea city echoed humanity's struggles, a poignant reminder that the problems facing the surface world were not unique.

As they prepared to leave Xylos, the team felt a profound sense of awe and responsibility. They had uncovered secrets that could change the fate of two worlds. The knowledge they gained, however, came at a cost. They had witnessed firsthand the consequences of neglecting the environment and the dangers of unchecked ambition.

As they ascended, the faint luminescence of Xylos receded into the darkness, leaving them to ponder the weight of their discoveries and the challenging path ahead.

The journey to the ancient city had not only unveiled lost technologies and ancient secrets but had also revealed a profound truth about the interconnectedness of life, the fragility of ecosystems, and the responsibility of all beings to protect the delicate balance of the world. Their return to the Luminese city was not merely a return to safety; it was a return to a new understanding of the interconnectedness of worlds and the weight of the knowledge they now possessed. The journey had just begun.

The Luminese city, Xylos, hummed with a quiet energy—a stark contrast to the frenetic activity that had marked their previous visits. The vibrant bioluminescence that painted the city's architecture felt softer, more subdued, as if the city itself was exhaling after a period of intense activity. The team, having returned from their expedition to the ancient city, shared a sense of exhaustion tempered by the thrill of their discoveries.

Dr. Thorne, his eyes still alight with the wonder of the underwater ruins, began to unpack the artifacts they had carefully salvaged.

"These," he announced, holding up a delicate, iridescent orb, "are unlike anything I've ever seen. The material is unlike any known terrestrial element. Its structure is crystalline, yet it seems to possess some kind of... bioluminescent energy signature far more sophisticated than anything we observed in the Luminese's everyday technology."

Sarah Chen, her connection to the Whispers growing stronger with each passing day, held out a small, intricately carved stone tablet. Its surface pulsed faintly with a light that seemed to mimic her own breathing.

"This tablet," she whispered, her voice filled with a mixture of awe and trepidation, "seems to respond to my touch. It resonates with... the Whispers. It's as if it's trying to communicate something."

Over the next few days, the team worked tirelessly, analyzing the artifacts under the watchful eyes of their Luminese hosts. The orb, Dr. Thorne discovered, contained a complex system of interconnected micro-crystals that pulsed with energy, creating a miniature, self-sustaining ecosystem within its confines. The energy source, he theorized, was a form of bioluminescent fusion far more efficient and environmentally friendly than anything humans had ever conceived. It seemed to draw power from the surrounding environment, converting the kinetic energy of ocean currents and even the subtle vibrations of the Whispers into usable power.

The stone tablet proved even more enigmatic. Initial scans revealed complex glyphs etched onto its surface, similar to those found in the ancient city. But unlike the city's more rudimentary technology, the tablet exhibited an almost sentient quality. As Sarah touched it, the glyphs rearranged themselves, forming new patterns and sequences, as if responding to her thoughts and emotions.

The Luminese elders, watching with a mixture of curiosity and reverence, explained that the tablet was a form of communication device—a conduit to a deeper understanding of the Whispers. The Whispers, they explained, were not just a phenomenon but a form of universal consciousness, a network of interconnected energy that permeated the entire underwater world. The ancient city, they revealed, was not merely a historical site but a vast energy reservoir capable of harnessing the power of the Whispers on an unprecedented scale. It was this very power, they believed, that had allowed the Luminese to develop their advanced technology, their mastery of bioluminescence, and their ability to thrive in this unique ecosystem.

The implications of this revelation were staggering. The

Luminese had not simply developed sustainable technologies; they had harnessed the very fabric of existence, creating a symbiotic relationship with their environment. Their technological prowess was not an isolated achievement but a reflection of their deep understanding and respect for the interconnectedness of all things. They weren't just manipulating the Whispers; they were listening to them, learning from them, and living in harmony with them.

Dr. Thorne, ever the meticulous scientist, began compiling a database of the Luminese technology, meticulously documenting their energy systems, architectural designs, and biological adaptations. He found that the Luminese buildings were not just aesthetically pleasing but also functional, designed to maximize energy efficiency and minimize environmental impact. Their cities seamlessly blended with the natural landscape, utilizing the ocean currents and bioluminescent organisms to their advantage. Their very existence was a testament to sustainable living—a stark contrast to the resource-depleting practices of the surface world.

Sarah, meanwhile, continued to explore her connection to the Whispers, her insights proving invaluable in deciphering the tablet's cryptic messages. The glyphs, she discovered, were not mere symbols but holographic representations of complex energy patterns. They could be manipulated, not just read, allowing her to send and receive information through the network of the Whispers themselves. It was a form of telepathic communication, instantaneous and far-reaching, potentially linking the underwater world to the surface world in ways that were previously unimaginable.

The team also discovered evidence of advanced bioengineering techniques within the ancient city, indicating that the Luminese had mastered genetic manipulation centuries ago. They had not only adapted to their environment but had shaped it, fostering biodiversity and creating an ecosystem that supported their advanced civilization. The Luminese weren't merely living sustainably; they were actively enhancing their world.

The bioluminescent corals that illuminated their cities were not merely decorative; they were carefully cultivated organisms that played a crucial role in the city's energy production and environmental regulation. The implications of these discoveries extended far beyond the scientific realm.

The Luminese's mastery of the Whispers raised profound philosophical questions about consciousness, interconnectedness, and the very nature of existence. Their society, governed by principles of cooperation and harmony, offered a compelling counterpoint to the often conflict-ridden societies of the surface world. Their commitment to sustainability provided a blueprint for a future where humanity might coexist peacefully with its environment.

As the team prepared to return to the surface, they carried with them not only artifacts and data but also a profound shift in perspective. The underwater world was not merely a separate realm but a vital part of the larger ecosystem. The Luminese's advanced technology was not simply a testament to their ingenuity but a reflection of their holistic approach to life. The Whispers, no longer a mere mystery, were now a potential bridge connecting two worlds, offering the chance for a shared future. The journey had transformed them; they were no longer just explorers but custodians of knowledge that held the potential to reshape the very destiny of humankind.

The *Triton's Kiss* ascended slowly, the bioluminescence of Xylos fading behind them as they returned to the surface. The memories of the Luminese, their technology, and their profound wisdom would remain—a beacon of hope and a reminder of the potential for a more harmonious and sustainable future. The challenge now lay in sharing this knowledge, bridging the divide between two worlds, and ensuring that the secrets of the underwater kingdom were not exploited but cherished and protected. The fate of both worlds hung in the balance, dependent not just on their understanding of the lost technologies but on their capacity for collective responsibility and global collaboration. The journey to uncover the lost technologies had only just begun; the far greater journey—to apply the knowledge wisely—lay ahead. The whispers of the ocean, once faint murmurs, were now a clarion call for change.

The *Triton's Kiss* shuddered slightly as it broke the surface, the transition from the hushed luminescence of the underwater world to the bright, harsh glare of the sun a jarring experience. The crew, however, barely registered the change. Their minds were still immersed in the breathtaking spectacle of the bioluminescent wonders they had witnessed during their exploration.

Dr. Thorne, ever the meticulous scientist, was already cataloging his observations. "The diversity is simply staggering," he murmured, his fingers flying across his datapad. "I've never encountered anything like it. The sheer range of bioluminescent organisms, the complexity of their light displays... it's rewriting our understanding of marine biology."

He described the shimmering fields of Luciflora, plants resembling giant kelp forests but emitting a pulsating, ethereal blue light that shifted in intensity with the ocean currents. "Imagine, Simon," he said, turning to me, "a forest that glows, its leaves whispering secrets in a language of light. And the patterns! They're not random; there's a certain rhythm, a synchronicity, as if the plants are communicating with each other."

His words conjured images of breathtaking beauty, an underwater galaxy composed of luminous stars. He then spoke of the Photozoa, microscopic organisms that formed living constellations in the water column. Their light, a vibrant emerald green, pulsed rhythmically, creating breathtaking, shifting patterns that mirrored the celestial formations above. He theorized that these tiny creatures played a vital role in the ocean's ecosystem—their light attracting prey and deterring predators. Their intricate dance of light was more than just a spectacle; it was a vital component of the underwater food web, a sophisticated communication system, and a mesmerizing display of natural artistry.

Captain Armstrong, ever pragmatic, interjected, "The sheer volume of energy produced by these creatures is astounding. We could learn a lot about energy efficiency from them." He gestured toward the ship's console. "We could practically power Xylos with the bioluminescence alone if we could figure out how to harness it efficiently."

My own observations during the expedition corroborated Thorne's and Armstrong's findings. I had witnessed the incredible diversity firsthand—from the miniature, twinkling fireflies of the deep to the gigantic, luminous jellyfish that pulsed with an otherworldly glow. One species, the Chromactinia, displayed an astonishing range of colors, shifting from deep violet to vibrant crimson in response to external stimuli—an unparalleled display of bioluminescent artistry that left even the jaded scientists of our team awestruck.

We encountered the Abyssalia, a bizarre species of bioluminescent fish that inhabited the deepest trenches. Their bodies, elongated and eel-like, emitted a faint, pulsating red light— a counterintuitive strategy considering the depth of their habitat, where red light doesn't penetrate. Their bioluminescence appeared to serve a completely different function than that of surfacedwelling species. It wasn't for attracting prey or mates; it was seemingly a form of internal communication, a system of signals that Thorne speculated was crucial to their social structure and adaptation to the extreme pressure and darkness of their habitat. Their bodies were marvels of natural engineering, their skin adapted to withstand the crushing pressure of the deep—a testament to the power of evolution.

Another extraordinary creature was the Lumisquama, a small, translucent fish with scales that shimmered with a dazzling array of colors. Each scale acted as an independent light source, creating a shimmering cascade of light that shifted and changed with the fish's movements. They were like living jewels, their beauty transcending the realm of mere functionality. Thorne theorized that their bioluminescence served a crucial role in camouflage, allowing them to blend seamlessly with the surrounding environment.

However, the bioluminescence wasn't always a spectacle of beauty. We discovered a species of anglerfish, the Malacoda, that employed bioluminescence as a sinister weapon. A glowing lure extended from its head, attracting unsuspecting prey into its gaping maw. The contrast between the beauty and the deadly efficiency of its hunting strategy highlighted the stark realities of survival in the deep ocean—a realm where beauty and danger existed side by side. Its bioluminescence, unlike that of other species, wasn't about communication or camouflage. It was solely about predation—a chilling reminder that nature's beauty could mask deadly intent.

Then there were the coral reefs. These weren't the vibrant, tropical reefs of the surface world; they were bioluminescent ecosystems of unparalleled complexity. The corals themselves glowed with a soft, pulsating light, their patterns varying depending on the species and the surrounding environment. The light was not merely ornamental; it attracted the microscopic plankton that formed the base of the food web within this unique habitat. The symbiotic relationship between the corals and their bioluminescent counterparts was a testament to the intricate interconnectedness of life in this alien world. The vibrant display of bioluminescent life on these reefs was a crucial part of their functionality—a carefully orchestrated dance of light and life that underscored the deep interdependence of these organisms.

But our journey into the bioluminescent wonders was not without peril. We encountered several aggressive species that employed bioluminescence as a defense mechanism or to ambush prey. One particularly memorable encounter was with a school of *Bioluminaria*, small, swift fish that emitted bursts of blinding light when threatened, momentarily disorienting predators. Their bioluminescence served as both a weapon and a defense mechanism, a testament to the diverse ways in which this remarkable phenomenon functioned within the underwater ecosystem. This highlighted the ongoing evolutionary arms race between predator and prey—where one species' defense mechanism drives the evolution of another species' attack strategy, and so on. The ecosystem was in a constant state of dynamic equilibrium, with bioluminescence playing a pivotal role in this ceaseless dance of survival and adaptation.

The sheer scale of the bioluminescent phenomena was almost overwhelming. It wasn't just about individual species; it was about entire ecosystems, entire landscapes illuminated by the light of countless organisms. It served as a reminder that we had only scratched the surface of understanding the complexities of this alien world—a world where the very definition of life was redefined by the interplay of light, chemistry, and evolution.

The experience left an indelible mark on all of us. It wasn't just about scientific discovery; it was a profound aesthetic and philosophical experience. The sheer beauty of the bioluminescent wonders was breathtaking, but it was also a testament to the interconnectedness of life, the delicate balance of ecosystems, and the ongoing evolutionary drama that played out in the depths of the ocean. The beauty and danger were interwoven, an intrinsic part of the rich fabric of life in this underwater world. The mysteries were still unfolding, prompting further explorations and promising revelations that would continue to challenge our understanding of life on Earth—and perhaps beyond. The implications extended beyond the purely scientific; they touched upon philosophy, aesthetics, and our overall place in the cosmos, enriching the human experience in profound ways. It was a journey that would stay with us long after we returned to the surface, a reminder of the wonders hidden beneath the waves and the boundless potential of the natural world.

The initial awe of the Luminese civilization gradually gave way to a growing unease. Our scientific instruments, recalibrated for the unique underwater environment, began to paint a picture far more complex and disturbing than we could have anticipated. The vibrant coral reefs, initially perceived as a testament to the Luminese's harmonious coexistence with nature, showed signs of significant stress. Sections of reef, once teeming with life, were now bleached and lifeless—the skeletal remains of countless marine organisms stark against the shimmering backdrop of the Luminese city.

Dr. Thorne, our team's resident marine biologist, was the first to notice the anomaly. Her initial readings were dismissed as equipment malfunctions, but as more data poured in, a grim reality emerged. The Luminese ocean, despite its unparalleled beauty, was suffering from acidification, a phenomenon eerily similar to what was devastating Earth's oceans.

"The levels are... alarming," Thorne muttered, her face pale in the soft, ambient light of the *Triton's Kiss*. "The pH is dropping faster than any natural process could account for. And the coral bleaching... it's widespread."

Further investigation revealed that the acidification wasn't uniform. Certain regions, particularly those close to the boundaries of Luminese territory, showed significantly higher levels of acidity. This pointed to a localized pollution source, a stark contrast to the overall impression of environmental harmony projected by the Luminese. Captain Armstrong, ever pragmatic, immediately suspected the Abyssals—the enigmatic, reclusive inhabitants of the deeper trenches. Their technology was shrouded in mystery, and their interactions with the Luminese were minimal, laced with a palpable tension. Could their activities be the source of this environmental catastrophe?

Our explorations took us deeper into the Luminese ocean, venturing further from the comforting proximity of their cities. We encountered breathtakingly diverse ecosystems, from towering kelp forests that swayed gently in the currents to vast plains of bioluminescent algae that shimmered like celestial constellations. Yet beneath the surface beauty, we found troubling evidence of ecological disruption. Certain species crucial to the balance of the underwater ecosystems were disappearing. The decline was not gradual; it was precipitous, suggesting a sudden and catastrophic environmental shift.

Thorne's team collected samples of water, sediment, and biological specimens, diligently analyzing them with our advanced equipment. The results were disheartening. Elevated levels of heavy metals, previously unseen in the Luminese ocean, were detected in areas far removed from the Luminese cities. These pollutants didn't just represent a localized problem—they were gradually spreading, poisoning the very heart of this vibrant underwater world.

Our encounters with the Luminese themselves proved equally revealing. Initially hesitant to discuss the environmental issues, they eventually opened up, revealing a long-standing conflict with the Cetea, a technologically advanced race known for their ruthlessness and disregard for the environment. The Cetea, it turned out, mined rare minerals vital for their technology, leaving behind a trail of destruction in their wake. Their mining operations, conducted with little regard for environmental consequences, were implicated in the heavy metal pollution plaguing the ocean.

The Luminese, pacifists at heart, lacked the military power to counter the Cetea's aggression. They were caught in a desperate struggle for survival—a silent battle waged between the preservation of their environment and the threat of annihilation.

The parallels to Earth's own environmental struggles were striking—a chilling reflection of our own self-destructive tendencies. We, too, had driven species to extinction, polluted our oceans with industrial waste, and ignored the warnings of our own scientists until the consequences became unavoidable. The Luminese ocean, a pristine world untouched by human intervention until our arrival, had become a mirror reflecting our own ecological sins. The discovery was not only scientifically significant but also profoundly unsettling. It forced us to confront our own role in the destruction of the environment—a role that, ironically, extended beyond Earth's boundaries.

Sarah Chen, whose connection to the "Whispers" grew stronger with each passing day, provided additional insights into the ecological crisis. She described visions of a cataclysmic event, a chain reaction triggered by the escalating environmental damage. The Whispers, she claimed, warned of a potential collapse of the entire underwater ecosystem, an event that would have devastating consequences for all inhabitants, including the Luminese and the human survivors. Her visions were not just warnings; they were glimpses into a possible future—a future we were actively shaping through our inaction and ignorance.

This realization forced a crucial shift in our priorities. The focus shifted from simply observing and documenting the environmental issues to actively seeking solutions. We worked closely with the Luminese scientists, sharing our knowledge of

Earth's environmental remediation techniques and adapting them to the unique conditions of their ocean. The task was immense, the challenges daunting. We were grappling with a problem that had festered for generations, a problem compounded by political tensions and technological limitations. Yet, the urgency of the situation spurred us on. We had witnessed the fragile beauty of this hidden world, the intricate dance of life in its depths. To stand idly by while it crumbled around us was unthinkable.

Our collective efforts were not without obstacles. The Abyssals remained enigmatic, their intentions unclear. The Cetea, fueled by greed and ambition, continued their destructive practices, oblivious or indifferent to the looming ecological disaster. We had to navigate a complex web of political alliances, forge fragile partnerships with the Luminese and the Abyssals, and challenge the power of the Cetea. It was a precarious balancing act, one that demanded diplomacy, cunning, and a profound understanding of the interconnectedness of life. The survival of the Luminese ocean— and perhaps even the future of humanity—rested on our ability to overcome these challenges. The whispers of impending doom became a constant reminder of the stakes involved, urging us to push our limits and strive for solutions. It was a battle not only for the survival of this hidden world but also a reflection of our own responsibility toward the planet we had left behind. The fate of two worlds, seemingly disparate yet intrinsically linked, hung precariously in the balance—a testament to the fragility of ecosystems and the profound consequences of our actions. Our journey into the depths had become a desperate race against time, a fight for survival that extended far beyond the confines of this hidden ocean and reached back to the very core of our own existence. The whispers echoed, a constant reminder that our actions, both past and present, had far-reaching consequences— consequences we could no longer afford to ignore.

The Luminese city, Avani, shimmered with a bioluminescent grace that belied the growing unease in our hearts. Dr. Thorne's grim pronouncements about the ocean's acidification hung heavy in the air, a constant reminder of the fragility of this hidden world. We'd established a tentative alliance with the Luminese, their advanced technology proving invaluable in our efforts to understand the Whispers and the ecological crisis unfolding around us. But the shadow of the Cetea loomed large, a constant threat to the precarious peace.

Our first direct encounter with the Cetea wasn't a planned expedition; it was an accident, a cruel twist of fate. We were mapping a previously unexplored section of the ocean floor, charting the extent of the acidification, when our submersible, the *Triton*, stumbled upon a Cetea mining operation. Giant, metallic claws, larger than any terrestrial mining equipment we'd ever seen, ripped through the seabed, leaving behind a trail of devastation. Coral formations were pulverized, the delicate ecosystems shattered, and clouds of sediment churned the once-clear water into a murky soup.

The *Triton's* sonar picked up several large, serpentine vessels— the Cetea's signature ships, sleek and menacing, their hulls reflecting the ambient light in an unsettling way. They were not merely mining; they were systematically stripping the ocean floor of its resources, leaving behind a barren wasteland. We watched, horrified, as bioluminescent creatures, usually vibrant and plentiful in this area, scattered in panicked flight, their ethereal glow briefly illuminating the destruction before vanishing into the gloom.

Captain Armstrong, his face grim, immediately ordered a silent retreat. Any direct confrontation would be suicidal. The Cetea's technology far surpassed ours. Their vessels were faster, more maneuverable, and armed with weapons we could only guess at. Our submersible, designed for scientific exploration, was no match for their war machines.

But as we tried to withdraw, a single Cetea vessel detached from the main group. It moved with unnerving speed, its metallic surface gleaming like polished obsidian. It pursued us relentlessly, its movements precise and predatory. The pursuit was a terrifying dance in the darkness, the *Triton's* lights casting fleeting shadows that played tricks on our senses.

The Cetea vessel didn't immediately attack. Instead, it shadowed us, its presence a chilling reminder of our vulnerability. We felt like prey, trapped in a vast, hostile ocean. The silence was broken only by the rhythmic hum of the *Triton's* engines and the faint, unsettling clicks and whistles emanating from the pursuing vessel—a kind of sonar, but far more sophisticated than anything we possessed.

Dr. Thorne, his face pale but determined, worked frantically at his consoles, trying to decipher the Cetea's communications. Their language was unlike anything we'd encountered before: a complex series of clicks, whistles, and low-frequency pulses. He suspected it was a form of bioacoustic communication, far more nuanced and efficient than human speech. The difficulty in decoding it underscored the technological gulf between us. Their technology was centuries, perhaps millennia, ahead of ours.

Hours stretched into what felt like an eternity. The pressure mounted with every passing moment. The relentless pursuit eroded our hope; our only solace lay in the faint glimmer of Avani, our refuge—still distant but a beacon of hope in this treacherous deep. We knew that if they chose to attack, it would be swift and devastating. The Triton's shielding was meant to withstand pressure, not direct weaponry.

Then, as suddenly as it had begun, the pursuit ended. The Cetea vessel abruptly broke off, disappearing into the darkness with unsettling speed. We were left alone—shaken but alive—to ponder the implications of our encounter. The silence returned, heavier and more ominous than before, a testament to the Cetea's power and their chilling indifference to our presence.

The incident had profound implications. It confirmed our worst fears: the Cetea were not just a rival faction; they were a force to be reckoned with. Their technological superiority, combined with their ruthless disregard for the environment, posed a grave threat to the entire underwater ecosystem—and by extension, to humanity's fragile hopes for a new beginning.

Our encounter also raised crucial questions about the nature of the Whispers. The Cetea's relentless mining activity seemed strangely focused, as if they were searching for something specific—something connected to the mysterious phenomenon that permeated this hidden world. Were the Whispers a source of power?

A technological marvel? Or something far more profound?

The immediate aftermath was a period of intense analysis and strategizing. We shared our findings with the Luminese, carefully weighing our words, trying to avoid provoking a larger conflict. The

Luminese, while peaceful, were not weak. They possessed a deep understanding of their world and their own unique technologies, but their approach was fundamentally different from the Cetea's aggressive, exploitative methods.

Captain Armstrong and Dr. Thorne engaged in tense discussions with the Luminese council, presenting the evidence of the Cetea's destructive activities and highlighting the potential for an ecological catastrophe. They stressed the urgent need for a unified front—an alliance between the Luminese and the human survivors to counter the Cetea's threat.

The Luminese, after a period of careful deliberation, agreed to cooperate, but their response was cautious and measured. Their history with the Cetea was long and complex—fraught with conflict and uneasy truces. They were wary of escalating the situation, understanding the immense power of their adversaries. Nevertheless, they agreed to provide us with intel, mapping data, and subtle technological assistance. It wasn't a full-blown alliance, but a crucial step toward a potential unified front against the looming danger.

Sarah Chen's connection to the Whispers became even more critical in this new context. Her ability to perceive and interpret the subtle energy shifts—the faint whispers that resonated through the ocean—offered a unique window into the Cetea's intentions and strategies. We realized that her role extended beyond that of a simple observer. She was becoming a key strategist, providing invaluable insights into the Cetea's movements and their enigmatic quest.

The days following our encounter were filled with a palpable sense of urgency. We knew that the Cetea's actions were not sustainable. Their reckless exploitation of the ocean's resources would eventually lead to a catastrophic collapse of the ecosystem, affecting everyone and everything in this hidden world. The peaceful coexistence we'd initially envisioned was being brutally challenged. The survival of this world—and perhaps even the fragile hope of a second chance for humanity—now hinged on our ability to understand and counter the power of the Cetea, a task that seemed daunting, almost impossible.

The whispers echoed—a constant reminder of the delicate balance hanging in the balance. The grim determination to protect the hidden world and its inhabitants filled our hearts and steeled our resolve. The fight had begun—a battle for survival in a breathtaking yet treacherous underwater realm, a world teetering on the brink of an ecological catastrophe.

CHAPTER 4

The shimmering bioluminescence of the Luminese city, once a source of wonder, now felt oppressive to Captain Armstrong. The initial euphoria of survival, the awe of a breathtaking alien world, had begun to crack under the strain of prolonged confinement and simmering resentments. Jian's sacrifice, while heroic, had exposed a fragility within the group, a vulnerability that went beyond the threats posed by the Abyssals or the Cetea. It was a vulnerability born of human nature itself: suspicion, self-interest, and the insidious erosion of trust.

The friction started subtly. Dr. Thorne, ever the meticulous scientist, chafed under Captain Armstrong's increasingly decisive— some would say dictatorial—leadership. His constant need for data, his insistence on methodical analysis, clashed with the Captain's pragmatic approach, born of years navigating the volatile currents of human conflict and survival at sea. Thorne's complaints, initially whispered to Sarah, began to leak into the wider group, poisoning the well of cooperation that had been so painstakingly built. He argued that Armstrong's decisions, while swift, lacked the long-term consideration necessary for navigating this complex, alien world. His words, carefully chosen but laced with thinly veiled criticism, found fertile ground among those who had lost loved ones or felt overlooked in the power dynamic.

Sarah, still grappling with her newfound ability to interpret the Whispers, became a focal point of contention. Her unique connection made her invaluable, but it also isolated her. The weight of the prophecies, the knowledge of impending threats, created a profound solitude that only deepened the growing schism. The others, struggling with their own anxieties and survival instincts, resented her privileged position, her almost mystical understanding of events they could barely comprehend. Whispers of her being a liability, a potential source of manipulation by the other factions, started circulating among the survivors. The quiet understanding, the mutual support that had been their lifeline, was unraveling thread by thread.

Rostova, typically a pillar of calm and competence, felt the strain. She had always been a leader who encouraged collaboration, believing in the strength of a united crew. Yet, witnessing the fracturing of her team, she found herself grappling with her own doubts and fears. The whispers of dissent were no longer confined to hushed conversations; they were seeping into the daily routine, creating an atmosphere of mistrust and suspicion. Simple tasks that once went without comment became fraught with passive-aggressive gestures and pointed remarks. The shared meals, initially a celebratory gathering, became strained affairs where every word, every glance, held a hidden meaning.

The tension culminated during a crucial mission to scavenge for vital resources in a treacherous, bioluminescent kelp forest. A disagreement over strategy, fueled by simmering resentments, nearly resulted in a catastrophic accident. Thorne's plan, cautious and methodical, clashed with Armstrong's more daring approach, which emphasized speed and efficiency. The heated argument, conducted amidst the swaying kelp and the eerie glow of the deep sea, revealed the depth of the divisions. Accusations flew, old grievances resurfaced, and the delicate balance of their uneasy alliance threatened to collapse entirely. Only Rostova's intervention, a forceful assertion of her authority, prevented a full-blown confrontation. But even her authority seemed to be weakening; a single crack in her command structure could trigger a full-scale implosion.

The incident highlighted the pressing need to resolve the internal conflicts. Rostova, realizing the gravity of the situation, called an emergency council. The atmosphere was heavy with unspoken tensions, the air thick with the scent of saltwater and the unspoken anxieties of survival. She attempted to mediate, to appeal to their shared experiences and their common goal of survival. But her words fell on deaf ears, or at least on ears selectively tuned to hear only what confirmed pre-existing biases. Thorne, fueled by a selfrighteous sense of scientific correctness, launched into a scathing critique of Armstrong's leadership, his words dripping with condescension. Others echoed his sentiments, each voicing their own grievances and suspicions.

The conflict was not merely about leadership styles or strategic differences. It reflected a deeper malaise, a fraying of the human spirit under the relentless pressure of their alien environment. The vastness and strangeness of this underwater world, the constant threat of the Abyssals and the Cetea, the ever-present weight of the Whispers—these were all contributing factors to the erosion of trust and camaraderie. Even the Luminese, once seen as allies, were now viewed with suspicion, their motivations questioned. A sense of paranoia began to engulf the survivors, each individual growing increasingly distrustful of the other.

The council ended in deadlock. Rostova's authority, though acknowledged, was not respected; her pleas for unity fell on stony ground. The underlying issue was not merely the lack of a unified approach but the failure of empathy, a failure to understand the burdens and fears of their fellow survivors. They were trapped not only in an alien world but also in the prison of their own emotional turmoil, their individual anxieties feeding the growing chasm between them.

The night following the council was a tense one. The onceshared quarters felt like separate islands of anxiety. The whispered conversations that had previously hinted at dissent now erupted into arguments, the harshness of the words reflecting the desperation born of isolation and mistrust. Each survivor retreated into their own shells, the sense of unity replaced by a haunting sense of impending doom that transcended the external threats posed by the Abyssals and the Cetea. The darkness of the deep ocean seemed to mirror the growing darkness within the human hearts, the bioluminescence offering only a fleeting glimpse of the beauty they were losing in their internal war.

The future seemed uncertain, not only from the threats lurking in the deep ocean trenches but also from within the fractured ranks of their own human fellowship. The idyllic image of survival together had crumbled, leaving behind a battleground of suspicion and self-preservation. The journey to discover the secrets of the Whispers had taken an unexpected and dangerous detour, into the shadowy depths of human nature itself. The once unified survivors were now fighting a silent, more insidious battle within their own ranks—a battle as fraught with danger as any confrontation with their formidable enemies.

The tremors that had shaken the Luminese city following Jian's desperate act still resonated deep within the ocean floor. The shimmering coral structures, normally vibrant with life, seemed dimmed, their bioluminescence a muted echo of the vibrant energy they once possessed. The silence that followed Jian's sacrifice was heavier than the crushing pressure of the deep ocean. It was a silence born of grief, of loss, and of the chilling realization of their own mortality in this alien world.

Dr. Thorne, usually a bastion of scientific composure, knelt beside the makeshift memorial—a cluster of phosphorescent Luminese flora arranged around a smooth, grey stone salvaged from a nearby reef. His fingers traced the intricate patterns on the stone, his gaze distant and haunted. The loss of Jian, a skilled engineer whose ingenuity had been crucial in their adaptation to this underwater world, was a blow they couldn't afford. His quiet competence, his unwavering loyalty, had become a stabilizing force in their fractured group. Now, a gaping hole remained, exposing the raw nerves of their fragile alliance.

Captain Armstrong, his face etched with a weariness that went beyond physical exhaustion, stood a few paces away, his arms crossed tightly over his chest. He hadn't spoken much since the incident. The weight of leadership, the burden of responsibility for these surviving souls, had become almost unbearable. Jian's sacrifice hadn't only taken a life; it had exposed the cracks in their collective strength, their shared vulnerability in the face of overwhelming odds. The initial relief at their escape from the surface world had been short-lived. They were survivors, yes, but now they were adrift in a sea of uncertainty, their ship damaged not only physically but also emotionally, their crew fractured by doubt and despair.

Sarah Chen, her eyes red-rimmed, approached Dr. Thorne. She had witnessed Jian's final moments—the selfless act that had saved her and several others from a collapsing section of the Luminese city. The memory burned in her mind, a testament to a courage that transcended the fear of death. Jian's connection to the Luminese, his uncanny understanding of their technology and culture, had already made him invaluable. His death felt like a betrayal, a cruel twist of fate that had snatched away a vital piece of their survival puzzle.

"He didn't have to," Sarah whispered, her voice choked with emotion. "He could have saved himself."

Dr. Thorne placed a comforting hand on her shoulder. "He chose to save others, Sarah. That's the measure of a man, of a truly selfless spirit." He paused, his gaze returning to the memorial. "His sacrifice revealed something else as well. It revealed our capacity for both great heroism and profound weakness."

The subsequent days were spent in a somber routine. The Luminese, normally welcoming and inquisitive, seemed subdued, their vibrant energy replaced by a quiet respect for the fallen human. They offered their condolences in their own way—intricate patterns of bioluminescence flickering across their bodies in a silent, elegant display of mourning. The human survivors, however, struggled to find solace in the Luminese rituals. The weight of guilt, the lingering sense of what could have been, cast a long shadow over their actions.

Captain Armstrong, wrestling with his own grief and the growing internal conflict within his group, organized a memorial service. It was a simple ceremony, lacking the grandeur of human traditions, yet imbued with a quiet dignity. They spoke of Jian's unwavering optimism, his calm demeanor in the face of danger, his infectious laughter that had once filled their cramped quarters. They spoke of his quiet courage, his selfless dedication. But even these words of remembrance couldn't fully bridge the chasm that had opened between them.

The whispers of suspicion, previously veiled, now grew louder.

Accusations, veiled in sorrow, were exchanged in hushed tones. Some questioned Jian's motives, suggesting that his actions were somehow a calculated move, a manipulation born of desperation. Others, consumed by their own anxieties, retreated into themselves, leaving a growing void of distrust within the already fractured group. The very fabric of their fragile alliance was unraveling, threatened not only by the external dangers lurking in the ocean depths but also by the corrosive power of internal conflict.

The incident with Jian had revealed a darker truth. Their shared experience, their common goal of survival, had not been enough to forge an unbreakable bond. Human nature, with its capacity for both profound altruism and ruthless self-preservation, had reared its head, threatening to undermine their chances of survival. The external threats posed by the Abyssals and the Cetea paled in comparison to the insidious threat of their own internal divisions.

Dr. Thorne, ever the scientist, found himself increasingly disturbed by this internal erosion. He began to see a parallel between their situation and the fragility of the underwater ecosystems surrounding them. The delicate balance of life, so easily disrupted by even minor changes, mirrored the fragility of their human relationships. The ocean, a world of stunning beauty and terrifying power, had become a microcosm of their own struggles—a place where the seemingly invincible could be brought low, where the most profound acts of kindness could be overshadowed by the insidious poison of suspicion.

The whispers of the ancient prophecies, once a source of hope, now seemed filled with foreboding. The ancient texts spoke of a time of great upheaval, a time when the balance of power would shift, when the very foundations of the underwater world would be tested. And now, their own internal struggles mirrored that impending cataclysm, threatening to bring about their downfall before they even understood the true nature of the "Whispers."

Sarah, grappling with her guilt and the weight of Jian's sacrifice, delved deeper into the Luminese archives. She discovered passages in the ancient texts that alluded to similar internal conflicts within the Luminese civilization—moments when the delicate balance of their society had been threatened from within. They had overcome those challenges, but only after enduring a period of profound upheaval and loss.

Her research unveiled a pattern, a recurring cycle of harmony and discord within the Luminese culture, mirroring the rise and fall of civilizations throughout history. The "Whispers" themselves seemed tied to this cycle, amplifying both the positive and negative aspects of societal interactions. The greater the harmony, the stronger the whispers, guiding the Luminese toward a path of progress and understanding. But the greater the internal discord, the more chaotic and unpredictable the whispers became, leading to uncertainty and conflict.

This discovery provided a crucial insight. Their internal conflicts were not just a human weakness; they were a reflection of a universal truth, a pattern embedded in the very fabric of existence. Overcoming this internal turmoil would not be a simple matter of patching up differences. It required a fundamental shift in perspective, a conscious effort to understand and transcend the limitations of human nature. It required them to embrace the interconnectedness of their lives, recognizing their interdependence in this alien world.

The journey toward survival had taken an unexpected turn. It was no longer just a matter of battling external threats. They had to confront an even greater threat within themselves—the deep-seated insecurities, the lingering distrust, and the insidious poison of suspicion. Jian's sacrifice, while a profound act of heroism, had also laid bare the vulnerabilities that threatened their existence. The path to survival, to unlocking the secrets of the "Whispers," and ultimately to returning to the surface world, lay in their ability to heal the wounds inflicted by their internal conflict, rebuild the broken trust, and forge a stronger, more unified front against the forces that threatened to consume them, both from within and without. The future hung in the balance, not just from the menacing shadows in the deep sea, but from the even more perilous currents within their human hearts. The weight of survival now rested on their ability to harness not only their scientific knowledge but also their capacity for empathy, understanding, and forgiveness.

The tremors subsided, leaving behind an unsettling stillness. The Luminese, normally so expressive in their fluid movements and shimmering bioluminescence, were withdrawn, their usually vibrant city cloaked in an almost somber light. Their intricate coral structures, usually pulsating with a gentle, internal light, seemed to have dimmed, reflecting the collective grief that hung heavy in the water. Elder Lyra, her usually radiant skin subdued, approached Captain Rostova. Her normally melodic voice was low, tinged with a sorrow that transcended language.

Through a combination of gestures, carefully chosen Luminese words, and Dr. Thorne's increasingly proficient translation, the extent of Jian's sacrifice was conveyed. The Luminese had witnessed the act, not as a barbaric display of violence, but as a selfless offering, a profound act of courage and sacrifice that went beyond their comprehension. Their technology, capable of translating the most complex biological and chemical signals, struggled to grasp the human concept of selfless altruism. Jian's act transcended the simple exchange of energy; it was a testament to the human spirit's capacity for love, loyalty, and selflessness.

Lyra explained, her voice laced with awe and respect, that Jian's life energy, rather than dissipating, had interwoven itself with the city's life support system. The energy wasn't merely absorbed; it had become a part of the intricate network that sustained the Luminese civilization. The dimming of the bioluminescence wasn't a sign of decline, but a temporary adjustment, a period of integration. Jian's energy, they explained, was recalibrating the city's bio-energetic field. It was a process of healing and adaptation, a subtle yet powerful transformation.

The Luminese's response wasn't merely emotional; it was deeply scientific. Teams of Luminese scientists, with their graceful, almost ethereal movements, began meticulously studying the changes in the city's energy grid. Their technology, far beyond anything on Earth, revealed a complex interplay of Jian's cellular energy and the city's own bio-luminescent structures. They discovered that Jian's sacrifice had inadvertently triggered a dormant mechanism within the city itself—a powerful, selfrepairing system that hadn't been activated in centuries. It was a symbiotic relationship, the human's sacrifice acting as the catalyst for the city's rejuvenation.

This scientific marvel, however, didn't diminish the sorrow felt by the Luminese. They had witnessed Jian's courage, his selfless act of protecting others. They had felt the impact of his sacrifice, not only on their city but on their understanding of life itself. Their relationship with the survivors shifted from one of cautious observation to one of profound respect and shared sorrow. The Luminese, in their grief, displayed a depth of empathy that transcended their advanced technology and their otherworldly existence. They mourned Jian, not as a stranger, but as someone who had become intricately linked to their very being.

The days that followed were filled with quiet contemplation. The survivors, overwhelmed by grief, found solace in the unexpected empathy of the Luminese. The Luminese, accustomed to life cycles that spanned centuries, possessed a perspective on mortality that was both humbling and strangely comforting. They offered their help in understanding the implications of Jian's sacrifice.

Dr. Thorne, though devastated by the loss of his friend, dedicated himself to comprehending the scientific ramifications of this extraordinary event. He worked alongside the Luminese scientists, analyzing the changes in the city's energy grid and the interaction between Jian's cellular structure and the city's bioenergetic field. Their collaborative efforts yielded astonishing insights into bio-energetic interconnectivity and the potential of symbiotic relationships between vastly different life forms. They began to unravel the secrets of the "Whispers," discovering that Jian's sacrifice had somehow amplified the subtle signals emanating from the deep ocean trench, providing them with clearer access to these mysterious communications. Jian's energy, it seemed, hadn't just enhanced the city's vitality; it had created a bridge, a conduit to a previously inaccessible level of information.

Captain Rostova, meanwhile, sought to reconcile the grief and the renewed hope. She focused on unifying the human survivors, addressing the internal tensions that had been exacerbated by Jian's sacrifice. She organized a memorial service, a poignant blend of human rituals and Luminese expressions of respect. The Luminese participated with reverence, demonstrating a profound understanding of loss and the importance of communal mourning. The ceremony served not only to honor Jian's memory but also to reinforce the bonds between the human survivors and their alien hosts.

Sarah Chen, who had felt a unique connection to the "Whispers" from the beginning, experienced an intensification of these signals following Jian's sacrifice. The "Whispers," previously vague and elusive, became clearer, offering more intricate insights into the ancient prophecies and the nature of the underwater world. Her connection to the "Whispers" had deepened, making her an invaluable asset in deciphering the ancient texts and understanding the intricate web of relationships between the various factions inhabiting this hidden realm. She began to see patterns, connections, and a deeper understanding of the ancient prophecies.

The Abyssals, sensing the shift in power and the enhanced connection to the "Whispers," became more active, their shadowy movements more frequent. Their interest in the human survivors, particularly in Sarah's connection to the "Whispers," was palpable.

The Luminese, however, were now more determined than ever to protect the survivors, having witnessed firsthand the strength and resilience of the human spirit. The alliance between the humans and the Luminese strengthened, forged in the crucible of shared loss and a shared understanding of a greater threat. The Luminese, always a peaceful civilization, showed their resolve, understanding that their future, and perhaps the fate of the entire underwater world, now rested upon their ability to protect the source of this newfound power and information.

The Cetea, known for their ruthlessness, sensed the potential for exploitation. They understood that the "Whispers" held the key to unimaginable power, and they wouldn't hesitate to use force to obtain it. Their attacks became more sophisticated, more targeted, utilizing their advanced aquatic technology to penetrate the Luminese defenses. The survivors found themselves in the midst of a strategic struggle, caught between the peaceful resolve of the Luminese and the relentless ambition of the Cetea. They knew that their survival, and the future of the underwater world, depended on their ability to navigate this dangerous new alliance, leverage their scientific knowledge, and understand the profound implications of Jian's sacrifice.

The underwater world, once a marvel of discovery, had become a battleground. The shimmering coral cities, once symbols of peace and tranquility, now stood as sentinels against the looming threat. The "Whispers," once an enigma, had become a source of both hope and danger. Jian's sacrifice, while profoundly sad, had unexpectedly unlocked a new chapter, a new understanding, and a new battle in this strange, beautiful, and dangerous underwater realm. The path ahead was fraught with peril, but the survivors, empowered by their alliance with the Luminese and guided by the intensified

"Whispers," prepared themselves for the challenges to come, carrying the weight of Jian's memory and the legacy of his selfless act. The fight for survival was far from over, but the sacrifice had inadvertently strengthened their resolve and offered a crucial advantage in the upcoming war for the future of this hidden world. The echoes of Jian's sacrifice resonated not just in the city's dimmed light but in the hearts of the survivors, a reminder of their shared destiny and the profound interconnectedness of all life, even across the vast chasm between human and Luminese understanding.

The aftermath of Jian's sacrifice hung heavy, a palpable silence replacing the usual vibrant hum of the Luminese city. The dimming of the bioluminescent coral, a reflection of their collective grief, served as a stark reminder of the fragility of their newfound peace. But even in mourning, the whispers persisted, a subtle hum beneath the surface, growing stronger, more insistent. It was as if the very ocean itself was urging them forward, whispering of impending battles and shifting alliances.

Elder Lyra, her normally radiant skin pale, approached Captain Rostova with strange urgency in her movements. "The tremors... they weren't natural," she communicated, her voice a low, resonant hum that vibrated within Rostova's chest. "The Abyssals... they've amplified the Whispers. They're using them, twisting them for their own purposes."

The Abyssals, previously an enigma, now emerged as a far more sinister threat. Their shadowy presence, once confined to the deepest trenches, was now felt throughout the underwater world. They were masters of the deep, creatures of immense power, their bodies adapted to the crushing pressures and eternal darkness of the abyss. Their motives, however, remained shrouded in mystery. Were they seeking to control the Whispers for power, or was there a more profound reason for their actions?

The revelation sent a ripple of fear through the survivors. The Luminese, with their peaceful nature, were ill-equipped for open warfare. The Cetea, on the other hand, were already a known enemy, their ruthless ambition fueled by a hunger for conquest and control. But the Abyssals were different, their motivations unclear, their methods unknown. This new enemy brought an unsettling uncertainty to the already precarious situation.

Dr. Thorne, ever the pragmatist, immediately began analyzing the data collected from the seismic readings. The tremors weren't random; they were concentrated near specific locations, points of immense energy where the Whispers were particularly strong. The Abyssals were systematically targeting these points, using the Whispers as a weapon. It wasn't a brute force attack; it was a subtle manipulation, a calculated unraveling of the delicate balance that held the underwater world together.

Sarah Chen, whose unique connection to the Whispers was now stronger than ever, felt the shift in their energy. They were no longer a soothing harmony; they were fractured, twisted, imbued with a dark energy that resonated with a deep, unsettling fear. She saw visions—fleeting glimpses of immense, shadowy creatures manipulating the very fabric of the ocean currents, harnessing the power of the Whispers to bend the underwater world to their will.

Amidst the growing fear and uncertainty, an unexpected alliance began to form. The Cetea, notorious for their ruthlessness, approached Captain Rostova with a proposal. Their leader, a hulking creature named Kraken, communicated through a series of clicks and bioluminescent flashes, his intentions surprisingly clear despite the communication difficulties. They, too, feared the Abyssals, recognizing their potential to destabilize the entire underwater ecosystem. Their common enemy, for the moment, overshadowed their differences. A temporary truce, a fragile alliance born from mutual fear and the desire for survival.

This newfound partnership, however precarious, gave them a crucial advantage. The Cetea, despite their brutality, possessed advanced underwater technology and a ruthless efficiency in combat. Their knowledge of the abyssal trenches and their strategic capabilities proved invaluable in tracking Abyssal activity. They shared information about specific locations where the Abyssals were actively manipulating the Whispers, allowing the Luminese and the human survivors to formulate a plan.

The plan was audacious, bordering on suicidal. It involved infiltrating the Abyssal territory, a place of perpetual darkness and crushing pressure, a realm where even the most advanced technology struggled to operate. Sarah, with her heightened connection to the Whispers, would act as a guide, her ability to sense their disruptions crucial for navigating the treacherous terrain. Captain Rostova, with her experience in underwater combat and strategic planning, would lead the attack. Dr. Thorne, always resourceful, would design specialized equipment capable of withstanding the extreme pressure and darkness of the abyss.

The Luminese, despite their aversion to violence, played a crucial role. Their advanced bioluminescent technology provided a beacon in the pitch-black darkness, enabling them to illuminate pathways and disorient the Abyssals. Their understanding of underwater currents allowed them to manipulate the flow of water, hindering the Abyssals' movements and creating tactical advantages.

The journey into the abyss was fraught with peril. Creatures, adapted to the extreme conditions, lurked in the shadows, their bioluminescent lures masking their predatory instincts. The pressure, intense and relentless, threatened to crush their submersibles, and the complete absence of light created a sense of disorientation and claustrophobia.

Sarah's connection to the Whispers proved essential. She sensed the subtle disturbances in the ocean currents, the vibrations caused by the Abyssals' activities, guiding them toward their target. The Abyssals' methods were sophisticated; they weren't simply using brute force. They were manipulating the delicate balance of the underwater ecosystem, using the Whispers to cause chaos and ultimately seize control. They were harnessing the power of the deep, bending it to their will, and their influence seemed to spread like a plague, infecting the very essence of the Whispers themselves.

The battle that ensued was unlike anything they had ever experienced. It wasn't a straightforward fight; it was a war waged in the darkest depths, a battle against the very essence of chaos and darkness. The Luminese's bioluminescent technology illuminated the darkness, creating momentary flashes of blinding light that disoriented the Abyssals. The Cetea's ruthlessly efficient tactics disrupted the Abyssals' plans, preventing them from further manipulating the Whispers. And Sarah, guided by her connection to the ocean's whispers, directed the human and Luminese forces, her insights proving crucial in their strategic countermeasures.

The battle was long and arduous, a test of endurance, resilience, and courage. They faced creatures beyond imagination, beings of immense power and terrifying intelligence. But in the end, fueled by Jian's sacrifice, driven by the shared hope for survival, and united by an unlikely alliance, they managed to push back against the darkness. They didn't destroy the Abyssals; they disrupted their plans, buying themselves time. The victory was pyrrhic; they sustained heavy losses, but they had averted a cataclysm.

Emerging from the abyss, battered but not broken, they returned to the Luminese city, carrying with them the weight of their victory and the haunting memory of their encounter with the terrifying power of the deep. The shifting alliances, the fragile truce, the nearcatastrophic battle—all underscored the ever-changing dynamics of the underwater world.

Their victory was temporary, a respite before the next battle. The Abyssals were not defeated, only subdued, their true motives still shrouded in mystery. The whispers still hummed, a constant reminder of the fragile balance of power and the everpresent threat lurking in the depths. The future remained uncertain, the fight for survival far from over. The journey, fraught with peril and loss, continued, their destination still far beyond the horizon.

The Luminese, still reeling from Jian's sacrifice, offered a somber welcome. Their city, usually a kaleidoscope of shifting bioluminescent light, felt muted. The vibrant hues were dimmed, as if mirroring their collective sorrow. Yet, amidst the quiet grief, a sense of urgency pulsed beneath the surface. The Whispers, those enigmatic hums that had guided them before, were growing stronger, more insistent, drawing them toward the ancient ruins that lay beyond the city's shimmering coral reefs.

Dr. Thorne, ever the pragmatist, saw the opportunity amidst the despair. "The Whispers... they're not just warnings," he stated, his voice low, almost reverent. "They're a roadmap. A key to understanding this world, and perhaps... our own." His eyes, usually twinkling with scientific curiosity, were now filled with a determined glint. He'd spent countless hours poring over the

Luminese's archaic texts, deciphering their intricate symbols and translating their whispered stories of a time before the separation of worlds.

Their journey took them through a labyrinth of underwater canyons, the walls adorned with phosphorescent flora that pulsed with an ethereal glow. Schools of bioluminescent fish, their scales shimmering like scattered stars, darted past, creating fleeting patterns of light and shadow. The ocean floor, usually teeming with life, felt strangely desolate in places, scarred by ancient battles— remnants of a war fought long ago between the Luminese, the Abyssals, and the Cetea.

The ruins themselves were breathtaking—colossal structures of a material unknown to them, sculpted into forms that defied earthly architecture. Giant arches, etched with intricate carvings, soared toward the surface, framing a view of the strange, altered sky above. The city, once a testament to an advanced civilization, now lay partially submerged, swallowed by the sea yet somehow preserved, almost frozen in time. The architecture blended seamlessly with the natural environment, suggesting a level of technological harmony far beyond human capabilities.

Inside the ruins, they discovered chambers filled with holographic projections, displaying scenes from a distant past. The projections depicted a unified world, where the surface and the underwater kingdoms existed in harmony, connected by a powerful energy source—the source of the Whispers. They learned of a cataclysmic event, a great upheaval that severed the connection between worlds, plunging both into chaos and separating the Luminese from their surface counterparts.

This event, according to the projections, was not a natural disaster but a deliberate act—a calculated destruction orchestrated by a faction seeking to control the Whispers' power for their own nefarious purposes, a faction that bore a striking resemblance to the Abyssals.

Sarah Chen, whose unique sensitivity to the Whispers had been instrumental in their previous successes, found herself drawn to a central chamber—a massive circular structure pulsating with an otherworldly energy. As she approached, the Whispers intensified, resonating deeply within her. Images flooded her mind—visions of a vast, interconnected network of energy flowing between the two worlds, a network disrupted, fractured, and now desperately seeking to reconnect.

The projections showed that the Whispers were not merely a source of energy; they were a form of communication—a sentient network connecting all life in both worlds. The cataclysm had not only severed this connection but had also severely damaged the delicate balance of both ecosystems. The surface world, as they now understood, had suffered from environmental collapse in the wake of the separation, mirroring the underwater world's own instability.

The ruins revealed a hidden technology—an intricate system of energy conduits that once harnessed the power of the Whispers.

The Luminese, in their peaceful existence, had lost the knowledge to reactivate this system, their technology having become largely organic and symbiotic with their environment. But the Abyssals, driven by greed and a thirst for power, sought to reclaim this technology—to weaponize the Whispers and dominate both worlds.

Captain Rostova, ever practical, saw the immediate implications. "If the Abyssals gain control of the Whispers," she said grimly, her voice carrying the weight of a thousand battles, "it won't just be an underwater conflict anymore. The surface will be at risk too." The reality of the situation hit them with the force of a tidal wave. Their fight for survival was no longer limited to this hidden world; it was a fight for the survival of both.

Thorne, poring over the recovered data, discovered clues hinting at a way to restore the connection between the two worlds—a way to heal the fractured network of the Whispers. It required an intricate process, involving the precise manipulation of the ancient energy conduits, a feat that demanded both advanced technological knowledge and a deep understanding of the Whispers' nature.

The task fell upon them—a ragtag team of survivors from a crashed plane, now thrust into the role of saviors of two worlds. They faced insurmountable odds, a technologically superior enemy, and a dwindling supply of hope. Yet, the knowledge gained from the ruins, the shared sorrow, and the unwavering bond forged in the face of adversity gave them the strength to continue.

The knowledge also revealed a chilling prophecy—a prophecy detailing the "Great Convergence," a moment when the Whispers would reach their peak power, capable of either healing both worlds or obliterating them entirely, depending on who controlled it. This

Convergence was fast approaching, adding a new layer of urgency to their mission.

They spent the following days meticulously studying the ancient texts, deciphering intricate diagrams, and experimenting with the recovered technology. They worked tirelessly, their hands blistered, their minds strained, fueled by a mixture of fear and determination. The Luminese, despite their grief, offered unwavering support, sharing their knowledge of the ocean's currents, the Whispers' patterns, and their own unique bioluminescent technologies that assisted them. The collective knowledge of two different species began to combine, forging new solutions and a renewed understanding of the delicate balance of nature.

The journey was not without its challenges. Subtle acts of sabotage hinted at the Abyssals' persistent presence, their spies infiltrating the Luminese city, sowing seeds of discord and uncertainty. They faced ambushes, near-miss encounters, and moments of despair, but the shared purpose, the weight of their responsibility, kept them going. They were not just fighting for survival; they were fighting to restore balance, to heal a broken world, and to fulfill a prophecy that could rewrite the fate of two worlds.

As the Great Convergence neared, the Whispers intensified, their hum vibrating through the very fabric of the ocean. The once serene underwater city pulsed with anticipation, a blend of fear and hope echoing in the hearts of all its inhabitants. Their journey had been fraught with betrayal, sacrifice, and the harrowing discovery of ancient secrets. But amidst the darkness, a flicker of hope remained—the hope of restoration, of healing, and of a future where the surface and underwater worlds could once again exist in harmony, connected by the powerful, life-giving hum of the Whispers.

The path ahead was uncertain, but for the first time, they were not merely reacting to events; they were proactively shaping their destiny, and the destiny of two worlds hanging in the balance. The fight had just begun, and the stakes were higher than ever.

CHAPTER 5

The Luminese, with their ethereal glow and serene demeanor, had initially presented the Whispers as both a source of power and prophecy, a force woven into the very fabric of their existence. However, understanding their true nature proved far more complex than simply deciphering ancient texts or observing their effects on Luminese society. Dr. Thorne, ever the scientist, pressed for a deeper understanding, seeking to move beyond the mystical interpretations and delve into the scientific mechanisms driving this enigmatic phenomenon.

Sarah Chen, with her unique sensitivity to the Whispers, became instrumental in this endeavor. Her ability wasn't simply about hearing or seeing; it was a visceral connection, a feeling that pulsed through her, mirroring the rhythms of the ocean itself. She described it as an overwhelming symphony of information, a torrent of data that was both beautiful and terrifying in its immensity. She could sense the ebb and flow of the Whispers' energy, its surges and lulls, almost as if it were a living entity breathing beneath the waves. Through carefully guided sessions with Dr. Thorne, she began to articulate patterns, map the fluctuating energy signatures, and translate them into a series of complex waveforms that the scientists could begin to analyze.

Thorne's team, a mix of Luminese scientists and human survivors, painstakingly collected data. They meticulously charted the Whispers' influence on the Luminese's technology, noting how their bioluminescent cities flickered and pulsed in response to the underlying currents of energy. They also studied the effects on marine life, observing subtle shifts in behavior, migratory patterns, and even the growth rates of certain species. The Whispers weren't merely a source of power; they seemed to be a fundamental component of the underwater ecosystem, influencing everything from the smallest microbe to the largest whale.

The data revealed surprising correlations. The Whispers' energy signature directly impacted the bioluminescent properties of the flora and fauna, causing shifts in color and intensity. They discovered that the Luminese's advanced technology, powered by a symbiotic relationship with the Whispers, was not merely harnessing the energy but actively interacting with it, creating a feedback loop that shaped and maintained the delicate balance of the entire ecosystem. This symbiotic relationship, however, was delicate. A disruption in the Whispers' flow, even a slight imbalance, could have catastrophic consequences.

CHAPTER 5
PART 2

This realization led to a deeper understanding of the Abyssals and Cetea. The Abyssals, dwelling in the deepest trenches, seemed intrinsically linked to a more primal, older aspect of the Whispers. Their technology, far more rudimentary than the Luminese's, appeared to be based on a direct, almost parasitic relationship with the Whispers' energy, exploiting it without understanding its intricacies. This stood in stark contrast to the Luminese, who had developed a sustainable and symbiotic partnership over centuries.

The Cetea, on the other hand, were driven by greed. They sought to control the Whispers' power, not for symbiosis or survival, but for domination, treating it as a weapon to be wielded against any who stood in their path. Their reckless attempts to manipulate this potent force threatened to unravel the entire ecosystem.

As the scientists pieced together the puzzle, a chilling possibility emerged. The Whispers weren't limited to the underwater world; they extended to the surface, subtly influencing Earth's climate and geological activity. The devastating changes observed on Earth after the survivors' arrival were not mere coincidence. The disruption of the underwater ecosystem, caused by the Cetea's actions, had sent ripple effects across the globe. The plane crash, the emergence of the underwater world—these weren't isolated incidents but pieces of a larger puzzle, all linked through the all-encompassing influence of the Whispers.

The ethical dilemma became starkly apparent. The Whispers held immense power, capable of both creation and destruction. Controlling this power offered the potential to restore the damaged Earth and heal the underwater ecosystem, but it also presented an immense temptation—a path to ultimate control with the potential for catastrophic misuse. The survivors found themselves at a precipice, burdened with the weight of this knowledge, facing a choice with global ramifications.

CHAPTER 5

PART 3

Sarah, her connection to the Whispers deepening, began experiencing vivid visions. These weren't mere prophetic glimpses into the future; they were intricate, multi-layered realities illustrating potential outcomes based on the choices they made. She saw scenarios of ecological devastation, societies collapsing under the weight of unchecked power, but also glimpses of a restored Earth—a world healed and unified through a harmonious understanding of the Whispers. Her ability to navigate these visions and interpret the subtle nuances of the Whispers' energy became essential to their strategy.

Captain Rostova, initially focused on survival, had to confront the immense responsibility that came with this new understanding. She had to balance the needs of the survivors with the fate of two worlds, making decisions that weighed heavily on her conscience. The weight of knowledge was a burden, but one they had to bear. The future of both worlds rested on their ability to understand and responsibly manage the Whispers' power. The seemingly simple task of understanding the Whispers' power had unfolded into a complex web of ecological interdependence, societal structures, and moral dilemmas. The team had to decipher not only the scientific principles behind the Whispers but also the ethical considerations of wielding such a potent force.

The task demanded a shift in perspective. The human survivors, accustomed to Earth's anthropocentric worldview, had to learn to respect the intrinsic value of the underwater ecosystem and its inhabitants. They had to understand the intricate web of relationships that sustained this vibrant world, recognizing the devastating consequences of disruption. This required humility—a willingness to acknowledge their limitations and to learn from the Luminese's wisdom, accumulated over centuries of coexistence with the Whispers.

The Luminese, initially hesitant to share their knowledge, began to trust the survivors, recognizing their genuine desire to understand and protect the underwater world. They shared ancient texts, revealing the history of their interaction with the Whispers, the lessons learned from past mistakes, and the strategies they had developed to maintain a harmonious balance. This sharing wasn't just about transferring information; it was about building bridges of trust and cooperation, acknowledging the interconnectedness of life across the two worlds.

The challenge was not merely scientific but also philosophical. The ability to control the Whispers wasn't just about mastering technology; it was about mastering oneself. It was about overcoming greed, ambition, and the innate human tendency to dominate. The survivors had to learn to respect the intrinsic value of the environment, recognizing that true power lay not in control but in understanding and harmony. The path forward lay not in conquering the Whispers, but in learning to coexist—to become part of the intricate dance of life that the Whispers themselves orchestrated. Their journey had taken a profound turn, transforming from a simple survival story into a quest for ecological balance and a struggle for responsible stewardship of immense power. The fate of two worlds hung in the balance, dependent on the wisdom and choices of those who now held the weight of knowledge.

The Luminese's understanding of the Whispers extended far beyond their immediate environment. Elder Lyra, a woman whose age seemed to defy the passage of time, spoke of a resonance—a subtle vibration that connected their underwater world to the surface. She described it not as a physical link, like a tunnel or a portal, but as a more fundamental interconnectedness—a symphony of energy that hummed through the planet's core, binding all life together. This resonated deeply with Dr. Thorne's scientific intuition. He hypothesized that the Whispers might be a form of planetary bio-electromagnetic field—an intricate network of energy flows influencing everything from tectonic activity to the very patterns of ocean currents. This field, he proposed, wasn't simply an environmental phenomenon; it was a living system, responding to and shaping the actions of all organisms within its sphere of influence.

Sarah Chen's unique sensitivity to the Whispers offered a critical window into this interconnectedness. Her dreams, initially filled with fragmented images and dissonant sounds, began to coalesce into a coherent narrative. She saw visions of the surface world—ravaged landscapes, polluted oceans, the skeletal remains of dead cities. These weren't just arbitrary images; they were interconnected to the health of the underwater world. As the surface world choked under the weight of its own pollution, the Whispers grew weaker, their subtle influence on the underwater ecosystems diminishing. The

Luminese, deeply reliant on the Whispers' harmonious rhythms, felt this weakening as a growing disharmony in their own environment. Their bioluminescence dimmed, their coral cities showed signs of stress, and even their usually placid demeanor seemed tinged with anxiety.

Captain Armstrong, ever the pragmatist, saw the immediate implications. If the surface world's destruction mirrored the decline of the underwater realm, then their survival was inextricably linked. This wasn't just about rescuing a few survivors from a plane crash; it was about forging a symbiotic relationship between two worlds teetering on the brink of collapse. He began to organize a detailed study of the relationship between the Whispers and the global ecosystems. They started with the obvious—analyzing ocean currents, measuring water temperature and salinity gradients, and mapping the distribution of bioluminescent organisms. But it quickly became clear that the Whispers weren't simply affecting the physical environment. They seemed to influence the behavior of marine life in ways that were far more complex than any known biological mechanism.

Dr. Thorne's research suggested a possible explanation. He theorized that the Whispers emitted subtle electromagnetic signals that influenced the behavior of organisms on a cellular level. These signals weren't merely controlling behavior, but coordinating it—creating intricate patterns of interaction across vast ecosystems. The Whispers acted as a planetary nervous system, regulating the flow of energy and nutrients, ensuring the stability of the entire biosphere. His observations aligned with Sarah's visions, showing how disturbances on the surface world—deforestation, climate change, industrial pollution—created ripples that echoed through the Whispers, destabilizing the underwater ecosystem. A rise in ocean acidity, a consequence of surface pollution, was mirrored by a decline in the coral reefs, while massive oil spills led to a drop in bioluminescence across vast swathes of the ocean floor.

The Abyssals, a reclusive species dwelling in the deepest trenches, held a piece of the puzzle. Their ancient knowledge, passed down through generations, spoke of a time before the separation—a time when the surface and underwater worlds were one, seamlessly integrated. The Abyssals regarded the Whispers as a sacred entity, a vital force that had been weakened by the surface world's actions. Their ancient prophecies hinted at a coming convergence—a point where the fate of both worlds would be determined. The Cetea, however, possessed a far more antagonistic view. They viewed the Whispers as a source of power to be exploited—a tool to enhance their dominance over the underwater realm. Their ambition threatened to disrupt the delicate balance, potentially causing catastrophic consequences for both worlds.

The survivors found themselves caught in the middle of this conflict, their own fate intertwined with the survival of two vastly different civilizations. They had to find a way to bridge the gap between scientific understanding and ancient prophecy—translating the language of physics and biology into a shared understanding of ecological responsibility. This wasn't a battle to be won, but a delicate dance to be mastered. They had to learn to listen to the whispers of the planet, to understand the intricate network of life that bound them together.

One evening, while exploring a vast, bioluminescent kelp forest, Sarah experienced a powerful surge of energy from the Whispers. The images in her visions intensified, showing not only the devastation of the surface world but also the intricate web of life that connected it to the underwater realm. She saw how the deforestation of rainforests led to erosion, impacting ocean currents, affecting plankton blooms, and ultimately harming the coral reefs. She saw how the industrial dumping of toxic chemicals poisoned the oceans, leading to the death of marine animals and affecting the delicate balance of the underwater ecosystem. This interconnectedness was undeniable. The act of poisoning one part of the system inevitably resulted in the poisoning of the whole.

This vision clarified the dire consequences of the Cetea's actions. Their reckless pursuit of power, fueled by their desire to control the Whispers, could destabilize the entire planetary system. The catastrophic consequences could include devastating earthquakes, volcanic eruptions, and tsunamis, affecting both the surface and the underwater worlds. The survivors realized that their primary goal wasn't just survival, but the preservation of this vital planetary system. They needed to convince both the Luminese and the Abyssals to work together, to find a way to heal the wounds caused by surface-world pollution, and to resist the Cetea's destructive ambitions.

Captain Armstrong, drawing on his experience as a seasoned naval officer, developed a strategy that combined diplomacy and strength. They would use their knowledge of the Whispers, combined with their understanding of the Cetea's weaknesses, to neutralize their threat. This involved forging a stronger alliance with the Luminese and the Abyssals, combining their respective strengths—the Luminese's technological prowess and the Abyssals' ancient wisdom. It was a long shot, but it was their only hope. They had to act fast; the Whispers were weakening, and with it, the stability of both worlds. The fate of two civilizations rested on their ability to learn from the past, understand the present, and work together for a future where the interconnectedness of all life was not just recognized but revered and protected. The weight of this knowledge, and the responsibility it implied, settled heavily on their shoulders.

The journey had taken them beyond the simple survival of a few survivors; it had become a fight for the survival of two worlds, a testament to the profound interconnectedness of life on this planet, a life that pulsed with a rhythm as subtle and powerful as the Whispers themselves. The fight for survival had become a fight for balance, and the weight of that knowledge threatened to crush them unless they could find a way to share it and act accordingly.

The discovery that the Whispers were not merely a phenomenon but a powerful, living energy field, capable of influencing both the underwater world and the surface, threw the survivors into a maelstrom of ethical dilemmas. Dr. Thorne, ever the scientist, saw the Whispers as a potential source of unimaginable energy—a clean, limitless power source that could solve the Earth's energy crisis, a crisis exacerbated by the cataclysmic events that had preceded their arrival in this underwater world. He envisioned a future where humanity could harness the Whispers' energy, ushering in an era of sustainable technology and unprecedented prosperity. The prospect was tantalizing, almost intoxicating. He could see the potential for healing the damage inflicted on Earth's ecosystems, a possibility that filled him with a sense of both excitement and immense responsibility.

However, Captain Armstrong, seasoned in the realities of power dynamics and military strategy, was far more cautious. He'd seen firsthand the destructive potential of unchecked ambition and the devastating consequences of wielding power without considering its ethical implications. He argued that controlling the Whispers was akin to holding the planet's fate in their hands, a responsibility too immense for any single group to bear. The consequences of misuse, he stressed, could be catastrophic, potentially disrupting the delicate balance of life not only in the underwater world but on the surface as well. The Whispers, he felt, were not merely a source of energy; they were the very lifeblood of this interconnected world, and any attempt to dominate them risked causing irreparable harm.

Sarah Chen, whose unique connection to the Whispers had proven invaluable, offered a different perspective. She spoke of the Whispers not as an object to be controlled, but as a sentient entity, a powerful force of nature deserving of respect and understanding. Her insights, though often cryptic and intuitive rather than scientifically quantifiable, resonated deeply with the Luminese, who viewed the Whispers with a reverence bordering on worship. She warned against the hubris of attempting to manipulate a force so profoundly interwoven with the fabric of existence. The potential for unintended consequences, she stressed, was simply too great. Her words echoed Elder Lyra's earlier pronouncements, reinforcing the ancient Luminese understanding of the interconnectedness of all things.

The debate raged for days, fueled by both the allure of immense power and the fear of unforeseen consequences. Dr. Thorne presented complex scientific models, meticulously detailing the potential for harnessing the Whispers' energy in a sustainable manner. He argued that with proper safeguards and careful monitoring, the risks could be mitigated, and the benefits would far outweigh any potential dangers. He envisioned a future where clean energy fueled not only human civilization but also aided in the healing of the damaged Earth's ecosystems. The idea of restoring balance to a world scarred by human greed and negligence filled him with a profound sense of purpose.

Captain Armstrong countered with his own projections, based on his knowledge of human history and the often-catastrophic consequences of wielding unchecked power. He pointed to past instances where humanity's pursuit of progress had led to unintended environmental devastation, mass extinctions, and even widespread societal collapse. He argued that the temptation to control the Whispers was a dangerous echo of humanity's past mistakes, a path fraught with peril that could lead to the annihilation of not just one, but two civilizations. He proposed instead a path of careful observation, a collaborative approach with the Luminese, and a deep commitment to understanding the Whispers' role within the overall planetary ecosystem before even considering any attempts at harnessing their energy.

The Abyssals, with their ancient wisdom and deep connection to the underwater world, offered a more nuanced perspective. They spoke of a delicate equilibrium, a cosmic balance maintained by the Whispers. They warned that interfering with this balance could trigger unforeseen consequences, possibly leading to a catastrophic destabilization of the entire planet. Their warnings, delivered in hushed tones, hinted at ancient prophecies and forgotten catastrophes, reinforcing the gravity of the ethical implications at stake. They spoke of a time long ago when a similar attempt to control a powerful, natural force had led to widespread destruction and the near-extinction of their own civilization.

The ethical dilemma extended beyond simply harnessing the Whispers' energy. The very act of gaining control over the Whispers would necessitate a shift in the power balance within the underwater world. The Luminese, who held a deep spiritual connection to the Whispers, would inevitably be displaced, their way of life threatened by human ambitions. Even cooperation, if it leaned towards human dominance, would still risk undermining the delicate equilibrium of the underwater civilization and, potentially, the surface world. The question became: Could human ingenuity and technological prowess coexist peacefully with the ancient wisdom and spiritual reverence of the Luminese, or was conflict inevitable?

Sarah Chen, acting as a bridge between the scientific understanding of Thorne and the spiritual understanding of the Luminese and Abyssals, proposed a compromise. She suggested a long-term research initiative focused on understanding the Whispers rather than controlling them. She advocated for a collaborative effort involving scientists, spiritual leaders, and representatives from all three civilizations. This approach, she felt, would prioritize knowledge and understanding over immediate gains, fostering a relationship built on respect and mutual benefit.

The challenge, however, was in overcoming ingrained human biases and the deeply embedded desire for control. The weight of responsibility, of understanding the profound interconnectedness of all things, was immense. The survivors were not just fighting for their own survival; they were grappling with the fate of two worlds, grappling with the ethical implications of wielding a power that exceeded human comprehension. The temptation to utilize the Whispers for technological advancement was strong, particularly in the context of rebuilding a devastated Earth. But the potential for devastating unintended consequences loomed large, fueling a debate that threatened to fracture the fragile alliances they had so carefully forged. The decision, they all knew, would shape not only their future but the fate of all life on the planet. It was a choice that would define the very meaning of responsibility in a world where the lines between science, spirituality, and the interconnectedness of all things were increasingly blurred. The journey, far from being over, had just entered its most treacherous, ethically complex phase.

Sarah's initial apprehension about her connection to the Whispers had quickly morphed into a cautious fascination, then a deep, almost unsettling understanding. It wasn't merely a passive observation; she felt the pulsating energy, the ebb and flow of its power, resonating within her very being. It was as if an ancient, ethereal language was being whispered directly into her soul, a language she was slowly beginning to decipher. She could sense the interconnectedness of all things, the intricate web of life that bound the Luminese civilization, the Abyssals, the Cetea, and even the ravaged surface world. It was a tapestry woven from light and shadow, harmony and conflict, a breathtaking panorama of existence that both thrilled and terrified her.

Initially, her connection manifested as fleeting glimpses—fragmented images and sensations. She'd see flashes of the past, echoes of events long forgotten, visions that seemed both real and unreal, like fragments of a shattered dream. These glimpses often came unbidden, striking her with the sudden force of a rogue wave. She'd find herself momentarily paralyzed, overwhelmed by the sheer volume of information flooding her senses. The images were often chaotic, a swirling kaleidoscope of colors and shapes, but slowly, gradually, patterns began to emerge, like stars coalescing into constellations.

One such vision revealed a catastrophic event—a seismic upheaval that shattered the surface world. She saw towering cities crumble into dust, the oceans rising to engulf the land—a scene of utter devastation. This vision was jarring, a stark reminder of the catastrophe that had thrust them into this underwater world. It deeply impacted her, fueling her determination to understand the Whispers, to grasp the true extent of their power and their potential to either heal or destroy.

Captain Armstrong, ever the pragmatist, recognized the significance of Sarah's abilities. While Dr. Thorne was consumed by the scientific possibilities of harnessing the Whispers' energy, Armstrong saw the potential for using Sarah's connection to gain a strategic advantage—to anticipate the moves of the Cetea or even to negotiate with the enigmatic Abyssals. He understood that her ability was not simply a scientific anomaly; it was a key—perhaps the only key—to unlocking the secrets of this hidden world.

As Sarah's understanding deepened, so did her role within the group. She wasn't just a survivor anymore; she was becoming a vital link between the human survivors and the underwater civilization. She began to act as a translator, interpreting the cryptic messages the Luminese conveyed through their intricate bioluminescent displays. Their communication wasn't based on sound or written language, but on a complex interplay of light patterns—a subtle dance of photons that only Sarah, through her connection to the Whispers, could truly understand. She relayed the Luminese concerns, their ancient prophecies, and their desperate pleas for help. Her translations became crucial in bridging the cultural and linguistic gap between the two worlds.

The Luminese, initially cautious and reserved, began to see Sarah not as an outsider but as a bridge—a connection to a world they feared they'd lost forever. They shared with her their history, their fears, and their hopes, revealing details of a civilization far more ancient and complex than anyone could have imagined. She learned of their intricate societal structure, their profound respect for the balance of the ecosystem, and their deep-seated fear of the Cetea—a ruthless faction driven by a hunger for power and control.

Through her connection, Sarah also gained insights into the Abyssals, a mysterious race that seemed to exist on the fringes of reality. They were shrouded in enigma, their intentions unclear, their motivations seemingly driven by forces beyond human comprehension. While the Luminese viewed them with a mixture of fear and reverence, Sarah perceived a certain sadness, a sense of lost potential, a tragic history untold. She sensed that the Abyssals, like the surface world, had once been a vibrant civilization, but a cataclysmic event—perhaps linked to the creation of the Whispers—had left them scarred and fragmented.

Sarah's expanded role also involved navigating the treacherous political landscape of the underwater world. She acted as an intermediary between the human survivors and the various factions, carefully fostering alliances and diffusing potential conflicts. She learned to use her connection subtly—to influence decisions, to guide events toward a peaceful resolution. This required not only a deep understanding of the Whispers but also a keen sense of diplomacy and tact. She had to walk a delicate line, ensuring that neither the humans nor the Luminese felt threatened or manipulated.

Her connection wasn't without its challenges. The overwhelming influx of information often left her exhausted, drained, and disoriented. There were times when the Whispers' energy felt oppressive—a burden almost too heavy to bear. The visions grew increasingly vivid and emotional, plunging her into the heart of ancient conflicts and exposing her to the raw pain and suffering of both past and present. She grappled with the moral ambiguities, the complex ethical dilemmas that emerged from her deeper understanding of the interconnectedness of all things. The weight of this knowledge, of this responsibility, was immense, but she bore it with quiet dignity and unwavering resolve.

One particular vision proved to be a turning point. She saw a cataclysmic event approaching—a convergence of energies that threatened to consume both the underwater world and the remnants of the surface. It was a prophecy of immense destruction, a foreshadowing of a future where the very fabric of existence was at stake. This vision served as a powerful catalyst, driving her to work tirelessly—to forge stronger alliances, to prepare for the impending disaster.

The weight of her knowledge became a burden shared with

Captain Armstrong and Dr. Thorne. They now understood that Sarah was not simply a conduit to the Whispers; she was the key to their survival. They had to protect her, support her, and trust her insights. They realized that Sarah's ability to connect with the Whispers wasn't a threat, but an opportunity—a chance to avert a global catastrophe, a chance to heal the wounds of a fractured world, and a chance to forge a better future for both the surface and underwater civilizations. The Whispers were no longer simply an energy source; they were a pathway to a deeper understanding—a key to the future of two worlds.

The Whispers had brought them together, forced them into an alliance born of necessity and shared peril. Now, Sarah's role was to help them navigate the treacherous currents ahead, to guide them toward a future that was uncertain, yet brimming with the potential for hope. The weight of knowledge, once overwhelming, now felt like a shared responsibility. And in that shared responsibility—in that collective effort to understand and to act—lay the fragile seeds of a new beginning. The future remained uncertain, but with Sarah at their side, interpreting the Whispers of the deep, they moved forward, together. The journey had become a quest not just for survival, but for understanding and, ultimately, for redemption. The weight of knowledge, once so crushing, now fueled their determination, forged their unity, and illuminated the path ahead.

The bioluminescent flora of the Abyssal city pulsed with an eerie rhythm—a counterpoint to the thrumming anxiety in Captain Armstrong's chest. He, Dr. Thorne, Sarah Chen, and a small contingent of Luminese guards stood before a colossal structure of obsidian and shimmering coral, its architecture both alien and breathtakingly intricate. This was the heart of the Abyssal kingdom, and they were here to negotiate—or at least to attempt to. The air crackled with an almost palpable tension, a silent pressure that weighed on them all.

The Whispers, Sarah felt, were not merely guiding her; they were screaming. A cacophony of warnings and foreboding pulsed within her, painting vivid images of impending conflict. She could sense the Abyssal leader's immense power—a dark tide of energy that threatened to engulf them all. It was a power that dwarfed even the Luminese's advanced technology—a power rooted in an ancient, almost primordial force.

Their escort, a Luminese elder named Xylos, his face etched with worry, spoke in hushed tones. "This is the domain of Xalzar, the most powerful of the Abyssal lords. He is... unpredictable. The Whispers say he is angered by our attempts to engage with the surface world."

Armstrong, ever the pragmatist, adjusted the strap of his makeshift underwater rifle. "Angered? Or perhaps... intrigued? The surface world holds many secrets the Abyssals might find valuable."

Dr. Thorne, her face pale beneath the filtered light, added, "The Whispers speak of an ancient technology—lost to both the Abyssals and the Luminese—a technology that could reshape the balance of power within this world, and perhaps even beyond." She glanced at Sarah, her eyes filled with a mixture of hope and apprehension. Sarah's ability to interpret the Whispers was their only real advantage. It was a dangerous gamble, relying on a young woman's connection to an unseen force, but they had no other option.

As they approached the main chamber, a wave of icy water washed over them—a physical manifestation of Xalzar's power.

The chamber itself was a vast cavern, lit by phosphorescent fungi and glowing crystals that cast long, dancing shadows. In the center, upon a throne crafted from the bones of some colossal, unknown creature, sat Xalzar.

He was a formidable sight—a being of immense size, his skin a dark, almost black hue, his eyes glowing with an internal luminescence. His form seemed to shift and writhe, hinting at a power that defied easy understanding. Around him, smaller Abyssal creatures—their forms contorted and grotesque—stood guard. They resembled enormous, bioluminescent crustaceans, their claws dripping with a viscous, shimmering fluid.

Xalzar's voice, when it came, resonated through the cavern—a deep, guttural sound that seemed to vibrate in their very bones. "You dare trespass in my domain, creatures of the shallows? The whispers have spoken of your presence. What brings you to the heart of my kingdom?"

Armstrong stepped forward, his voice calm but firm despite the tremor in his heart. "We come in peace, Xalzar. We seek understanding, a way to coexist, to share knowledge."

A low chuckle rumbled from Xalzar's throat. "Knowledge? You speak of knowledge like a child playing with fire. Knowledge is power, and power corrupts. You humans have proven that more than once." He gestured with a massive claw toward a wall of the chamber, revealing a series of intricate carvings that depicted a cataclysmic event—a scene of fiery destruction and upheaval. "This is what your kind brought to the surface world. Do you believe you can avoid the same fate here?"

Dr. Thorne responded swiftly, trying to bridge the chasm between their conflicting views. "The past cannot be changed, Xalzar. But the future can be shaped. We have learned from our mistakes. We seek to understand the Whispers, to harness their power for the good of all, not just our own."

Xalzar remained unconvinced. "The Whispers are a force beyond your comprehension. They are a legacy, a burden, not a gift to be wielded. You have already interfered with their natural rhythm, disrupting the balance of this world."

Sarah stepped forward, her voice barely a whisper, yet somehow carrying across the vast cavern. "The Whispers speak of a prophecy, Xalzar. A prophecy of unity, of a future where all creatures of this world can coexist." Her connection to the Whispers allowed her to see, to understand, and to translate the chaotic whispers into a clearer message. She could sense a deep-seated fear within Xalzar—a fear of the unknown consequences of this power.

Xalzar's glowing eyes narrowed, his gaze fixed on Sarah. He seemed to be considering her words, a hint of uncertainty creeping into his formidable demeanor. "This... prophecy," he rumbled. "It speaks of a merging of worlds, a reconciliation of forces. Is this what you believe?"

Sarah nodded, her confidence growing. "The Whispers tell me that there is a way to harness the power, not to control it, but to understand it—to guide it toward a future where there is balance, cooperation, not conflict." She revealed a fragment of information gleaned from the Whispers—a hidden location, a place where the power of the Whispers was most potent, a place that could potentially unite the warring factions.

Xalzar's massive form shifted. For a long moment, silence reigned in the cavern, broken only by the soft glow of the phosphorescent fungi. Then, slowly, he nodded. "The prophecy... it offers a different path. A path... less destructive."

The confrontation was far from over, but a crack had formed in the wall of antagonism. The weight of knowledge and the potential for catastrophic consequences weighed heavily on them all. But now, a glimmer of hope emerged from the deep, dark abyss. The shared understanding, however fragile, was a step toward a future where knowledge was not a weapon but a tool for survival, cooperation, and perhaps even redemption. The journey continued, fraught with peril, but with a newly forged alliance, a path toward a future of hope—however tenuous—had been revealed.

The agreement, however, came with a price. Xalzar demanded proof of the humans' commitment to peaceful coexistence. He requested a demonstration of their understanding of the Whispers— a test of their ability to navigate the subtle energies that pulsed through the underwater world. Sarah, guided by the Whispers, led a small group on a perilous journey through the treacherous currents, navigating swirling vortexes of energy and avoiding the wrathful guardians of the Abyssal realm. This demonstration of their ability to interact with the Whispers, to understand and respect their power, served to solidify the alliance—albeit a fragile one.

The return to the Luminese city was not without incident. A scouting party of the Cetea, another faction vying for control of the

Whispers' power, attacked their group. The battle was fierce—a clash of advanced Luminese weaponry against the brute strength and cunning tactics of the Cetea. The fight underscored the tenuous nature of the newly forged alliance and the constant threat of conflict. Yet, despite the dangers, the newfound understanding between the humans and the Abyssals held.

The events of the confrontation with Xalzar and the subsequent skirmishes with the Cetea laid bare the complexities of power dynamics in the underwater world. It emphasized the importance of forging alliances, of navigating the treacherous waters of politics and warfare within this newly discovered realm. But it also revealed something far more profound—the inherent interconnectedness of all life. The Whispers, Sarah understood, were not simply a source of power; they were a binding force, a thread that connected all beings, all factions, all worlds. Harnessing this power, understanding this connection, was not simply about survival but about shaping a future where all creatures could coexist—a future where knowledge was not a tool for domination but a key to understanding, collaboration, and lasting peace. The weight of that knowledge, once almost unbearable, now fueled their determination, guiding them through the darkness toward a light they hoped would eventually dawn.

CHAPTER 6

The flickering bioluminescence of the Luminese city cast long, dancing shadows as Captain Rostova, Dr. Thorne, and the remaining survivors huddled in a makeshift war room. The air thrummed with nervous energy, a palpable tension that vibrated through the very floor beneath their feet. The recent skirmishes with the Cetea had been brutal, showcasing the enemy's superior technology and ruthless efficiency. The Luminese, though technologically advanced in their own right, lacked the firepower to effectively counter the Cetea's devastating weaponry. Their peaceful nature, once a source of strength, now felt like a crippling vulnerability.

"We're running out of time," Captain Rostova stated, her voice tight with urgency. Her usually sharp, commanding presence was tempered by a weariness that reflected the weight of their desperate situation. Days bled into nights, each sunrise bringing a fresh wave of anxieties. The constant threat of Cetea attacks hung heavy over them, a suffocating cloud of fear that threatened to extinguish any remaining hope.

Dr. Thorne, ever the pragmatist, tapped a series of complex equations onto a Luminese data pad, its surface glowing with an ethereal, soft light. "Their energy source," he explained, his voice hushed, "It's based on a highly unstable isotope. A single, precisely placed disruption could trigger a catastrophic chain reaction." He paused, the implications of his words hanging in the silent chamber. "It's a risky gamble, but it might be our only option."

The room fell silent as the gravity of Thorne's words sunk in. The plan was audacious, bordering on suicidal. It required a delicate insertion of a specifically engineered destabilizing device deep within the Cetea's primary energy core. A failure would not only result in the annihilation of the Cetea, but also the Luminese city, the survivors' only sanctuary in this alien world.

Sarah Chen, her face pale but resolute, spoke softly, her voice barely a whisper. "The Whispers... they... they show me a path. A narrow, treacherous one, but it leads to a possible victory." Her unique connection to the Whispers, the ancient prophecies woven into the fabric of this underwater realm, had become an invaluable asset, providing glimpses into potential strategies and hidden vulnerabilities. But her visions were fragmented, cryptic flashes of light and shadow, requiring careful interpretation and immense courage to follow.

The plan involved a daring infiltration mission, spearheaded by Captain Armstrong, a Luminese warrior known for his unparalleled combat skills and unwavering loyalty. His team would be composed of a select group of Luminese soldiers, carefully chosen for their experience and proficiency in stealth operations. Supporting them would be the human survivors, each contributing their unique skills to the complex mission. Rostova would provide tactical support, utilizing her vast knowledge of military strategy and unconventional warfare. Thorne's expertise in understanding the Cetea's technology would be critical in navigating the enemy stronghold and deploying the destabilizing device. And Sarah, with her connection to the Whispers, would serve as their unseen guide, her ethereal insights providing crucial tactical advantages.

The mission presented a multitude of challenges. The Cetea's defenses were formidable, layered with advanced sensor grids and automated weapon systems. Navigating the labyrinthine corridors of their underwater fortress would require precision and absolute secrecy. Any misstep could trigger an immediate and devastating response. The risks were enormous, the odds stacked against them.

Yet, despite the inherent dangers, a quiet sense of determination settled upon the group. They were facing annihilation, not just for themselves, but for the entire Luminese civilization. Their survival, and the future of this unique underwater world, hinged on the success of this audacious gambit.

Over the next few days, the survivors and their Luminese allies meticulously planned every detail of the operation. They studied schematics of the Cetea fortress, analyzing its defensive systems and identifying potential weaknesses. Thorne worked tirelessly, refining the destabilizing device, making it smaller, more efficient, and easier to deploy. Sarah spent hours in meditation, her mind attuned to the Whispers, seeking guidance and warning signs.

The Luminese engineers crafted a specialized submersible, cloaked in a unique bioluminescent camouflage that mimicked the surrounding environment. It was a marvel of engineering, a silent vessel designed to slip through the Cetea's defenses undetected. The vessel, dubbed the "Silent Shadow," was fitted with state-of-the-art sensors and countermeasures, designed to circumvent the enemy's detection systems.

The operation's timeline was critical. The Cetea were planning a massive offensive, aiming to seize control of the Whispers once and for all. If the survivors failed, the Luminese would face an almost certain extinction. This was not just a battle for survival; it was a fight for the very soul of this hidden underwater world.

As the day of the mission dawned, a palpable sense of dread and anticipation filled the air. Each member of the team knew the stakes; failure meant certain death, not just for themselves but for countless others who depended on their success. But they also understood the potential for a glorious victory, a chance to secure a future for this vibrant, breathtaking world they had come to call their home.

The Silent Shadow slipped into the deep, its bioluminescent camouflage blending seamlessly with the surrounding environment. Armstrong, leading the charge, navigated the treacherous currents and complex underwater architecture. Thorne monitored the ship's sensors, his eyes glued to the data streams, alert to any signs of Cetea detection. Sarah, her mind connected to the Whispers, guided them through hidden passages and warned them of impending dangers. Rostova, stationed on a separate support vessel, kept a watchful eye, providing tactical advice and adjusting their strategy as needed.

The journey was fraught with peril. They evaded automated sentries, navigated minefields, and outwitted advanced detection systems. At times, it felt as if their very luck was running out; every encounter brought them closer to a catastrophic failure. But they pressed on, propelled by a shared determination that refused to be extinguished. The Whispers guided them, their ethereal voice leading them towards their ultimate goal.

Finally, after what seemed like an eternity, they reached the heart of the Cetea fortress. The energy core pulsed with dangerous energy, a throbbing heart of destruction that threatened to consume them all. Thorne prepared to deploy the destabilizing device. The moment held their collective breath. The success or failure of the entire mission rested on this single, critical act.

The device was carefully placed, its activation sequence initiated. A moment of agonizing suspense followed before a brilliant flash of light erupted from the energy core. A shockwave rippled through the fortress, shaking the very foundation of the Cetea stronghold. The air crackled with energy, the sound of destruction echoing through the deep ocean. They had succeeded.

The aftermath was chaotic. The Cetea's infrastructure collapsed, their advanced technology rendered useless. The survivors and their Luminese allies escaped the collapsing fortress, their mission accomplished. The underwater world had been saved, but at a great cost. The battle had left its mark, scars etched into the very fabric of this unique ecosystem. The future remained uncertain, but for now, the immediate threat had been neutralized. The Whispers had been silenced, at least for a while. The fight for survival, however, was far from over. The consequences of their actions, the environmental damage, and the lingering threats all pointed towards a new chapter, filled with new challenges and uncertainties. The desperate gamble had paid off, but the victory was only the beginning of a long and arduous journey to rebuild and heal this extraordinary world.

The chilling silence that followed the tumultuous battle hung heavy in the air. The victory felt hollow, a pyrrhic triumph etched in the ghostly glow of bioluminescent coral. The once-vibrant city of the Luminese now lay in ruins, a testament to the Cetea's destructive power and the desperate gamble that had just barely paid off. Captain Rostova, her face streaked with grime and exhaustion, surveyed the damage. The air, thick with the scent of ozone and decaying sea flora, stung her nostrils. Dr. Thorne, ever the pragmatist, was already organizing the survivors, assigning tasks with a grim determination that belied his weariness.

Their immediate concern was the wounded. Many of the Luminese, despite their advanced healing techniques, were critically injured. The human survivors fared relatively better, though several suffered severe burns and concussions from the collapsing Cetea fortress. Sarah Chen, her connection to the Whispers still a mystery, sat quietly tending to a Luminese elder, her hands moving with an almost supernatural gentleness. The loss of Jian, a sacrifice that echoed through their hearts, cast a long shadow over their efforts. "We need to consolidate our forces," Captain Rostova declared, her voice carrying over the muted groans of the injured. "The Cetea may be weakened, but they are far from defeated. We've bought ourselves time, but not enough."

Dr. Thorne nodded, his gaze sweeping across the ravaged landscape. "The Abyssals... they hold the key. Their technology, while different from the Cetea's, is equally advanced, perhaps even more so. If we can convince them to join us, our chances of survival will increase dramatically."

The Abyssals, a reclusive race dwelling in the deepest trenches of this underwater world, were known for their enigmatic nature and their mastery of manipulating the very fabric of the ocean currents. Their motivations remained a complete enigma, their interactions with other factions few and far between. Some whispered they were ancient beings, guardians of this hidden world; others feared them as malevolent entities controlling the ocean's most powerful forces. Reaching them, persuading them, would be a challenge of monumental proportions.

"How do we reach them?" asked one of the survivors, a former marine engineer named Lieutenant Miller. "Their territory is treacherous, guarded by natural defenses that would crush even the most advanced submersible."

"We'll need a Luminese guide," Captain Rostova replied. "Someone who knows the Abyssal territories, their customs, their weaknesses."

A hush fell over the group. The Luminese, traumatized by the recent conflict, were hesitant to venture into the Abyssal depths, a place steeped in legends of unspeakable horrors. Yet, the urgency of the situation demanded action. A young Luminese scientist, Elara, stepped forward. Her eyes, usually bright with curiosity, were now filled with a steely resolve.

"I know the way," she said, her voice barely a whisper but firm. "My grandfather studied the Abyssal currents, their patterns, their energy signatures. He left behind a detailed chart, a risky path, but it might work."

Elara's knowledge proved invaluable. Using her grandfather's chart, the group carefully navigated the treacherous currents, dodging whirlpools and navigating through underwater canyons that seemed to press in on them from all sides. The silence of the abyssal plains was punctuated only by the rhythmic hum of their submersible and the occasional unsettling creak of the vessel's hull. The pressure was immense, a constant reminder of the unforgiving environment.

They reached the Abyssal city, a breathtaking spectacle of organically grown structures, glowing with an eerie, internal light. The city pulsed with a strange energy, a rhythm that resonated deep within their bones. The Abyssals themselves were unlike anything they had encountered before—tall, slender beings with translucent skin and luminous eyes, their movements fluid and graceful like those of the ocean currents themselves.

Their initial contact was tense, fraught with suspicion. The Abyssals, communicating through a series of intricate bioluminescent patterns, conveyed their distrust. But Sarah Chen, her unique connection to the Whispers unexpectedly useful, stepped forward. She communicated, not through words, but through a subtle manipulation of the underwater currents, a silent language understood by both humans and Abyssals. She conveyed the Cetea's threat, the shared devastation, the need for a unified front.

The Abyssals, initially aloof, began to listen. They were ancient guardians, deeply connected to the ocean's delicate balance. The Cetea's destructive actions had threatened this balance, and the Abyssals, despite their reclusive nature, recognized the common enemy. They agreed to help, though their aid wouldn't come in the form of soldiers, but rather, in the form of technology and strategic guidance.

The Abyssal technology was unlike anything the humans or Luminese had ever witnessed. It wasn't based on weaponry, but on harnessing the raw power of the ocean—manipulating currents, creating powerful tidal waves, and even controlling bioluminescence on a massive scale. The Abyssals provided the survivors with devices that could amplify the Luminese's own technology, creating a defensive shield capable of withstanding the Cetea's weaponry. They also shared knowledge of the Cetea's weaknesses, exploiting their reliance on a particular type of energy source that was surprisingly vulnerable to manipulation of the ocean currents.

With the Abyssals' assistance, the survivors embarked on a desperate, painstaking effort to gather more allies. They contacted smaller, less technologically advanced factions, highlighting the looming threat and appealing to their shared survival instinct. Word spread through the interconnected underwater communities, a silent wave of defiance against the Cetea. Each new ally, however small, added to the growing coalition, a fragile tapestry woven together by the shared peril and the promise of a future where all could coexist peacefully.

The preparations for the final stand were grueling, each moment filled with tension and anticipation. The survivors, now a diverse coalition united by a common goal, worked tirelessly. The Luminese rebuilt their defenses, reinforced with Abyssal technology. The humans, with their engineering expertise, perfected the strategic defense systems. The Abyssals, though mysterious, provided invaluable strategic guidance.

As the final confrontation approached, a renewed sense of hope, born from unity and shared sacrifice, rippled through the coalition. The desperate gamble, that once seemed foolhardy, was transforming into a glimmer of hope, a testament to the power of resilience and the strength that comes from uniting against a common threat. The underwater world, a place of wonder and peril, held its breath. The final battle was about to begin.

The faint, rhythmic pulse of the Whispers, once a subtle hum, now throbbed with a menacing intensity. It resonated not just in the depths of the ocean but seemed to vibrate within the very bones of the survivors. Dr. Thorne, his usually meticulous demeanor replaced by a grim focus, explained the escalating threat. The Whispers, he theorized, weren't merely a source of energy or communication; they were a fundamental component of the underwater ecosystem—a delicate balance that the Cetea's actions were irrevocably disrupting.

"The increased intensity," Thorne explained, his voice low and urgent as he gestured toward the complex holographic projection shimmering above a makeshift table crafted from salvaged Luminese technology, "indicates a catastrophic shift. We're talking about a chain reaction, a cascading failure of the bioluminescent processes that underpin this entire environment. The light, the very lifeblood of this world, is fading."

The projection showed a disturbing trend. The vibrant, pulsating energy signature of the Whispers, normally a chaotic yet harmonious dance of light and energy, was now fracturing, exhibiting erratic spikes and alarming dips. Areas once teeming with life were plunged into darkness, the bioluminescent organisms flickering weakly before succumbing to an eerie stillness. The implications were chilling. The Luminese cities, reliant on the Whispers for energy and sustenance, were already struggling. The delicate balance of the underwater ecosystem, already strained by the Cetea's attacks, was teetering on the brink of collapse.

Captain Rostova, her face etched with worry, looked at the assembled survivors. "What can we do? We've barely survived the Cetea's onslaught; we can't possibly prevent this..." Her voice trailed off, the weight of the impending disaster heavy in the air.

Sarah Chen, her connection to the Whispers still a mystery even to herself, stepped forward, her normally bright eyes clouded with concern. "The Whispers... they're reacting to something. Something bigger than the Cetea." She closed her eyes, her brow furrowed in concentration. "I... I feel a disturbance. A powerful surge of negative energy, emanating from deep within the Abyssal trenches."

Thorne nodded grimly. "The Abyssals," he muttered, "we always suspected they had a hand in this, but we never understood the extent of their influence. Their technology, their understanding of the Whispers... it's far beyond what we've encountered."

The realization struck them like a physical blow. The Cetea were a destructive force, but they were acting out of greed and ambition. The Abyssals, however, seemed to be manipulating the Whispers, harnessing their power for a purpose none of them could fathom. The impending catastrophe wasn't just an environmental crisis; it was a deliberate act of sabotage, orchestrated by a shadowy force lurking in the deepest, darkest recesses of the ocean.

Preparing for this cataclysm wasn't a question of military strategy; it was about survival against the forces of nature, amplified and weaponized by unknown entities. Their plan, hastily formulated in the flickering light of salvaged bioluminescent lamps, was threefold.

First, they needed to understand the nature of the Abyssal influence. Sarah's connection to the Whispers would be crucial, but Thorne knew they couldn't rely on her alone. He proposed constructing a device—a sort of sensory array—that could capture and analyze the subtle fluctuations of the Whispers, perhaps even allowing them to communicate with the source of the disruption. This required scavenging the remnants of Luminese technology, a daunting task considering the damage inflicted during the battle.

Second, they had to prepare for the environmental consequences. The dwindling bioluminescence meant dwindling oxygen levels, a collapsing food chain, and the potential for widespread ecological collapse. They would need to establish emergency oxygen supplies, find alternative food sources, and prepare for mass migration. This meant venturing into unknown and potentially hostile territories, a risky endeavor even in the best of circumstances.

Third, and perhaps most importantly, they had to strengthen their alliance with any remaining Luminese. Trust had been earned through blood and sacrifice, but maintaining unity amidst the impending chaos would be a constant struggle. The Luminese, already weakened and grieving, needed not just protection but hope—a promise that their world, and their future, wasn't completely lost.

The next few days were a blur of frantic activity. The survivors, fueled by a potent cocktail of adrenaline, fear, and a stubborn refusal to surrender, worked tirelessly. They salvaged damaged Luminese technology, piecing together fragments of intricate machinery, their hands raw and bleeding. They explored the ruined city, searching for edible plants and any remaining stores of oxygen. They even found a hidden chamber containing ancient texts that hinted at the history of the Whispers, their power, and their vulnerabilities.

Sarah, under Thorne's watchful guidance, began to hone her connection to the Whispers. She would lie in a specially constructed chamber, her body bathed in the faint, pulsating light of salvaged bioluminescent organisms, her mind attuned to the subtle vibrations that permeated the underwater world. Her readings were erratic, often punctuated by waves of intense energy that left her breathless and exhausted. But gradually, she began to discern patterns, to perceive the source of the disturbance, not as a chaotic force, but as a deliberate, malevolent manipulation.

The construction of Thorne's sensory array proved to be a herculean task. It involved intricate wiring, the delicate calibration of salvaged Luminese components, and a careful understanding of the Whispers' energy signature. The device was a marvel of improvised engineering, a testament to human ingenuity and the desperate need for survival. Its completion was a watershed moment—a tangible symbol of hope amidst the encroaching darkness.

As the sensory array neared completion, the environmental changes became more pronounced. The bioluminescence was rapidly diminishing, plunging vast sections of the underwater world into an unsettling darkness. Schools of fish, normally vibrant and teeming with life, were listless and disoriented. Coral reefs, once dazzling displays of color and life, were turning ghostly white, a grim reminder of the impending ecological collapse. Even the air, once crisp and clean, was becoming thick and heavy, laced with the stench of decay.

The Luminese, already traumatized by the Cetea's attack, were now faced with a far greater threat—the imminent death of their world. Their once vibrant and hopeful eyes now held a deep weariness, a quiet resignation. Yet, despite the palpable despair, a flicker of defiance still burned within them. They assisted the survivors in their efforts, their collective sorrow fueling a determined resolve. Their unity with the human survivors, born from shared suffering and a common goal, became their greatest strength.

The final confrontation was no longer just about survival; it was about safeguarding the very essence of their shared home—a testament to the resilience of life in the face of overwhelming odds.

The desperate gamble wasn't just about winning a battle; it was about protecting the very fabric of existence in this extraordinary underwater world. The future hung precariously in the balance, a fragile hope flickering against the backdrop of an impending cataclysm.

The Luminese, despite their advanced technology, possessed a limited understanding of the Whispers' full potential. Their efforts to mitigate the escalating energy surge were proving futile. The rhythmic pulse, once a comforting lullaby of their world, had transformed into a terrifying heartbeat, threatening to shatter their existence. Despair hung heavy in the air, thick and suffocating, like the pressure of the abyssal depths. Even Captain Armstrong, ever the optimist, felt a chill creep into his resolve.

Then, from the least expected quarter, came a glimmer of hope. A colossal form, larger than any creature they had encountered thus far, emerged from the swirling currents near the edge of the Luminese city. It was a creature of myth, a being spoken of in hushed tones by the elders—the Leviathan.

The Leviathan was not a creature of aggression. Its immense size, a living mountain of bioluminescent scales shifting through a spectrum of blues and greens, inspired awe rather than fear. Its presence filled the underwater city with an unexpected sense of calm, a counterpoint to the rising panic. As it approached, intricate patterns pulsed across its skin, communicating in a language beyond human comprehension yet somehow understood by the Luminese.

Dr. Thorne, ever the scientist, recognized the patterns as a complex form of bioluminescent communication, a language based on shifting light intensities and wave frequencies. With Sarah Chen's unique sensitivity to the Whispers, he hypothesized that the Leviathan might be somehow attuned to it, capable of influencing or even controlling its power. Sarah, who had been strangely subdued since Jian's sacrifice, felt a surge of energy coursing through her—a connection to this ancient being that resonated with the Whispers themselves. It was a feeling of profound understanding, a shared consciousness that transcended language and species.

The Leviathan, seemingly sensing the desperation of the Luminese and the human survivors, extended a tentacle, its surface covered in sensory organs that pulsed with light. The tentacle gently touched the edge of the city's energy grid, a network of shimmering crystals that were struggling to contain the overwhelming power of the Whispers. An almost imperceptible shift occurred. The erratic pulses of the Whispers began to stabilize, the chaotic energy finding a conduit, a path to be channeled and controlled.

The Leviathan's intervention was not a simple act of brute force but a delicate act of manipulation. It was as if the creature understood the subtle intricacies of the Whispers, the need to harmonize the energy rather than suppress it. It was a testament to the interconnectedness of life in this underwater world, a demonstration of a symbiotic relationship that transcended the limitations of human understanding.

The Luminese, witnessing this unprecedented event, erupted in a chorus of joyous sounds, their voices resonating through the water.

Hope, which had seemed lost, rekindled with the Leviathan's arrival, flickering brightly like a bioluminescent beacon. Captain Armstrong, his face etched with relief, turned to Dr. Thorne.

"We thought we were alone in this fight," he said, his voice tinged with wonder. "But it seems the ocean has its own guardians."

Dr. Thorne, his scientific mind racing, began to formulate hypotheses. "The Leviathan," he mused, "it's possible that this creature is a keystone species, a vital component of this ecosystem's balance. Perhaps its role has been crucial in managing the Whispers' energy throughout millennia, a role now disrupted by the Cetea's actions."

Their newfound alliance, however, was not without its challenges. The Leviathan's communication, even with Sarah's help, was difficult to interpret. Its intentions were clear, its actions benevolent, but the specifics of its method remained shrouded in mystery. They needed to understand how the Leviathan was interacting with the Whispers, how it was channeling the energy, and whether this assistance was sustainable.

The Cetea, meanwhile, were unaware of the Leviathan's intervention. Their relentless attacks on the Luminese city continued, though with less ferocity than before. The subtle shift in the Whispers' energy, seemingly imperceptible to them, had inadvertently weakened their offensive capabilities. Their advanced weaponry, fueled by the Whispers themselves, was operating at reduced efficiency. This unexpected setback, however, only served to infuriate them further, fueling their determination to seize control of the Whispers completely, regardless of the cataclysmic consequences.

The human survivors, aided by the Luminese and the Leviathan, began to strategize their next move. They knew that the Leviathan's assistance was crucial but temporary. The creature couldn't indefinitely stabilize the Whispers' energy; it needed a sustainable solution. They also knew that the Cetea wouldn't remain passive. They needed to strike decisively, utilizing the Leviathan's assistance to their advantage.

Dr. Thorne, working alongside the Luminese scientists, developed a plan. They would use the Leviathan's influence to create a localized field, shielding the city from the most destructive effects of the Whispers' surge. This would buy them time, allowing them to mount a counteroffensive. The plan was risky, the margin of error razor-thin. If they failed, the consequences would be devastating—not just for the Luminese, but for the entire underwater ecosystem.

The operation required precise coordination and timing. The Luminese, guided by Sarah's insights and the Leviathan's subtle cues, adjusted their energy grids. The human survivors, equipped with modified weapons that interacted with the Whispers' energy fields, prepared for a final, desperate assault on the Cetea's stronghold.

As the plan was set into motion, a new worry emerged. The

Whispers weren't merely a source of energy or communication; they were interwoven with the very fabric of the underwater world. Their manipulation, even with the Leviathan's help, might have unintended and far-reaching consequences. The delicate balance of the ecosystem, already teetering on the brink, hung precariously in the balance. Every action, every decision, carried the weight of untold consequences.

The confrontation wasn't a battle of brute force, but a delicate dance of energy manipulation—a battle waged not only on the physical plane but on a metaphysical level, a realm where the Whispers themselves reigned supreme. The success of this desperate gamble rested not just on strategy and skill, but on a deep understanding of the interconnectedness of this extraordinary underwater world and the delicate balance that held it together.

The fate of two worlds—the hidden one beneath the waves and the surface world left reeling from the mysterious disappearance of the plane and its passengers—hung in the balance, a testament to the unpredictable, yet ultimately awe-inspiring, wonders of nature and the mysteries that still lay hidden in the depths. The next move would determine not only survival but the very future of this extraordinary hidden world, a legacy that would echo through time.

The air crackled with anticipation, a tangible tension that vibrated through the Luminese city of Xylos. The rhythmic pulse of the Whispers, once a gentle hum, now throbbed with a menacing intensity, a chaotic symphony of energy threatening to tear the very fabric of their world apart. Captain Armstrong, his face etched with grim determination, surveyed the assembled forces. He stood beside Dr. Thorne, whose usually bright eyes held a flicker of fear, but her resolve remained unshaken. Sarah Chen, her connection to the Whispers stronger than ever, stood a little apart, her hands gently resting on a smooth, obsidian orb, pulsing faintly with the same chaotic energy that thrummed through the city.

The Abyssals, enigmatic beings of immense power, were present, but their intentions remained unclear. Their shimmering forms, ethereal and unsettling, moved with a fluidity that defied the laws of physics, their silent presence a constant reminder of the unpredictable nature of this underwater world. They had offered an alliance, but their motives were shrouded in secrecy, a chilling uncertainty that added to the already volatile situation.

The Cetea, on the other hand, showed no such ambiguity. Their immense, bioluminescent bodies, resembling colossal, predatory whales, pulsed with a malevolent energy. They were driven by a relentless hunger for power, their eyes glowing with a predatory gleam, focused on harnessing the Whispers for their own nefarious ends. Their leader, a creature of immense size and terrifying power, known only as the Leviathan, surveyed the scene with cold, calculating eyes.

The battle wouldn't be fought with conventional weapons. This was a war of energy, a contest of wills, a struggle to control the very essence of this hidden world. The Luminese, despite their technological prowess, were ill-equipped for this kind of conflict.

Their defenses were designed to protect against physical threats, not the volatile, metaphysical power of the Whispers.

The strategy was audacious, bordering on suicidal. Sarah, guided by her unique connection to the Whispers, would act as a conduit, attempting to redirect the chaotic energy flow. Dr. Thorne, utilizing her knowledge of both human and Luminese technology, had devised a complex system of energy dampeners, designed to lessen the impact of the surges. Captain Armstrong, along with a hand-picked team of Luminese warriors, would act as a defensive force, protecting Sarah and the dampeners from the relentless attacks of the Cetea. The Abyssals remained an unknown variable— a wild card that could shift the balance of power at any moment.

The first assault came with a blinding flash of light and a deafening roar. The Cetea launched their attack, their bioluminescent bodies a wave of pulsating energy. The city of Xylos was bathed in an unearthly glow, the very structures of the city trembling under the force of the attack. Captain Armstrong's team fought valiantly, their energy weapons a feeble counter to the raw power of the Cetea. But their defense was holding, buying precious time for Sarah and Dr. Thorne.

Sarah, her face pale with exertion, focused all her concentration on the obsidian orb. Sweat beaded on her forehead, her breathing ragged, as she channeled the chaotic energy of the Whispers. The orb glowed brighter, mirroring the intensity of the battle raging around her. The energy surged through her, threatening to

overwhelm her, but she held on, her determination fueled by knowledge that the fate of two worlds rested on her shoulders.

Dr. Thorne, her fingers dancing over the controls of the energy dampeners, worked tirelessly. The system strained under the immense pressure, alarms blared, and sparks flew from the overloaded circuits. Yet, she persevered, her scientific mind calculating, adjusting, and fighting to maintain control. Each adjustment was a delicate dance, a gamble with the precarious balance of the Whispers. A miscalculation could result in catastrophic consequences, unleashing a wave of energy that would obliterate not only Xylos but potentially the entire underwater world.

The Leviathan, its massive form looming over the fray, unleashed a wave of raw, destructive energy. It struck the energy dampeners, sending shockwaves that threatened to rip the system apart. Dr. Thorne fought back, but the energy was too powerful, pushing her to her limits.

The Abyssals, who had remained silent observers until now, suddenly intervened. Their ethereal forms pulsed with a powerful counter-energy, a wave of calming influence that diffused the Leviathan's attack. Their intervention was unexpected, a sudden shift in the tide of battle, their motives still unclear. Were they allies, or were they merely playing a deeper game, manipulating the conflict for their own inscrutable purposes?

The battle raged on, a chaotic maelstrom of energy and destruction. Sarah, fueled by adrenaline and a desperate hope, continued to channel the Whispers. Slowly, painstakingly, she began to redirect the chaotic energy, weaving a new pattern, a calming rhythm in the midst of the storm. The pulsating orb in her hands glowed with a new, steady light, its energy now controlled, focused, and harmonious.

As Sarah's efforts bore fruit, the chaotic energy of the Whispers began to subside. The pulsating rhythm slowed, its intensity diminished, and a sense of calm began to spread throughout Xylos. The Cetea, their power waning, retreated, their bioluminescent bodies dimming, leaving behind a trail of devastation. The Leviathan, its aura of menace diminished, retreated into the abyss, its retreat a grudging admission of defeat.

The battle was won, but the victory was hard-fought, its cost evident in the damaged city, the exhausted faces of the Luminese warriors, and the deep weariness that settled upon Sarah and Dr. Thorne. The fate of two worlds had hung precariously in the balance, held together by the threads of courage, determination, and a deep understanding of the interconnectedness of life, both above and below the waves. The Whispers were still a mystery, their full potential yet to be understood, but for now, they were under control. The future remained uncertain, but the shadows of despair had lifted, replaced by a fragile hope for a brighter tomorrow.

The silence that followed the battle was heavy, filled with unspoken knowledge of what they had just endured. The scars remained, both physical and emotional, but the shared experience had forged a bond of unity that stretched across species and worlds.

The Abyssals, their involvement still a mystery, observed from the periphery, their enigmatic presence a lingering question mark. Their reasons for intervening remained unknown. Were they true allies, or did their actions serve a deeper, more complex purpose— one that only time would reveal?

The surface world, oblivious to the battle raging beneath the waves, continued its existence, unaware of the critical role it played in the delicate balance of this hidden, wondrous world. The survival of both worlds was intrinsically linked, a fact that the survivors now understood more profoundly than ever before.

The whispers of the deep, once a source of both wonder and terror, now held the potential for both destruction and salvation. The next step, the long road to understanding and healing, lay ahead.

Their journey was far from over.

CHAPTER 7

The aftermath of the battle hung heavy in the water, a stark contrast to the vibrant bioluminescence that had once illuminated the Luminese city. The once-pristine coral reefs, teeming with life, were now fractured and scarred. Vast swathes of the seabed lay barren, the vibrant hues replaced by a desolate gray. The air—or rather, the water—tasted of salt and something acrid, a metallic tang that clung to the gills and stung the eyes. The battle for the Whispers had been won, but at a terrible cost.

The Cetea's relentless assault, combined with the sheer destructive power of the Whispers themselves, had unleashed a cascade of environmental devastation. The sonic weaponry employed by the Cetea had created pressure waves that shattered delicate coral structures, leaving behind a trail of destruction. The underwater volcanoes, usually dormant, had been awakened by the seismic activity, spewing plumes of ash and superheated water into the ocean, further poisoning the already stressed ecosystem. The bioluminescent flora, the source of the Luminese's energy and the city's breathtaking beauty, had been decimated. Large sections of the glowing kelp forests were bleached white, their life force extinguished. The once-harmonious symphony of bioluminescence was now a fragmented, dying chorus.

Dr. Thorne, ever the meticulous scientist, documented the damage. He swam through the ravaged landscape, collecting samples of the contaminated water and surveying the extent of destruction. His usually bright eyes were clouded with a deep sadness as he observed the lifeless coral, the ghostly remnants of once-thriving ecosystems. He understood the intricate balance of the underwater world, the delicate web of life that had been so brutally disrupted. The consequences, he knew, would be far-reaching, affecting not only the Luminese but the entire underwater ecosystem.

Captain Rostova, hardened by years of commanding vessels through treacherous seas, felt a different kind of despair. The losses in the battle were staggering, not just in terms of lives but of the beauty and wonder they had come to know. The faces of fallen Luminese warriors, their bioluminescent skin dimmed and lifeless, haunted her. She had seen war before, but nothing had prepared her for the sheer scale of destruction witnessed in the battle. The victory felt hollow, overshadowed by the environmental catastrophe they had inadvertently unleashed.

Sarah Chen, her connection to the Whispers stronger than ever, felt the deep sorrow of the ocean itself. The Whispers, usually a source of guidance and wisdom, were now a mournful lament, echoing the devastation across the underwater world. She sensed a lingering, malevolent energy—a residue of the battle's violence— that threatened to further destabilize the delicate ecosystem.

The immediate priority was survival. The remaining Luminese, their once-proud city now a fractured shell, worked tirelessly to salvage what they could. They created makeshift shelters, utilizing salvaged materials from their damaged structures. They tended to the injured, both Luminese and human. Their resilience, their unwavering determination to rebuild, was both inspiring and heartbreaking.

The survivors, humbled by the experience, understood the weight of their actions. They had come to this world as outsiders, seeking refuge and knowledge, but they had become entangled in a conflict that had irrevocably altered the balance of life. The initial thrill of discovery was replaced by a heavy burden of responsibility.

News of the underwater battle, fragmented and distorted, eventually reached the surface world. Initial reactions were a mixture of disbelief and fear. Governments, initially dismissive of the reports of a hidden underwater civilization, now faced a crisis of a different kind—an environmental catastrophe of unprecedented scale. The impact of the battle extended beyond the underwater world, subtly altering weather patterns and ocean currents. The potential for global consequences was clear, and the world held its breath, anticipating the unfolding repercussions.

The Luminese, aided by the survivors, initiated a desperate effort at environmental restoration. They utilized their advanced technology to create artificial reefs, stimulate the growth of bioluminescent flora, and purify the contaminated water. But the task was immense, the damage widespread. Recovery would take generations, perhaps centuries.

The process was painstaking, each step requiring careful planning and execution. Dr. Thorne, drawing upon his extensive knowledge of marine biology and environmental science, oversaw the restoration efforts. He worked alongside Luminese scientists, sharing his expertise and learning from their innovative approaches. Their collaboration, a testament to the strength of their newly forged alliance, offered a glimmer of hope amidst the despair.

The search for survivors in the aftermath of the battle unveiled surprising information. They discovered several pockets of resistance, where Luminese and human survivors had banded together, holding off smaller Cetea squads. These unexpected encounters revealed hidden reservoirs of resilience and the power of unity against adversity.

As the dust settled, both literally and metaphorically, the survivors faced the difficult task of confronting the emotional and physical toll of the battle. The weight of loss, the trauma of witnessing such devastation, left an indelible mark on each of them. Grief was shared, wounds were tended to—both physical and emotional. The bonds forged through hardship proved stronger than the devastation surrounding them. A new understanding, a deeper appreciation for the fragility of life and the importance of preservation, began to blossom.

The surface world's response was slow and hesitant, reflecting the initial skepticism toward the stories emerging from the depths. Yet, as evidence of environmental change mounted, a reluctant acceptance began to dawn. International collaboration became necessary—not to conquer a new world, but to help heal a damaged one. The scientific community became intensely interested in the Luminese technology and their ecological expertise, hoping to learn from their advanced methods of environmental restoration.

The battle had not only revealed a hidden world but also highlighted the interconnectedness of all life on Earth, both above and below the waves. The environmental damage caused by the conflict served as a stark reminder of the potential consequences of unchecked ambition and the need for stewardship of the planet's delicate ecosystems.

The final chapter of the battle was not a clean victory or a complete defeat, but a somber understanding that nature is a powerful force, and humanity, even with its technology, must tread cautiously in its presence. The Whispers, once a source of mystery and power, had become a silent testament to the consequences of greed and war. The journey to restoration was long, arduous, and uncertain. However, it was a journey they must embark on, together, or face further devastation. The future, however uncertain, was not entirely hopeless. The seeds of a new beginning had been sown in the ravaged seabed, nurtured by a fragile yet tenacious hope.

The initial silence from the surface world was deafening. Days bled into weeks, the underwater world holding its breath, waiting for a sign—any sign—from the world above. The absence of communication was a chilling counterpoint to the devastation they had witnessed. Had the surface world even noticed their absence? Or worse, had the cataclysmic events that had transpired beneath the waves somehow reached the surface, triggering a global catastrophe of their own? The questions gnawed at them, feeding the anxiety that simmered beneath the surface of their fragile hope.

Then, sporadic, fragmented signals began to arrive—faint, distorted transmissions, barely intelligible whispers from a dying world. These weren't the sophisticated, coordinated broadcasts of the pre-disaster era; these were desperate cries for help, garbled pleas that spoke of chaos and unimaginable loss. The survivors gathered around the salvaged communication array, their faces grim as they pieced together the horrific truth.

The Whispers, it turned out, weren't contained to the underwater realm. Their power, their influence, stretched far beyond the ocean floor, reaching into the very fabric of the planet. The initial disruption—the unexplained atmospheric disturbances that had preceded the plane crash—weren't isolated incidents. They were the first tremors of a planetary upheaval, the prelude to a global environmental crisis of epic proportions.

The surface world's initial reports were fragmented and chaotic. Massive earthquakes, tsunamis of unprecedented scale, and volcanic eruptions of unimaginable fury had ravaged coastal regions. The weather patterns had gone haywire, with extreme storms and unpredictable temperature fluctuations wreaking havoc across the globe. Entire ecosystems had collapsed, turning once-fertile lands into desolate wastelands. The delicate balance of nature, so easily disturbed, had crumbled under the weight of the whispers' uncontrolled energy.

The reports painted a grim picture: mass extinctions, widespread famine, and societal collapse. The technologically advanced world, with its hubris and disregard for the environment, had been brought to its knees, its intricate systems shattered by forces it had neither understood nor been able to control. The irony was not lost on the survivors. They had escaped a disaster only to find themselves facing the consequences of a far greater one.

Among the scattered transmissions, they picked up faint echoes of scientific reports—desperate attempts to understand the magnitude of the catastrophe. The scientists spoke of a global disruption of the electromagnetic field, of unusual energy signatures emanating from the ocean depths, of a mysterious phenomenon that seemed to be manipulating the very core of the planet. Their words confirmed their worst fears: the cataclysm wasn't random; it was directly linked to the whispers, the same source of energy they had fought so desperately to control.

Captain Armstrong, ever the pragmatist, saw beyond the immediate horror. He understood that their survival, the survival of the underwater world, was inextricably linked to the fate of the surface. The Whispers, for all their destructive power, held the key to both destruction and restoration. Their uncontrolled energy was causing havoc, but if harnessed correctly, it could potentially heal the wounds it had inflicted. This meant that their journey wasn't simply about survival, but about a desperate, almost impossible mission: to find a way to stabilize the whispers and restore the balance of the planet.

Dr. Thorne, meanwhile, dedicated herself to analyzing the fragmented scientific data, searching for clues to understand the mechanisms behind the global catastrophe. She poured over the reports, cross-referencing them with her own knowledge of the underwater world, attempting to create a coherent picture of the unfolding disaster. She discovered that the whispers weren't simply a source of energy, but a highly sensitive and complex system, responding to environmental changes in unpredictable ways. Their instability was amplified by the very actions humanity had taken to exploit natural resources, disrupting the planet's delicate balance and triggering the cataclysm.

Sarah Chen, with her unique connection to the whispers, became a vital component of their efforts. Her insights, though fragmented and often difficult to interpret, offered glimpses into the system's inner workings. She described visions of a planetary network of energy pathways—a delicate web of interconnected forces that the whispers controlled. Disrupting this network, as humanity had inadvertently done, caused a cascade effect, leading to the global environmental catastrophe. Her visions also revealed potential solutions—fragile pathways to re-establish equilibrium, albeit at immense risk.

The survivors were faced with an insurmountable challenge. They had to find a way to not only stabilize the whispers but also to communicate with the fractured remnants of the surface world, sharing their knowledge and guiding them toward a path of restoration. This meant venturing into the ravaged surface world, facing the dangers of a hostile and unpredictable environment, all while carrying the weight of the planet's fate upon their shoulders.

The undertaking was monumental, the odds overwhelmingly stacked against them. Yet, the survivors, scarred but not broken, forged ahead. They knew that failure was not an option. The future of two worlds—the underwater realm they had come to call home and the ravaged surface world they had left behind—depended on their success. Their journey from the underwater world to the devastated surface was not just a physical one but a journey into the unknown, a desperate race against time to undo the damage caused by humanity's unchecked ambition and to learn the profound lesson of interconnectedness and respect for the delicate balance of nature. The surface world's reaction was a testament to that disruption, a horrifying mirror reflecting humanity's own devastating impact. Now, they had to find a way to heal not just the wounds on the planet but the fractured spirit of humanity itself. The journey was fraught with peril, both from the environment and the fragmented, desperate pockets of human civilization that remained, but their hope, however fragile, remained their guiding light. They were not just survivors; they were the custodians of a dying planet, entrusted with a mission of impossible proportions. The fate of two worlds, and the profound lesson of interconnectedness, lay in their hands.

The ravaged landscape of the former world stretched before them, a stark contrast to the vibrant underwater haven they had left behind. Dust devils danced across cracked earth, the skeletal remains of cities clawing at the bruised sky. The air, thick with the scent of ash and decay, stung their lungs. This wasn't the planet they had known, not the one they had left behind in the chaos of the Bermuda Triangle anomaly. This was a world gasping its last breath, a testament to humanity's unchecked ambition and its devastating consequences.

Their first priority was establishing a base—a sanctuary from the harsh elements and a hub for their ambitious restoration project. They settled on a relatively intact coastal area, utilizing what remained of a pre-catastrophe research facility. Its partial shielding and pre-existing infrastructure provided a much-needed advantage. Power generation was a critical challenge; the widespread destruction of conventional power sources meant they had to rely on alternative energy solutions. Dr. Thorne, ever resourceful, spearheaded the effort. They harnessed geothermal energy, a sustainable and potent source, tapping into the planet's inherent heat. Ocean thermal energy conversion—utilizing the temperature difference between the surface and deep ocean waters—was also explored, a testament to their adaptation and the knowledge gleaned from their time with the Luminese.

The immediate challenge, however, was the contamination. The air was thick with pollutants, and the water sources were dangerously tainted. Thorne's expertise, combined with the advanced technology scavenged from the Luminese city, proved invaluable. Specialized filtration systems capable of removing even the most insidious toxins were constructed. Water purification became a relentless, round-the-clock operation, ensuring a clean supply for both drinking and agricultural purposes.

Air purification was a more significant undertaking, requiring large-scale atmospheric scrubbers. Using a combination of bioengineered algae, capable of absorbing pollutants, and advanced filtration technology adapted from the Luminese, they slowly began to cleanse the air. This painstaking process demanded constant vigilance and innovation.

Food production was another major hurdle. The decimated agricultural lands yielded nothing. Hydroponic and aeroponic systems, mirroring techniques the Luminese used in their underwater farms, were implemented. Specialized nutrient solutions, meticulously formulated by Thorne, nourished the plants in controlled environments. This ensured a relatively stable food supply, though at a scale insufficient for a large population. They needed to reclaim agricultural lands—a daunting task, considering the widespread soil degradation. This required a multi-pronged approach.

Bioremediation techniques, borrowed from the Luminese's advanced ecological engineering, became central to their strategy. Specifically bred microorganisms were deployed to break down harmful pollutants in the soil, making it suitable for cultivation once more. These microorganisms, genetically modified for maximum efficiency and resilience, played a crucial role in their efforts. Their resilience was tested, however, by the unpredictable environmental conditions and the lingering radiation in certain areas.

The reforestation project presented an equally formidable challenge. The forests, once the lungs of the planet, were reduced to ashen wastelands. The Luminese's technology provided them with a breakthrough. They acquired seeds and saplings of fast-growing, resilient tree species, genetically modified to thrive in the ravaged environment. These trees were also engineered to absorb toxins more effectively than their natural counterparts.

Using drones and specialized planting equipment, they began reforesting devastated areas—a slow but steady process of reclaiming the land. The reforestation process was meticulous, requiring detailed soil analysis and careful species selection to ensure the plants could survive and flourish. The use of drones for monitoring progress and planting in remote areas—technology acquired from the Luminese—was an invaluable asset.

Meanwhile, Sarah Chen's unique connection to the "Whispers"—the mysterious energy field they discovered in the underwater world—proved unexpectedly useful. Her ability to manipulate the energy to a limited extent allowed for the accelerated growth of the plants and a more efficient cleansing of the polluted areas. However, her powers were unpredictable, often draining her physically and mentally. They learned to balance her abilities with a meticulously planned approach to ensure she didn't overextend herself while still utilizing her gift to its fullest potential.

Their efforts, however, were not without setbacks. The lingering radiation from the initial catastrophe caused mutations in the flora and fauna, creating new challenges and unforeseen dangers. They had to develop new strategies to combat these mutated organisms, modifying their methods and adapting to an environment constantly in flux.

They faced further setbacks in the form of unpredictable weather patterns exacerbated by climate change. Intense heatwaves, followed by sudden and violent storms, threatened to undo their painstaking progress, prompting the team to constantly refine their strategies and develop a more resilient infrastructure.

The psychological toll on the survivors was equally significant. They faced not only the daunting environmental challenges but also the grief of a lost world and the uncertainty of the future. The constant struggle against the elements, coupled with the burden of their responsibility, tested their resilience. They supported each other, sharing both their successes and their failures, bolstering their spirits and maintaining hope in the face of overwhelming odds.

Their bond, forged in the crucible of survival, proved invaluable in their efforts to heal a fractured planet. Regular counseling sessions, led by a psychologist among their number, were essential in helping them cope with the psychological trauma.

But amidst the hardship, small victories began to emerge. The first green shoots pushing through the contaminated soil, the first breaths of cleaner air, and the first harvests from their hydroponic farms—these were milestones that fueled their determination. The reforestation efforts started to show tangible results; small patches of vibrant green began to reclaim the wasteland. The air, though still far from pristine, was gradually becoming cleaner and more breathable. Rivers and lakes, once barren and lifeless, started to show signs of revival. It was a slow, arduous process, filled with setbacks and disappointments, but their relentless work was slowly turning the tide.

Their success wasn't solely dependent on technological advancement; it also relied on a fundamental shift in their relationship with the environment. They learned to work with nature, rather than against it. The respect they had developed for the interconnectedness of life, fostered by their experiences in the underwater world, guided their every decision. They recognized the delicate balance of ecosystems and the importance of biodiversity in restoring the planet's health. It was not simply about reclaiming the land, but about nurturing and fostering a new harmonious relationship with the planet.

The story of their environmental restoration wasn't just a tale of scientific innovation and technological prowess, but also one of resilience, hope, and profound understanding. It was a testament to the human spirit's ability to overcome adversity, learn from its mistakes, and find the strength to heal a fractured world. The long road ahead remained fraught with challenges, but as they looked upon the burgeoning green shoots pushing through the ashen landscape, they knew that they were on the right path—a path illuminated by the fragile yet unwavering hope for a brighter future. A future where humanity and nature could coexist in a balanced and harmonious relationship. The scars of the past remained, a constant reminder of the devastation they had witnessed, but those scars would also serve as a testament to their unwavering resolve—their determination to build a better future for generations to come.

The acrid smell of ozone hung heavy in the air, a phantom scent clinging to the survivors even as they distanced themselves from the ravaged surface world. The landscape, a testament to the cataclysmic events that had reshaped their reality, was a stark reminder of their fragility. Dust storms, whipped up by unpredictable winds, scoured the cracked earth, obscuring the skeletal remains of cities in a perpetual twilight. The once-vibrant blue of the sky was now a muted grey, a canvas streaked with the scars of atmospheric disruption.

Captain Armstrong, his face etched with exhaustion and worry lines that hadn't been there before the descent into the underwater realm, surveyed the scene with a heavy heart. The battle against the Cetea had been brutal, a clash of advanced technology and desperate survival. The victory had been hard-won, purchased with the

ultimate sacrifice of Jian, whose selfless act echoed in the silence of the ravaged world. His loss was a wound that would not easily heal.

Dr. Thorne, despite her usual steely resolve, was visibly shaken, her eyes reflecting the horror she had witnessed. The advanced technology of the Luminese, once a marvel, had felt inadequate in the face of the Cetea's relentless assault. The battle had exposed the limitations of even their sophisticated weaponry.

Sarah Chen, her connection to the "Whispers" strained but not broken, was withdrawn, the weight of her newfound understanding pressing heavily on her young shoulders. The prophecies she had glimpsed hinted at a far greater threat lurking in the shadows—one that extended far beyond the immediate conflict. She had seen visions of an ecological collapse even more devastating than what they currently witnessed, a future where the delicate balance of the planet was irretrievably shattered. The whispers of impending doom haunted her, a constant reminder of the precariousness of their situation.

The emotional toll of the battle was as devastating as the physical damage. Each survivor carried the invisible scars of trauma: the haunting memories of fallen comrades and the relentless pressure of fighting for survival. Captain Rostova, usually a pillar of strength, was struggling to reconcile the horrors she had witnessed with her unwavering faith in the Luminese's peaceful nature. The stark contrast between the idyllic underwater city and the desolate surface world had shattered her perception of reality. She grappled with the realization that even the most advanced civilizations were vulnerable to internal conflicts and external threats.

The physical injuries were less visible but equally debilitating. Many of the survivors suffered from radiation sickness, the aftereffects of the weapons employed in the battle. The exposure to the altered atmosphere further complicated their recovery. Dr. Thorne worked tirelessly to treat them, her medical expertise a beacon of hope in the face of overwhelming adversity. She rationed the precious medical supplies that had survived the journey, prioritizing the most severe cases. Her efforts were a constant race against time and dwindling resources. She found herself relying on both advanced technology salvaged from the wreckage and rudimentary techniques, piecing together solutions with whatever she could find. The lack of proper medical facilities compounded the problem, forcing her to improvise solutions in the harsh and unforgiving environment.

Beyond the immediate physical and emotional wounds, the survivors faced the daunting task of rebuilding a shattered world. The environmental damage was catastrophic—an unrelenting assault on the biosphere. The atmosphere was toxic, poisoned by the fallout of the conflict and years of unchecked pollution. The land was scarred and barren, the soil contaminated with harmful substances. The ecosystem, once rich and diverse, was on the brink of collapse. The oceans themselves, once a source of life and abundance, were now plagued by harmful algal blooms and dead zones. The once vibrant coral reefs, marvels of nature, lay bleached and lifeless.

The sheer scale of the devastation was daunting, prompting an existential crisis amongst the survivors. Doubt gnawed at them, casting shadows on their resolve. Could they truly rebuild a world so profoundly damaged? Was it even worth the effort? The weight of responsibility pressed down upon them, threatening to crush their spirits. Captain Armstrong, however, refused to surrender to despair. He knew that surrender meant certain extinction. He called a meeting, addressing the survivors with a strength and resolve that belied his weariness.

"We have lost much," he acknowledged, his voice gravelly but resolute. "We have suffered losses beyond measure. But we are not broken. We have survived the battle, and we will survive the aftermath. We may not have the answers to every challenge, but we have each other. We have the knowledge gleaned from the Luminese. We have the resilience of the human spirit. The road ahead will be long and arduous, but we will not falter. We will rebuild. We will heal this world. We will honor Jian's sacrifice by creating a future worthy of his memory."

His words resonated deeply within the survivors, rekindling a flicker of hope in their weary hearts. Sarah Chen, regaining her composure, stepped forward. Her connection to the "Whispers" had given her a glimpse of possible solutions, a path toward healing the planet. She shared her visions, outlining specific areas where intervention could yield the most significant results. Her insights, combined with the advanced technology salvaged from the underwater world and the Luminese's scientific expertise, formed the foundation of their plan.

The rebuilding process was a meticulous and painstaking task, a blend of ancient wisdom and cutting-edge technology. Dr. Thorne, drawing upon her expertise in environmental science, worked alongside Luminese scientists to develop innovative solutions for restoring the damaged ecosystem. They harnessed the power of bioremediation, using genetically engineered microorganisms to clean up the contaminated soil and water. They employed advanced atmospheric technologies to repair the ozone layer and cleanse the air. The task was monumental, but each small victory—each sprouting plant, each returning bird—instilled a renewed sense of hope and purpose.

The survivors discovered that the "Whispers" were not just prophecies, but a form of advanced communication—a network connecting the planet's ecosystems. Sarah, acting as a conduit, learned to interpret these subtle signals, receiving guidance on how to restore balance to the environment. She discovered that the planet itself was striving toward self-healing, but it required human intervention, guided by understanding and respect for the natural world. Through this profound understanding, they learned the true meaning of interconnectedness—the intricate web of life that held together the planet.

The journey toward healing was a testament to human resilience and ingenuity, a process of learning and adaptation. They discovered new sustainable technologies that allowed them to harness renewable energy, reducing reliance on harmful fossil fuels. They developed innovative farming techniques that preserved and replenished the soil, enabling the cultivation of food crops even in the harsh conditions. They re-established biodiversity, reintroducing native species to their former habitats, carefully monitoring their progress.

The process was slow and challenging, filled with setbacks and unexpected difficulties, but the survivors persevered, driven by their shared vision of a future where humanity and nature could coexist in harmony. They learned the profound lesson that destruction and healing were not mutually exclusive. They were intimately intertwined, each shaped by the other, reminding them that the true measure of human success was not domination over nature, but the establishment of a symbiotic relationship that preserved the delicate balance of life. As they looked toward the horizon, a faint blush of pink coloring the ashen sky—a silent promise of a new dawn—they knew their journey was far from over, but the path forward, however uncertain, was now illuminated by the unwavering light of hope. The scars of the past, though indelible, served as a stark reminder of the fragility of their world and the importance of safeguarding the delicate balance of life. The battle for survival was won, but the journey toward a sustainable future had just begun.

The air, thick with the scent of burnt earth and ozone, offered little comfort. The ravaged landscape, a grotesque parody of its former self, stretched before them—a testament to the environmental catastrophe that had reshaped their world. Captain Armstrong, his face etched with grim determination, surveyed the scene. The battle had been won, but at a terrible cost. Scattered amidst the debris of collapsed buildings and twisted metal were the remnants of the conflict—shattered vehicles, scorched earth, and a chilling silence punctuated only by the mournful sigh of the wind.

Their immediate priority was the search for survivors. The initial aerial survey had revealed pockets of potential survivors, but the ground reality was far more complex. Communication was spotty at best, the remnants of the communication infrastructure rendered useless by the cataclysm. Dr. Thorne, his normally meticulous demeanor tinged with anxiety, oversaw the deployment of search teams. He had developed a rudimentary communication system using salvaged parts and repurposed Luminese technology, a testament to his resourcefulness. Small teams, each equipped with basic medical supplies and portable communication devices, fanned out across the devastated terrain.

Their search led them through a maze of rubble, a landscape rendered unrecognizable. They navigated precarious pathways, carefully avoiding unstable structures that threatened to collapse at any moment. The silence was oppressive, punctuated only by the crunch of their boots on broken glass and the occasional groan of a shifting building. The air was thick with dust, making breathing difficult and obscuring vision. Protective masks, scavenged from abandoned vehicles, offered little respite, the dust finding its way through any crack.

The first discovery was a small group huddled in a partially collapsed subway station. They were civilians, mostly elderly people and children, who had found refuge from the chaos. They were dehydrated and traumatized, but alive. Dr. Thorne and his team quickly administered first aid, offering them water, food, and a sense of security. Their rescue was a beacon of hope, a stark contrast to the desolation surrounding them.

As the search progressed, however, the reality of the situation became more grim. They encountered more casualties than survivors, a sobering reminder of the brutal reality of the conflict. Many bodies lay where they had fallen, untouched by scavengers, their stillness a chilling testament to the swiftness and brutality of the cataclysm. The discovery of a makeshift hospital, overwhelmed and abandoned, was particularly heartbreaking. Medical supplies lay scattered, along with the heartbreaking personal belongings of both patients and staff.

One team, led by Sarah Chen, stumbled upon a hidden bunker, almost miraculously untouched. Inside, they discovered a surprising group of survivors—a mix of soldiers, scientists, and civilians. The group, led by a resilient woman named Anya Petrova, had managed to withstand the onslaught. They were well-organized and wellsupplied, having created a self-sufficient ecosystem within the bunker, utilizing hydroponic systems and advanced filtration technology. They possessed crucial information—data that could help them understand the environmental changes and possibly reverse them. Anya had been a leading environmental scientist before the cataclysm, her knowledge proving invaluable in adapting to the new harsh realities.

Among their supplies, however, they also unearthed something entirely unexpected: sealed containers labeled "Project Chimera." These contained biological samples, research notes, and advanced genetic engineering equipment. The information indicated that a clandestine project had been underway—a desperate attempt to engineer resilient species capable of thriving in the altered environment. The project had been kept secret, even from many of the high-ranking officials. This revelation raised disturbing questions about the true nature of the cataclysm and whether it was entirely accidental. The possibility of a deliberate act—a desperate attempt to reshape the environment for a specific agenda—cast a shadow over their newfound hope.

The discovery of Project Chimera prompted a heated debate among the survivors. Some argued for immediate disclosure, believing the world needed to know the truth, even if it was unpleasant. Others, however, believed that the information was too dangerous to release, fearing the potential consequences. Captain Armstrong, after careful consideration, decreed that the information be shared with the leadership of the Luminese. Their wisdom and technological expertise might offer valuable insights into the implications of Project Chimera, a critical next step in their journey toward a sustainable future.

The ongoing investigation into Project Chimera revealed a darker side to the environmental crisis. Further analysis of the data indicated that the project was not solely focused on engineering resilient species. The research notes revealed an attempt to manipulate the very fabric of the planet's ecosystems—a dangerous gamble with unpredictable consequences. The goal, according to the fragmented documents, was to accelerate a natural selection process, favoring species capable of adapting to extreme environments. But the approach was ethically questionable, involving genetic manipulation and the potential for unintended consequences. Dr. Thorne, his scientific curiosity battling with moral apprehension, expressed his concerns about the long-term implications of such reckless intervention in the delicate balance of nature.

The implications were staggering. The cataclysm, once attributed solely to environmental factors, now appeared to be a consequence of human hubris—a tragic testament to the unintended consequences of scientific experimentation. The survivors were left to grapple with the weight of this revelation, questioning the very essence of human progress and responsibility toward the planet. They realized that the battle for survival extended beyond the immediate threat; it encompassed a deeper struggle against a pattern of reckless exploitation of the environment. Their quest for a sustainable future now had a more profound urgency, driven by the need to learn from the mistakes of the past.

The journey had shifted from mere survival to a commitment to restoring the ecological balance—a quest that demanded not just resilience, but profound introspection. The fight for a sustainable future was far from over; it had just begun, shrouded in the complexities of Project Chimera's revelation. The weight of the discovery hung heavy in the air, a profound challenge to their collective understanding of human responsibility and the delicate balance of the world around them. As they moved forward, the path ahead was fraught with challenges, both known and unknown. But the quest for a sustainable future was propelled by a new sense of purpose, shaped by the lessons learned from the depths of Project Chimera.

CHAPTER 8

The immediate aftermath of the battle was a scene of devastation. Bioluminescent wreckage littered the ocean floor, a stark contrast to the vibrant coral reefs that had once thrived in this area. The once-pristine Luminese city, a testament to their advanced technology and harmonious existence, bore the scars of conflict. Sections of its shimmering, bioluminescent structures lay shattered, and the intricate network of glowing pathways was disrupted. The air, or rather, the water, hung heavy with the lingering metallic tang of damaged technology and the faint, unsettling odor of scorched coral.

The Luminese, resilient and adaptable as they were, immediately began the arduous process of rebuilding. Their intricate understanding of their environment and their advanced technology, even amidst the wreckage, was evident. Teams of Luminese, their bodies shimmering with a soft, internal light, worked tirelessly, utilizing a combination of bio-engineered materials and salvaged technology to repair damaged structures. Floating platforms, propelled by gentle currents harnessed by ingenious bio-mechanical devices, transported building materials and workers with balletic grace—a testament to their advanced engineering. These were not mere repairs; they were acts of restoration, driven by a deep-seated respect for their environment and a commitment to maintaining the delicate balance of their underwater ecosystem.

Human survivors, humbled by their own near-destruction, joined the Luminese in their efforts. Captain Rostova, though physically weary, led her team with unwavering determination. Dr. Thorne, ever the scientist, meticulously documented the damage and began researching methods of accelerating coral regrowth and restoring the disrupted ecological balance. Their combined efforts with the Luminese highlighted a growing understanding and mutual respect—a foundation for a new era of collaboration.

The process of ecological restoration was complex and painstaking. Dr. Thorne discovered that the battle had not only caused physical damage to the coral reefs but had also disrupted the delicate balance of the underwater ecosystem. The "Whispers," despite their immense power, had proven to be a double-edged sword, capable of causing widespread environmental devastation if mishandled. Thorne's research revealed that the energy surges from the battle had disrupted the intricate symbiotic relationships between various species, threatening the biodiversity of the entire ecosystem. It was a critical moment, not just for the survival of the Luminese, but for the overall health of this unique underwater world.

Utilizing their advanced technology, the Luminese, guided by Thorne's research, initiated a comprehensive restoration plan. They employed bio-engineered microorganisms designed to accelerate coral growth and repopulate damaged areas. These microorganisms, infused with Luminese technology, could even absorb and neutralize pollutants left behind by the battle. The process was slow and required constant monitoring, but the results were slowly becoming visible. The once-bleached coral began to regain its vibrant color, and new life slowly started to appear in the previously desolate areas.

Beyond the physical reconstruction, healing was also essential for the emotional well-being of both Luminese and humans. The trauma of the battle was palpable, leaving a lasting impact on both sides. The Luminese, who had lived for millennia in peace and harmony, had experienced violence on a scale previously unimaginable. The human survivors, too, were grappling with the loss of their homeworld, the trauma of the crash, and the challenges of adapting to a completely new environment.

The Luminese approached healing through communal meditation and therapeutic practices that harnessed the power of their bioluminescence. Their tranquil underwater cities became sanctuaries where both Luminese and humans could find solace and engage in restorative activities. The rhythmic pulse of their bioluminescent structures offered a soothing rhythm, and the gentle currents seemed to carry away the burden of their shared trauma. The humans, in turn, shared their own coping mechanisms, offering support and fostering a newfound sense of unity.

The formation of new alliances, built on mutual respect and a shared understanding of the fragility of their environment, was a crucial step in the healing process. While trust remained fragile, the common goal of rebuilding and protecting their shared homeworld fostered unprecedented cooperation. The Abyssals, having witnessed the destructive power of the Cetea, proved unexpectedly willing to cooperate, at least for the time being. Their understanding of the deep ocean and its currents offered invaluable assistance in the ecological restoration efforts.

A communication link was established with the surface world, which had also undergone significant changes during the survivors' absence. News of this underwater world, once a figment of imagination, filtered through, sparking a wave of global wonder and concern. The survivors, led by Captain Rostova and Dr. Thorne, acted as emissaries, sharing their knowledge and urging for international cooperation in environmental protection and sustainable practices. The shared experience served as a stark reminder of the interconnectedness of all life and the urgent need for global action.

The sharing of knowledge proved to be a turning point. The advanced technology of the Luminese, combined with human ingenuity, opened up new possibilities for sustainable living. The Luminese's bioluminescent energy sources, once solely powering their cities, could provide a clean, renewable energy solution for the surface world. Their mastery of marine bioengineering offered a chance to address global warming and restore depleted ecosystems. The sharing of knowledge was not merely an exchange of information, but a testament to the power of collaboration and a profound shift in the relationship between the surface world and the underwater realm.

The underwater world, once a hidden secret, now held a pivotal role in shaping the future of the planet. The catastrophic events of the recent past served as a stark warning and a catalyst for change. The newfound alliances, the shared understanding of the delicate balance of ecosystems, and the combined knowledge of both worlds laid the foundation for a future characterized by cooperation, sustainability, and a shared responsibility for the planet. The path to a new beginning was long and arduous, but the shared journey of rebuilding and recovery offered a glimmer of hope—a testament to the resilience of life and the power of interconnectedness. The whispers of the past now held a promise for the future, a future where the once-separate worlds were joined together, not by conflict, but by shared purpose and a determination to heal the planet, both above and below the waves.

The immediate priority was salvage and rescue. Luminese healers, with their astonishing regenerative technology, worked tirelessly alongside the human medical team, patching wounds and stabilizing the injured. The shared grief over losses—both Luminese and human—fostered a strange kind of unity, a common understanding forged in the crucible of shared trauma. The sight of Luminese technicians working shoulder-to-shoulder with Captain

Armstrong's engineers, sharing schematics and repairing damaged equipment, was a powerful symbol of this burgeoning alliance.

Dr. Thorne, ever the pragmatist, focused on understanding the technology. The Luminese readily shared their knowledge, their advanced understanding of bioluminescence and energy

manipulation proving invaluable. He learned of their sophisticated system of underwater agriculture, their methods of sustainable energy harvesting from hydrothermal vents, and their intricate network of underwater communication. The exchange was mutually beneficial: the Luminese gained access to human scientific knowledge, particularly in areas like medicine and materials science, while humans gained a profound understanding of a civilization that had mastered the delicate balance of technology and nature.

The Abyssals, initially perceived as enigmatic and untrustworthy, proved to be a more complex entity. Their initial hostility stemmed, it turned out, from a deep-seated fear of the Cetea's expansionist ambitions. The Cetea, with their aggressive tactics and ruthless pursuit of power, had long been a threat to the delicate balance of the underwater world. The recent conflict, however, had revealed the true extent of the Cetea's destructive potential, prompting a reassessment of alliances. Several Abyssal clans, witnessing the Luminese's resilience and the humans' unexpected technological prowess, cautiously extended tentative offers of cooperation. This wasn't a sudden shift of allegiance, but rather a slow, careful dance of mutual interest, born from a shared fear of the common enemy.

Sarah Chen's connection to the Whispers proved crucial in navigating these complex relationships. Her ability to interpret and understand the subtle vibrations emanating from the ancient ruins and the deep ocean trenches offered a unique perspective on the underwater world's history and the prophecies interwoven with its fate. She discovered that the Whispers weren't merely voices from the past but a complex, interconnected network of energy—a kind of subterranean internet woven into the very fabric of the ocean floor. This network held the key to understanding not only the underwater world but also the strange changes occurring on the surface.

The surface world, as the survivors learned through sporadic radio transmissions, was in chaos. The disappearance of the plane, followed by the seemingly impossible emergence of a sophisticated underwater civilization, had thrown global politics into disarray. Conspiracy theories ran rampant, and governments were in crisis.

The scientific community, initially skeptical, was now grappling with the implications of a world far more complex and interconnected than they had ever imagined. The shared knowledge, cautiously relayed through encrypted transmissions, slowly began to bridge the gap between the surface and underwater worlds. The previously impossible concept of cooperation now seemed not only possible but necessary for the survival of both.

The challenge of rebuilding was immense. The Luminese city, while advanced, had suffered significant damage. The human survivors, with their unique skills and resources, pitched in, their engineering expertise complementing the Luminese's advanced technology. The rebuilding process became a collaborative effort, a testament to the burgeoning friendship and mutual respect that was blooming between the two civilizations. This wasn't merely a physical reconstruction; it was a rebuilding of trust and a forging of a shared future.

The Abyssal clans, once isolated and distrustful, also contributed their unique knowledge. Their expertise in deep-sea engineering and their understanding of the ocean currents proved invaluable in the design of new, sustainable habitats. They shared their knowledge of bioluminescent algae cultivation, a critical component of the underwater ecosystem and a source of both light and energy. The Abyssals, long isolated in their dark, deep-sea cities, discovered a new appreciation for the vibrant surface and the potential for cooperation.

The process of establishing sustainable systems of governance also presented a challenge. The Luminese council, while benevolent, needed to incorporate the humans and the Abyssals into their decision-making process. A complex system of representation was devised, involving representatives from each faction to ensure that all voices were heard. This wasn't an easy process; tensions remained, particularly between the more traditional Luminese elders and the more progressive factions, but the common goal of survival and the shared desire for a peaceful future fostered compromise.

The human survivors, initially overwhelmed by the strangeness of their new environment, played a critical role in this governance evolution. Captain Armstrong, with his military background, brought an organizational structure and a sense of discipline, while Dr. Thorne provided the scientific expertise needed to build a sustainable future. Sarah Chen, with her unique connection to the Whispers, served as a bridge between the past, present, and future, offering guidance and insights into the interconnectedness of the underwater and surface worlds.

Meanwhile, the understanding of the Whispers continued to grow. It wasn't merely a source of prophecies; it was a powerful communication system, a vast network of energy that connected the entire planet, both above and below the waves. Sarah's ability to interpret its signals became crucial in anticipating natural disasters, managing resource allocation, and even predicting the movements of the Cetea. This network was far more than just a form of communication; it was a means of understanding the delicate balance of life on Earth. The Whispers provided a glimpse into the interconnectedness of all things, revealing the profound impact human actions had on the entire planet, highlighting the responsibility for stewardship.

The threat of the Cetea, however, remained. While weakened by their defeat, they hadn't vanished. Their ruthlessness and their determination to control the Whispers meant they posed a constant, insidious danger. The newly formed alliance—the Luminese, the humans, and several Abyssal clans—had to remain vigilant, constantly adapting and preparing for any potential attack. This wasn't a time for complacency but a time for unity and shared responsibility.

The shared experience of rebuilding, confronting the Cetea, and learning to live together in harmony had profoundly changed the survivors. They were no longer just human beings; they were guardians of a world far larger and more complex than they had ever imagined. They were custodians of the delicate balance of life, not only in the underwater kingdom but on the planet as a whole. The path ahead was uncertain, riddled with challenges, but the foundation for a new beginning had been laid. A new dawn was breaking, not only on the underwater world but on the entire planet. The Whispers of the past were now a beacon, guiding them toward a future where technology and nature could coexist, where different civilizations could learn to understand and respect each other, and where the shared responsibility for the planet's well-being could finally prevail. The future was not merely about survival; it was about thriving, about creating a world where all could flourish—a world born from the ashes of conflict and nurtured by the seeds of hope and understanding. The journey was far from over; this was merely the first step toward creating a new equilibrium, a new harmony, a new beginning.

The shared experience of near-death, the collaborative effort to rebuild after the devastation wrought by the Cetea attack, and the ongoing threat of the Abyssals—all had forged an unprecedented bond between the human survivors and the Luminese. This wasn't mere tolerance; it was a profound understanding, a recognition of shared vulnerability and a mutual dependence that transcended species. The Luminese, with their advanced technology and deep understanding of the ocean's intricate ecosystem, provided the crucial scientific and technological expertise. The humans, in turn, offered their diverse skills—from engineering and medicine to leadership and diplomacy—skills honed in a vastly different environment, yet surprisingly applicable in this strange new world.

Captain Armstrong, initially skeptical of the Luminese's pacifistic nature, had witnessed firsthand their courage and ingenuity in the face of adversity. He had seen their healers mend wounds that seemed beyond repair, their engineers solve problems with an elegant simplicity he found awe-inspiring. He now understood that their peaceful demeanor wasn't weakness; it was a strength born from a deep respect for life and a sophisticated understanding of interconnectedness. His initial military strategy, based on dominance and control, had been replaced by a more nuanced approach—one that prioritized cooperation and mutual respect. He began to see the value of diplomacy, the power of understanding, and the potential for synergistic collaboration. He had learned to appreciate that true strength wasn't about conquering, but about co-existing.

Dr. Thorne, ever the scientist, had discovered a boundless source of inspiration in the Luminese's approach to science. Their understanding of marine biology, their mastery of bioluminescent technology, and their harmonious relationship with the ocean's diverse life forms offered a stark contrast to the exploitative practices prevalent on the surface world. The Luminese didn't conquer nature; they worked with it, understanding its complexities and respecting its limits. Thorne found himself immersed in collaborative research projects, sharing his knowledge of human medicine and technology while absorbing the Luminese's wisdom. Their joint efforts led to breakthroughs in regenerative medicine, the development of sustainable energy sources, and a deeper understanding of the ocean's delicate balance.

Sarah Chen's connection to the Whispers proved invaluable. Initially a source of fear and confusion, her unique ability to interpret the ocean's subtle cues became a vital tool for communication and understanding. She could sense the emotional state of the ocean, predict environmental changes, and even decipher the cryptic messages embedded within the Whispers. This ability was particularly helpful in navigating the treacherous currents and identifying potential dangers. The Luminese, who had a limited understanding of this phenomenon, embraced Sarah's unique gift, recognizing its potential to foster a deeper connection with the ocean's vast consciousness. Their collaborative research into the Whispers yielded remarkable insights into the ocean's history, its future, and its profound interconnectedness with all life on Earth.

The cooperation wasn't confined to the human-Luminese alliance. The experience of facing the common threat of the Cetea had unexpectedly fostered a fragile truce with some of the more moderate Abyssal factions. These enigmatic beings, once perceived as purely hostile, were now seen as possessing a wisdom born from their ancient connection to the ocean. Their understanding of the deep sea's secrets, their mastery of ancient technologies, and their unique perspective on the Whispers proved invaluable in comprehending the full scope of the underwater world's history. This understanding was built slowly, cautiously, through shared experiences and a willingness to listen and learn, to overcome ingrained prejudices and mistrust. It highlighted the importance of patience and empathy, of recognizing shared humanity despite profound differences.

The challenges were immense. Cultural differences, contrasting worldviews, and lingering suspicions posed ongoing obstacles. Misunderstandings and conflicts arose frequently, but the shared commitment to a better future continually propelled them forward.

They learned to find common ground, to navigate disagreements with respect and understanding, and to appreciate the value of diversity. The common goal – survival and the preservation of their shared home – outweighed their differences. The process involved compromises, concessions, and a willingness to relinquish preconceived notions. They had to learn to see beyond their own limited perspectives, to embrace a wider, more inclusive worldview.

This cooperation extended to the practical aspects of rebuilding. The Luminese's advanced technology accelerated the repair of damaged structures and the construction of new settlements. They developed sustainable farming techniques that capitalized on the unique properties of the underwater environment. They harnessed renewable energy sources, creating a self-sufficient ecosystem that minimized the impact on the delicate marine life. The humans, with their practical ingenuity and diverse skill sets, adapted their knowledge to this novel environment, creating innovative solutions and bridging the technological gap. The joint effort resulted in a sustainable, thriving civilization that seamlessly blended the advanced technology of the Luminese with the human spirit of resilience and ingenuity.

The process of cooperation was not always smooth. There were moments of friction, disagreements over strategy, and clashes of personalities. But the overriding sense of shared fate, the understanding that their survival depended on their ability to work together, prevented these conflicts from derailing their efforts. Disagreements were addressed through open dialogue, mutual respect, and a willingness to compromise. They had learned that effective cooperation required patience, empathy, and a deep understanding of each other's perspectives and motivations.

The creation of a unified council, composed of representatives from both the Luminese and the human survivors, marked a significant milestone in their journey toward harmony. This council, though initially unwieldy, gradually developed effective mechanisms for decision-making and conflict resolution. The shared commitment to transparency and accountability fostered trust and mutual respect. The council's decisions were not always unanimous, but the process itself became a symbol of their shared determination to build a better future, a future where cooperation and understanding were the foundation of their society.

The cooperation extended beyond simple survival; it encompassed a shared responsibility for protecting their environment. The Luminese's deep respect for the ocean's delicate ecosystem became a guiding principle for the unified community. They implemented strict environmental regulations, developed sustainable technologies, and prioritized the preservation of biodiversity. The humans, initially more focused on technological solutions, came to understand the importance of harmonious coexistence with nature. The result was a society that thrived in balance, where technological advancement and environmental stewardship were not mutually exclusive but intertwined, complementary facets of their existence.

The lessons learned during this period of collaboration were profound. It wasn't just about working together; it was about understanding, respecting, and celebrating diversity. They discovered the strength that comes from embracing different perspectives, from integrating unique skills and knowledge, and from recognizing the value of empathy and compassion. This newfound unity was not merely a political alliance or a temporary truce. It represented a fundamental shift in perspective, a paradigm shift that recognized the profound interconnectedness of all life and the shared responsibility for protecting the planet. This new beginning wasn't just about building a new civilization; it was about fostering a new way of life, a way of life based on mutual respect, cooperation, and a deep understanding of the delicate balance between humanity and nature. It was a testament to the power of collaboration, a beacon of hope in a world that had once seemed hopelessly divided. The journey was far from over, yet the foundation for a truly harmonious future had been laid. The whispers of the past now echoed with the promise of a future built on unity, cooperation, and a profound respect for the interconnectedness of all life.

The successful repair of the Luminese communication array was a monumental achievement, a beacon of hope piercing the veil of isolation that had separated this underwater world from the surface. The initial signal, a faint pulse of energy detected by a repurposed satellite fragment orbiting high above, sent shivers of anticipation through both the human and Luminese communities. The ensuing weeks were a blur of feverish activity. Dr. Thorne, working alongside a team of Luminese scientists whose understanding of electromagnetic fields far surpassed anything he'd encountered, meticulously calibrated the array, ensuring a clear, stable transmission. Captain Armstrong, ever practical, organized the gathering and transmission of information, a task requiring a delicate balance between maintaining secrecy – they still couldn't be certain of the surface world's reaction – and the urgency of sharing their discoveries.

The first message, a simple, coded greeting, was met with stunned silence. Days turned into weeks as they waited for a response. The tension was palpable. Had the signal been intercepted? Had the surface world even survived the cataclysmic events that had preceded their arrival in this hidden realm? The uncertainty was agonizing. Finally, a response arrived, a scrambled message laden with static, yet undeniably a response. The initial contact was tentative, cautious, laced with disbelief and wonder.

Subsequent messages, however, revealed a world transformed.

The surface world had endured profound ecological devastation. The very fabric of the planet's ecosystems had been altered, a consequence of unchecked industrialization and a catastrophic climate shift. Vast swathes of land were uninhabitable, cities lay in ruins, and the global population had been decimated. The descriptions painted a grim picture, a stark contrast to the vibrant, relatively pristine underwater world they had found. Yet, amidst the despair, there was a flicker of hope. The message spoke of resilience, of humanity's tenacity in the face of adversity, of pockets of survival and the slow, arduous process of rebuilding. The surface world's message resonated with the humans' own experiences; they understood the fragility of life, the importance of cooperation, and the weight of responsibility.

The ensuing communication exchange involved the painstaking transmission of data. The Luminese shared their advanced knowledge of sustainable energy sources, of bio-remediation techniques capable of restoring damaged ecosystems, and of technologies far beyond anything the surface world had ever imagined. The humans, in return, provided their detailed knowledge of terrestrial ecosystems, of past mistakes and lessons learned, a crucial piece of information to prevent future catastrophic ecological collapse. This was a two-way street, a symbiotic exchange of knowledge designed not just for survival, but for the creation of a better future for both worlds.

Sarah Chen, whose unique sensitivity to the "Whispers" had played such a crucial role in navigating their underwater world, found herself at the heart of this communication exchange. Her ability to perceive subtle shifts in energy, to interpret the hidden language of the ocean, proved invaluable. She could sense the emotional currents flowing through the transmissions, the anxieties, the hopes, and the shared longing for a peaceful and sustainable future. She became a vital bridge between two worlds, interpreting subtle nuances and helping to smooth out any misunderstandings, offering emotional context that raw data alone could not convey.

The exchange wasn't without its challenges. Cultural differences proved to be a significant hurdle. The Luminese, with their deeply interconnected society and harmonious relationship with their environment, found it challenging to grasp the concept of human individualism—the often-destructive pursuit of personal gain and unchecked ambition. The surface world, scarred by centuries of conflict and exploitation, struggled to comprehend the Luminese's pacifistic philosophy and their innate respect for all life forms. But slowly, patiently, through countless transmissions, a shared understanding began to emerge.

The discussions went far beyond the exchange of technical data. They touched upon philosophical questions of responsibility and the delicate balance between progress and preservation. The Luminese shared ancient prophecies that spoke of a time of great upheaval, a time when the balance of the planet would be tested, when both the surface and underwater worlds would be called upon to unite or perish. The humans, in turn, shared their own accounts of past conflicts, the devastating consequences of environmental degradation, and the hope they now found in the possibility of a shared future.

The collaborative efforts extended beyond simple information exchange. The Luminese scientists provided detailed schematics and instructions for constructing bio-regenerative structures—buildings that harnessed the power of the ocean to create sustainable habitats. They shared knowledge of advanced agricultural techniques that could revitalize depleted soils and produce abundant harvests with minimal environmental impact. The humans, leveraging their knowledge of human physiology and medicine, offered aid in treating chronic diseases prevalent in the devastated surface world, sharing medical technologies and techniques. They also worked to interpret and disseminate the Luminese's advanced scientific concepts into formats accessible to the surface world's damaged scientific infrastructure.

The communication also brought about a shift in power dynamics. The surface world, once the dominant force in its own realm, now found itself relying on the expertise of a hidden civilization. This change sparked a significant shift in perspective— a humbling acknowledgment of humanity's limited knowledge and its capacity for self-destruction. It also brought an unexpected sense of unity. Facing a shared predicament of global-scale ecological devastation, nations previously driven by self-interest began to cooperate more effectively.

There were moments of frustration and setbacks. The damaged satellite networks of the surface world struggled with the sheer volume of information being transmitted. The Luminese's advanced technology was not always compatible with existing surface-world infrastructure. There were occasions of misinterpreted messages, resulting in periods of anxious silence before understanding was restored. But amidst these challenges, the shared commitment to a better future persevered.

The success of this communication exchange wasn't just about exchanging data; it was about fostering a relationship—a bond of shared destiny. The surface world now looked to the underwater realm not as a mysterious anomaly, but as a source of hope, a potential partner in the monumental task of rebuilding and creating a sustainable future. And, in turn, the Luminese, who once existed in peaceful isolation, now found themselves not only accepting but actively participating in the fate of a planet far beyond the luminous depths of their hidden world. The whispers of the past, once a source of apprehension, now resonated with the harmonious song of hope—a melody composed of a shared language of survival, collaboration, and a profound respect for the intricate web of life that interconnected all. The future remained uncertain, but for the first time, it felt possible—even probable—that both the surface world and the underwater kingdom would not only survive but thrive, together.

The initial contact was tentative—a hesitant exchange of images and simple messages. The surface world, scarred and reeling from the ecological catastrophes that had preceded the plane crash, responded with cautious optimism. Images of ravaged coastlines, depleted resources, and desperate populations were met with equally stark depictions of the Luminese cities, their vibrant coral architecture a stark contrast to the grey desolation depicted from above. Yet, underlying the visual differences was a shared urgency, a mutual recognition of the fragility of life and the interconnectedness of all ecosystems.

Dr. Thorne, ever the scientist, focused on the practicalities of the exchange. He meticulously documented the Luminese technologies, their innovative approaches to sustainable energy and resource management, sharing data that could revolutionize surface-world practices. The Luminese, in return, eagerly absorbed information about the devastating effects of human industrialization, the depletion of the ozone layer, and the rise of global temperatures. This exchange wasn't simply a transfer of information; it was a collaborative learning process, a shared exploration of solutions.

The Luminese engineers, particularly skilled in bio-engineering and energy manipulation, were instrumental in developing advanced desalination systems using bioluminescent organisms to filter and purify vast quantities of seawater, providing a crucial solution to the surface world's dwindling freshwater reserves. In return, surfaceworld engineers, utilizing salvaged components from the downed aircraft and Luminese technology, helped develop more efficient methods of harnessing the power of the "Whispers"—the mysterious energy field that underpinned the underwater world's advanced technology.

This collaboration extended beyond the purely technological. Cultural exchange became a key component of the burgeoning relationship. Luminese artists shared their mesmerizing bioluminescent sculptures, their intricate designs reflecting a deep understanding of natural rhythms and symbiotic relationships. Surface-world musicians, adapting their instruments to the underwater environment, responded with compositions inspired by the Luminese melodies, creating a fusion of sounds that echoed the bridging of two worlds. This exchange of art and music helped transcend the language barrier, forging a deeper connection based on shared emotions and experiences.

However, this newfound harmony wasn't without its challenges. The Abyssals, a reclusive and enigmatic faction inhabiting the deepest trenches of the ocean, remained largely unknown, their motives shrouded in mystery. Their infrequent, cryptic communications hinted at a history interwoven with the Luminese, a history fraught with conflict and ancient grudges. Captain Armstrong, ever vigilant, maintained a close watch, navigating the delicate balance between fostering collaboration and guarding against potential threats.

The Cetea, on the other hand, presented a more immediate danger. Their ruthless pursuit of power, their exploitation of the "Whispers" for their own selfish gains, posed a direct threat to both the Luminese and the surface world. Intelligence gathered through the newly established communication link revealed the Cetea's plans to weaponize the "Whispers," their ambition threatening to plunge both worlds into a devastating conflict. A coordinated effort, involving both the Luminese military and surface-world experts in counter-terrorism and strategic defense, was put in place to counter this imminent threat.

Sarah Chen's unique connection to the "Whispers" played a pivotal role in navigating this complex situation. Her ability to sense and interpret the subtle fluctuations in the energy field provided crucial insights into the Cetea's plans, allowing for preemptive measures and strategic alliances. Her intuition, coupled with the scientific analysis of Dr. Thorne and the Luminese scientists, revealed hidden patterns and vulnerabilities in the Cetea's technology, paving the way for a carefully crafted counter-strategy.

The collaborative effort involved not just military might but also diplomatic maneuvers. Messages were sent to neutral factions in the underwater world, appealing to their sense of self-preservation and urging them to reconsider their neutrality in the face of the Cetea's escalating aggression. This diplomatic approach, built upon the foundation of trust and mutual respect established in the initial communication exchange, proved remarkably effective, garnering support from unexpected quarters.

The battle that followed wasn't a straightforward military conflict. It was a complex interplay of strategies, a combination of technological prowess and diplomatic finesse. The Luminese, with their superior understanding of the underwater environment and their advanced bio-engineered weaponry, disrupted the Cetea's operations, while surface-world forces provided crucial support through long-range surveillance and targeted interventions. Sarah Chen's ability to manipulate the "Whispers" on a localized scale proved instrumental in disabling key Cetea installations, turning their own technology against them.

The outcome was a decisive victory, yet it came at a cost. Several Luminese warriors and surface-world personnel made the ultimate sacrifice, their courage and dedication a testament to the growing bond between the two worlds. The fallen were honored with ceremonies reflecting both Luminese and human traditions, a poignant reminder of the shared loss and the shared commitment to a future built on cooperation and respect.

The aftermath of the conflict saw a significant shift in the power dynamics of the underwater world. The Cetea's influence was severely curtailed, their aggressive expansionism replaced by a reluctant acceptance of collaboration. The Abyssals, having witnessed the combined strength of the Luminese and the surface world, adopted a more cautious, less enigmatic stance, initiating tentative communications that suggested a possible path toward peaceful coexistence.

This newly forged alliance between the surface world and the underwater kingdom was more than a simple treaty; it was a fundamental change in the relationship between two distinct worlds, two profoundly different civilizations. It represented a shared understanding of the intricate interconnectedness of life, the realization that the fate of one was inextricably linked to the other. The future remained uncertain, with numerous challenges still to be overcome, but the foundation had been laid for a sustainable and prosperous future—a future where the song of hope, once a hesitant melody, now resonated with a powerful, unified chorus.

The whispers of the past, once foreboding, now carried the promise of a new beginning, a harmonious symphony played by two worlds, finally in tune. The success wasn't just about survival; it was about forging a new understanding, a new responsibility, a new world built on cooperation and mutual respect. The journey had been fraught with peril, but the destination, however distant, seemed achievable. The echo of Jian's selfless act still resonated in the hearts of all, a constant reminder of the sacrifices made and the strength of the human spirit.

The underwater world, once a mystery, now held the potential for a revolutionary future—a future brighter than anyone could have imagined before the plane crash, a future where technology and nature, surface and deep, humanity and Luminese could coexist in harmony. It was a future written not in the whispers of the past, but in the resounding echoes of a new beginning.

CHAPTER 9

The air shimmered above the ocean's surface, a heat haze distorting the already surreal landscape. The Bermuda Triangle, once a byword for mystery and disappearance, now held a different kind of secret.

The Whispers—a phenomenon that had threatened to unravel the delicate balance between the underwater world of Luminese and the surface—had left an indelible mark. The cataclysmic events of the past months—the battles, the betrayals, the sacrifices—had reshaped everything.

In the immediate aftermath, survival was a chaotic scramble. The environmental devastation caused by the final confrontation with the Cetea had scarred the Luminese reefs. Vast swathes of bioluminescent coral, once vibrant and teeming with life, were now bleached and lifeless—ghostly reminders of the war's destructive power. The delicate symbiotic relationships that sustained the ecosystem had been fractured, leaving many species struggling. Even the Luminese, with their advanced technology, grappled with the scale of the damage.

But the long-term effects of the Whispers were more subtle, more pervasive. The very fabric of reality seemed altered. Once a chaotic force, the Whispers now resonated with a subdued hum—a low thrum that permeated the water, a silent song of change. This was evident in the Luminese themselves. Their technology, once seemingly limitless, now operated with a newfound efficiency, a streamlined elegance born from necessity.

They had learned to harness the residual energy of the Whispers, integrating it into their architecture and daily life. Their cities, though bearing the scars of battle, shimmered with renewed vitality. Bioluminescent lights pulsed with rhythmic intensity, echoing the subdued hum of the Whispers.

Sarah Chen, whose unique connection to the Whispers had been instrumental in the victory over the Cetea, found herself at the center of this transformation. Her understanding of the Whispers' energy had deepened, allowing her not only to interpret its subtle fluctuations but also to influence them. She worked alongside Luminese scientists, using her abilities to aid in the restoration of the damaged coral reefs. Guided by the Whispers, her touch seemed to accelerate coral growth, coaxing life back into the barren stretches of ocean floor.

The process wasn't instantaneous. It was slow, painstaking, but progress was evident. New species, resilient and adapted to the altered environment, began to emerge—a testament to the

persistence of life in the face of adversity. Sarah's role was no longer just that of a survivor; she had become a catalyst for healing, a bridge between the human world and Luminese civilization.

The surface world, too, felt the ripples of the Whispers' legacy. The sudden disappearance and reappearance of the crashed plane, the tales of a hidden underwater civilization, and the ensuing battle had left a profound impact on global consciousness.

Governments and scientific institutions initially dismissed the reports as fantastical, but irrefutable evidence—the salvaged Luminese technology, the firsthand accounts of survivors—forced a reevaluation. International collaborations, spurred by this newfound awareness of interconnectedness, were initiated to study the Whispers and understand their potential.

The Luminese technology, carefully shared with select scientists, sparked an unprecedented revolution in sustainable energy and environmental remediation. Their mastery of bioluminescence and ability to harness the ocean's inherent energy provided a blueprint for a future free from fossil fuels. Advances in materials science, inspired by deep-sea organisms, led to the development of biocompatible materials and self-healing infrastructure.

This knowledge transfer extended beyond technology—it fostered a profound shift in global environmental policy. The collective trauma of near-catastrophe became a catalyst for change, fueling international efforts to address climate change and protect marine ecosystems.

However, the legacy of the Whispers was not without its shadows. The power they held, once wielded as a weapon, now posed new ethical dilemmas. The temptation to manipulate the very fabric of reality remained a constant concern. Strict protocols were established, both within Luminese society and the international scientific community, to ensure the responsible use of the Whispers' energy.

Dedicated research centers were founded to monitor the Whispers long-term and prevent potential threats. The understanding that unchecked power could lead to devastating consequences became a central tenet of the post-Whispers era.

Years after the initial cataclysm, Captain Rostova—now an elder stateswoman of the underwater world—reflected on the journey. The scars on her body, both physical and emotional, served as constant reminders of the battles fought and the sacrifices made. Yet her eyes held a spark of hope, a testament to the resilience of the human spirit.

She had witnessed firsthand the power of collaboration, the beauty of unexpected alliances, and the extraordinary ability of life to adapt and thrive. The Whispers' legacy was not solely one of destruction and chaos; it was also a testament to human innovation, resilience, and the capacity to find hope even in the face of insurmountable odds.

Dr. Thorne, once a cynical scientist, had undergone a profound transformation. His initial skepticism had given way to a deep reverence for the interconnectedness of life, the delicate balance of ecosystems, and humanity's profound responsibility toward the planet. Dedicating his life to Whispers research, he sought to understand their full potential while remaining acutely aware of their inherent dangers.

He knew the Whispers held the key to a future both technologically advanced and environmentally sustainable—but only if humanity approached this power with humility and wisdom.

The relationship between the surface and underwater worlds continued to evolve—a partnership forged in the crucible of shared adversity. Regular exchanges of knowledge and resources fostered mutual respect and understanding. The Luminese, once a hidden civilization, had emerged as a beacon of hope, demonstrating a path toward harmonious coexistence between technology and nature.

Still, vigilance remained. The potential for future threats, whether from within or without, was a constant reminder of the fragility of peace and the importance of continued caution.

The Whispers' legacy extended beyond the immediate aftermath. The changed world shaped subsequent generations. The children of survivors, raised in this era of unprecedented cooperation, inherited a profound sense of responsibility toward the environment and a deeper appreciation for the interconnectedness of all living things.

The stories of the past, passed down through generations, served as cautionary tales but also as inspirational narratives, reminding them of the remarkable power of human resilience and the potential for creating a truly sustainable future.

Even Simon Pierce, the narrator of this incredible saga, felt the lingering effects of the Whispers. His writing, shaped by his experiences in the underwater world, carried a profound sense of environmental awareness and a deeper appreciation for the complexity of life. His words, disseminated through the global network, played a significant role in shaping public opinion and furthering the international commitment to environmental protection.

He, too, stood as a testament to the Whispers' legacy—a testament to how even a single human life could be irrevocably altered by a powerful force of nature, leaving an enduring mark on the world and shaping the future in unforeseen ways. The story of the Whispers was far from over; it was a story of ongoing change, adaptation, and the enduring quest for a more sustainable and interconnected future.

The Whispers of the deep, once a source of fear and destruction, had become a catalyst for change—a testament to the indomitable spirit of both humankind and the wondrous creatures of the deep.

The cataclysmic events surrounding the Whispers had profoundly reshaped Luminese society. Before the near-apocalyptic upheaval, their civilization, while advanced, possessed a certain... stagnancy. Their technology, though elegant and seamlessly integrated with their environment, lacked the dynamism of a society constantly striving for innovation, driven by external pressures. The Whispers, in their destructive wake, had inadvertently shattered this complacency.

The initial impact was devastating. The underwater cities, built with a delicate balance of bioluminescent coral and engineered structures, suffered significant damage. Entire districts were lost to the unpredictable surges of energy that accompanied the Whispers' peak intensity.

The Luminese, with their inherent pacifism, were ill-prepared for such a widespread catastrophe. Their sophisticated defense systems, primarily focused on maintaining the delicate ecosystem, proved inadequate against a force that seemed to defy their understanding of the natural world.

The immediate aftermath saw a surge in communal effort. The Luminese, despite their losses, demonstrated remarkable resilience. Their innate connection to their environment, honed over millennia, allowed them to quickly assess the damage and initiate repairs.

Specialized bioluminescent algae, cultivated for centuries for illumination and energy, were strategically deployed to accelerate the regeneration of damaged coral reefs, forming the foundation for rebuilding their cities. This collaborative effort, born out of necessity, fostered a sense of unity unseen in their previous history.

The rebuilding process, however, highlighted a critical weakness: their reliance on traditional methods. Their technology, while efficient, was deeply rooted in their understanding of the natural world. The unpredictable and destructive nature of the Whispers demonstrated a profound gap in their knowledge, spurring a significant shift in their scientific and technological pursuits.

A new generation of Luminese scientists emerged, driven by a desire to understand and even harness the power of the Whispers. Research into previously neglected fields, such as energy manipulation and advanced prediction models, intensified.

Collaboration with the human survivors, particularly Dr. Thorne and her team, proved invaluable. Dr. Thorne's knowledge of human technology, though vastly different from the Luminese approach, opened up new avenues of exploration. The fusion of Luminese bioengineering and human technological prowess produced remarkable results.

The development of new energy sources, based on a deeper understanding of the Whispers' energy signatures, became a priority. The Luminese had long relied on harnessing the bioluminescence of their environment, but the Whispers had revealed a far greater potential. These new energy sources were not just more powerful; they were cleaner and more sustainable, further integrating with the existing ecosystem rather than exploiting it.

The cultural impact was equally profound. Their pacifistic nature, previously a source of strength and stability, was now questioned. The vulnerability exposed by the Whispers forced a reevaluation of their defense strategies.

While violence remained antithetical to their core values, they began to develop sophisticated early warning systems and defensive technologies that were far more proactive than their previous passive approach. This did not signify a shift toward aggression; rather, it was a necessary adaptation for survival—about protecting their society and ensuring the continued existence of their unique culture.

The relationship with other factions also underwent a dramatic change. The Abyssals, previously viewed with a mixture of curiosity and apprehension, became potential allies in the face of a common threat. The Cetea, however, remained an implacable enemy, their ambitions unchanged by the cataclysmic events.

The Luminese understood the need for strategic alliances, a concept largely foreign to their previous diplomatic practices. Negotiations, often tense and fraught with difficulties, were conducted with a newfound resolve, driven by the shared goal of protecting their underwater world.

The integration of human survivors into Luminese society also had unforeseen consequences. While initially viewed with a mixture of caution and wonder, the humans—particularly Sarah Chen, with her unique connection to the Whispers—became integral to their society.

Sarah's ability to sense and even subtly influence the Whispers provided valuable insights into the phenomenon, accelerating the pace of scientific breakthroughs. The Luminese, ever adaptable, found new ways to incorporate human knowledge and perspectives, leading to a more diverse and innovative society.

The educational system underwent a significant overhaul. The curriculum expanded to incorporate a deeper understanding of the natural world, specifically focusing on the unpredictability of powerful natural forces.

The past emphasis on harmony and balance was retained, but now it was tempered with a pragmatic approach to preparedness and proactive defense. The younger generations were taught not only about the peaceful coexistence of their species but also about the importance of resilience and adaptation in the face of unforeseen challenges.

The Whispers' legacy was not just about destruction; it was about transformation. The Luminese society, once characterized by its harmonious stagnation, was now a dynamic and adaptable civilization. Their technological advancements, spurred by adversity, paved the way for a more sustainable and resilient future.

They had learned to harness the very force that had once threatened to destroy them, transforming it into a source of power and knowledge. This transformation, though born from tragedy, ultimately strengthened their society, enriching their culture and securing a future that was both prosperous and harmonious.

The whispers of the past had resonated deeply, changing the course of their history, but they emerged stronger, wiser, and more prepared to face whatever the future held. The memory of the destruction served as a constant reminder of the importance of preparedness, fostering a societal structure both peaceful and resilient.

The Luminese society had not only survived; it had thrived, proving that even in the face of unimaginable adversity, adaptation and collaboration could lead to growth and innovation. Their story became a testament to the enduring strength of a civilization deeply rooted in its environment, yet capable of embracing change and forging a new path toward a future brighter than ever before.

The echoes of the Whispers continued to ripple through their collective consciousness, a constant reminder of the delicate balance between peace and preparedness—one they were now adept at maintaining. The future remained uncertain, but the Luminese, shaped by the crucible of the Whispers, stood ready to face it.

Sarah Chen, barely more than a wisp of a girl when the plane plunged into the iridescent depths, had become an unlikely linchpin in the fragile alliance between the surface world and the Luminese.

Her initial connection to the Whispers—a strange resonance felt deep within her bones—had been dismissed as youthful imagination by some, a dangerous anomaly by others. But the truth, as it often did, lay somewhere in between. Her ability wasn't merely a sensitivity; it was a form of communication. Not spoken words, but a deeper understanding—a sense of the Whispers' essence, their power, their sorrow, and their inherent unpredictability.

This ability, initially terrifying, evolved into a crucial tool. She could sense shifts in the underwater currents, subtle changes in the bioluminescent flora that often preceded the Whispers' unpredictable surges of energy.

Her interpretations, initially tentative and hesitant, became increasingly precise and insightful. She learned to anticipate the Whispers' patterns, to predict the times of relative calm, and to warn the Luminese and the remaining human survivors of impending disturbances. Her early fears were replaced with a cautious confidence, tempered by a profound respect for the immense power she could now partially understand.

Her influence extended beyond simple warnings. She began to decipher fragmented glyphs discovered within the ruins of ancient Luminese cities—glyphs that spoke of the Whispers' origins and the catastrophic events that had shaped this world. These ancient texts, indecipherable to others, resonated with a similar frequency to Sarah's connection, slowly revealing their cryptic secrets.

The glyphs detailed a history far richer and more complex than the Luminese had previously understood, a history that intertwined with the surface world in ways no one could have imagined. They spoke of a time before the separation—a time of shared ecosystems and symbiotic relationships between the two realms, now tragically severed.

This knowledge became pivotal in rebuilding the fractured relationship between the Luminese and the humans. The initial mistrust, born of fear and cultural differences, gradually gave way to a tentative understanding, fueled by Sarah's translations of the ancient texts.

She highlighted passages detailing the common ancestry of both worlds, suggesting that the separation wasn't a matter of conquest or conflict but a catastrophic natural event, possibly triggered by the very same forces that had brought the plane to this hidden world. This revelation eased the tension, fostering a collaborative spirit previously unimaginable.

Sarah's unique abilities also played a critical role in the ongoing exploration of the underwater world. Captain Armstrong, initially skeptical of her gift, eventually came to rely on Sarah's intuition, often incorporating her insights into the mission's planning.

Her ability to sense disturbances in the Whispers' energy allowed them to navigate treacherous zones, avoiding areas of intense energy that could prove fatal. She became an indispensable part of their expeditions, her youthful energy and unwavering determination providing a counterpoint to the more cautious and analytical approach of Dr. Thorne.

The relationship between Sarah and Dr. Thorne, in particular, underwent a subtle yet profound transformation. Initially, Dr. Thorne viewed Sarah with a mixture of professional curiosity and paternal concern. He saw in her a rare, untamed talent that needed careful nurturing and guidance.

However, as Sarah's understanding of the Whispers deepened, so did Dr. Thorne's respect for her insight and abilities. He began to see beyond the young woman and recognize the powerful force of nature she had become. He learned to trust her instincts, acknowledging the limitations of purely scientific analysis when faced with forces that defied conventional understanding.

Their collaboration led to a groundbreaking discovery—a hidden chamber deep within the ruins of an ancient city. This chamber, protected by complex energy fields, was revealed only when Sarah's unique connection to the Whispers resonated with a specific sequence of bioluminescent patterns.

Inside, they found not only ancient artifacts but also functional technology, far surpassing anything the Luminese had been able to replicate. This technology hinted at a lost era of remarkable scientific achievement—a testament to the potential that lay dormant within the combined knowledge of both worlds.

This discovery, however, also brought forth new challenges. The technology possessed immense power, capable of influencing the Whispers themselves—manipulating their energy, potentially controlling their destructive potential.

This revelation raised ethical questions of immense consequence: Should they attempt to control such a powerful force, or was it best to leave it untouched, respecting the delicate balance of the ecosystem?

The decision was far from simple, dividing the human survivors and the Luminese into factions with differing opinions. Sarah, caught in the crossfire, found herself advocating for a cautious approach, warning of unforeseen consequences and the potential for misuse.

Sarah's voice, once softly spoken, had now gained a powerful resonance. Her understanding of the Whispers extended beyond the scientific and technological; she possessed an intuitive grasp of their spiritual essence—their connection to the very fabric of the underwater world.

She argued that controlling the Whispers would be akin to controlling the very heart of their world—a transgression that would inevitably result in unintended consequences. She appealed to a sense of responsibility, a recognition of the interconnectedness of life, an understanding that their survival was intricately woven into the fate of this hidden world.

The debate raged, threatening to fracture the nascent alliance. But Sarah's persistent warnings, coupled with her growing influence within both the Luminese and human communities, ultimately swayed the majority toward a path of cautious observation and respectful coexistence.

The decision was not a simple surrender to the Whispers' power but a conscious acknowledgment of the need for harmony with nature—a realization that progress shouldn't come at the expense of the delicate balance that sustained life in this hidden world. Her influence solidified her position as a pivotal figure, a bridge between two worlds, a voice of reason in the face of overwhelming power.

As the story progressed, Sarah's role evolved. She was no longer merely a young woman with an unusual connection to a mysterious phenomenon; she became a leader—a visionary—guiding both societies toward a shared future built on respect, understanding, and a profound appreciation for the interconnectedness of all life.

Her journey became a testament to the extraordinary power of empathy, intuition, and the courage to stand up for what one believes in. It wasn't just her understanding of the Whispers that changed the fate of two worlds; it was her willingness to listen to their silent whispers, to interpret their energy, and to share her wisdom with a world desperate for a guide.

Her legacy wouldn't be measured in technological achievements but in the peaceful coexistence she helped foster—a beacon of hope for a future where human ingenuity and environmental harmony could exist side by side.

Her influence continued to ripple outward, shaping not only the immediate future of the two worlds but also hinting at a larger, perhaps even cosmic, significance.

Her story, intertwined with the mysteries of the Whispers, was far from over, promising future chapters of even greater discoveries and even more profound challenges. The journey had only just begun.

The Luminese, with their mastery of bioluminescence and their symbiotic relationship with the ocean's ecosystems, possessed a technology far beyond human comprehension. Their cities, carved from living coral and powered by harnessed bioelectricity, were marvels of sustainable engineering.

We had initially focused on their energy sources—a network of glowing polyps that converted chemical energy into a clean, potent electrical current. Dr. Thorne, ever the pragmatist, immediately recognized the potential.

"This," he'd declared, his eyes shining brighter than any Luminese polyp, "could revolutionize energy production on Earth. No more reliance on fossil fuels, no more greenhouse gas emissions."

The implications were staggering. The Luminese's bio-electrical grids were not only efficient but also self-regulating, adapting to fluctuations in demand and integrating seamlessly with the surrounding environment. We painstakingly documented their systems, collecting samples of the polyps, analyzing their genetic makeup, and studying the intricate architecture of their energy networks.

Initial attempts to replicate the process on Earth proved challenging. The polyps, it turned out, were highly sensitive to changes in salinity, temperature, and pressure—parameters that were difficult to perfectly mimic in a laboratory setting. But the breakthroughs were coming. Teams of scientists, inspired by the Luminese model, were developing artificial bioluminescent organisms, genetically engineered to produce electricity with similar efficiency.

Beyond energy, the Luminese possessed an advanced understanding of marine biology and genetic engineering. Their ability to manipulate coral growth to create intricate structures was astonishing. We discovered they used a complex system of pheromones and bioluminescent signals to direct coral growth, creating living buildings, bridges, and even vehicles.

This **bio-architecture** held immense potential for sustainable construction, offering a far more environmentally friendly alternative to traditional methods. Imagine skyscrapers that grew from the ground, adapting to their surroundings and requiring minimal maintenance. Or bridges that repaired themselves, responding to stress and wear. This level of biological integration, unheard of on Earth, opened up new avenues of architectural design and construction.

Their medical technologies were equally impressive. The Luminese had developed sophisticated treatments based on marine organisms, using compounds extracted from deep-sea creatures to heal injuries and combat diseases. One particular compound, derived from a bioluminescent jellyfish, showed remarkable promise in treating certain types of cancers.

Dr. Thorne's team was already collaborating with Luminese scientists to understand the mechanism of action, hoping to replicate the treatment on Earth. The possibilities were vast; a new era of marine-based pharmaceuticals was on the horizon. We could potentially unlock cures for diseases that had plagued humanity for centuries.

Perhaps the most fascinating aspect of Luminese technology was their communication system. It wasn't a system of spoken words or even written symbols but a complex interplay of bioluminescent flashes, subtle changes in water pressure, and pheromonal signals.

The communication wasn't merely conveying information—it was a form of symbiotic interaction, an exchange of energy and intentions. It was a far cry from our clumsy radio waves and digital signals. Understanding this system proved to be a significant challenge.

Sarah's connection to the Whispers, initially viewed as an anomaly, became a crucial element in decoding the Luminese communication system. Her ability to interpret the subtle shifts in energy and the nuances of the bioluminescent patterns allowed us to bridge the gap between two vastly different forms of communication.

This opened up a whole new world of possibilities in humancomputer interaction. Imagine computers that could communicate with us not through a screen or keyboard, but through subtle energy shifts—anticipating our needs and responding to our emotions. It would be a symbiotic relationship, a true merging of human intention and technological capabilities.

The implications were profound, from revolutionizing assistive technologies for people with disabilities to creating intuitive interfaces for complex systems.

But the Luminese technology wasn't without its ethical considerations. Their mastery of genetic engineering, while beneficial in many ways, raised concerns about the potential for unintended consequences.

The possibility of creating new species, manipulating ecosystems, and altering the fundamental balance of nature demanded careful consideration. We, the human visitors, had a responsibility to learn from the Luminese—not just to exploit their advancements.

This realization wasn't just scientific; it was philosophical.

Our interaction with the Luminese forced us to confront our own technological hubris. We had always viewed technology as a tool for domination, for conquering nature and bending it to our will. The Luminese, on the other hand, demonstrated a philosophy of harmony and symbiosis—a way of living in balance with the natural world.

This new perspective profoundly impacted our understanding of technological progress. It was a paradigm shift, forcing us to rethink our approach to innovation and development. We had to learn to integrate technology with nature, not subjugate it.

The Abyssals, a reclusive civilization residing in the deepest trenches, presented a different technological challenge. Their technology was less about overt displays of power and more about subtle manipulation of the environment. They possessed a deep understanding of geological processes, capable of triggering underwater volcanoes and manipulating tectonic plates.

Their technology, while frightening, was based on an understanding of Earth's underlying processes that was centuries ahead of our own. Studying the Abyssals wasn't about replicating their technology; it was about understanding the profound power they wielded and learning from their mastery of the Earth's geological forces.

It offered a chance to better understand and potentially mitigate the effects of earthquakes and tsunamis—events that have devastated humanity for millennia. Understanding their abilities could save countless lives and usher in an era of far greater predictive accuracy in geological events.

The Cetea, a technologically advanced aquatic species with a ruthless ambition to control the Whispers' power, employed sophisticated sonar and bio-acoustic technologies to track and manipulate marine life.

Their weapons, utilizing focused sonic blasts, could shatter underwater structures and incapacitate anything within their range. Deciphering their technology was not a matter of mere scientific curiosity—it was a matter of survival.

We had to understand their methods to defend against them, to protect the Luminese, and to ensure our own survival. But understanding their destructive technologies also meant learning to harness the power of sound in a positive way.

The Cetea's mastery of sonar could be studied to develop more advanced underwater navigation systems, improved sonar imaging for medical and geological applications, and sophisticated methods for acoustic communication.

The Whispers themselves, a mysterious energy force, presented the ultimate technological enigma. Their influence was evident in the abilities of the Luminese, their effect on the ecosystem, and the seemingly supernatural events that occurred throughout the underwater world.

It became clear that the Whispers were not simply a force of nature; they were a source of immense, untapped energy—a force capable of reshaping the very fabric of reality. Understanding the Whispers would be the greatest technological leap imaginable: access to a source of clean energy beyond our wildest dreams, a source of healing beyond our current capacity to comprehend.

It would be energy that was not exploitative but intrinsically linked to the planet's natural systems.

The journey had just begun. The discoveries in this submerged world were not just technological marvels, but philosophical milestones. They presented challenges and opportunities that redefined our understanding of life, technology, and our place in the vast, interconnected ecosystem of the planet.

The Whispers' legacy was not just a story of survival—it was a story of transformation, one that would redefine the future of both the underwater world and the surface. The knowledge and discoveries made would shape humanity for centuries to come.

The delicate balance of ecosystems, once a theoretical concept, had become a stark reality—a lesson learned in the shimmering depths of the ocean, a lesson that would ultimately determine the fate of two worlds.

The Luminese's approach to environmental stewardship wasn't merely a set of practices—it was woven into the very fabric of their society. Their reverence for the ocean wasn't just a philosophical ideal but a practical necessity, a life-sustaining principle. Observing their methods, we began to grasp the depth of their understanding— an understanding forged over millennia of coexistence with the ocean's delicate ecosystems.

Dr. Thorne, fueled by a potent mix of scientific curiosity and a growing sense of responsibility, spearheaded the effort to document and understand their techniques. He meticulously cataloged their methods, focusing on three key areas: sustainable energy production, waste management, and ecosystem preservation.

The Luminese's energy source, as we'd already discovered, relied on a vast network of bioluminescent polyps. These weren't simply organisms; they were sophisticated bio-batteries, converting chemical energy from the ocean's currents and nutrients into a clean, powerful electrical current with almost no waste.

Dr. Thorne's team worked tirelessly to understand the intricate biochemical processes involved, hoping to replicate this marvel of natural engineering on Earth. The implications were staggering—a renewable, sustainable energy source that could power entire cities, eliminating our reliance on fossil fuels and reducing pollution and climate change.

The challenge, however, was immense. The polyps were part of a complex, interconnected web of life, and mimicking their functionality required a deeper understanding of their symbiotic relationships within the ecosystem.

Their waste management system was equally astonishing. Instead of discarding waste as pollutants, the Luminese integrated it back into the ecosystem. Organic waste, for instance, was used to feed specialized microorganisms that, in turn, provided nutrients for the coral reefs and other marine life.

Non-organic waste was processed using a combination of biological and chemical methods, transforming it into inert substances harmless to the environment. This circular economy, where nothing was truly wasted, stood in stark contrast to our linear

"take-make-dispose" model. The implications for reducing pollution on Earth, particularly in our oceans, were profound.

Dr. Thorne and his team collaborated with Luminese scientists, translating their complex biochemical processes into a framework that could be adapted for terrestrial environments. The task was monumental, requiring a global shift in our mindset and infrastructure.

However, perhaps the most impressive aspect of the Luminese's environmental protection measures was their approach to ecosystem preservation. They didn't merely protect individual species; they maintained the intricate web of life that sustained their civilization. They understood the interconnectedness of organisms and their environment on a level far beyond our current grasp.

Their cities weren't simply built within the ecosystem; they were an integral part of it, designed to enhance biodiversity rather than diminish it. Living coral formed the foundations of their structures, providing habitat for countless marine species.

The city's architecture was carefully planned to create diverse microhabitats, encouraging the proliferation of various life forms. Even their agriculture, if it could be called that, was integrated seamlessly into the natural environment. They cultivated nutrientrich algae farms in carefully designated areas, using the waste products to fertilize surrounding ecosystems.

These farms provided a source of food, but more importantly, they maintained the delicate balance of the local food web. Their agricultural practices avoided monoculture, opting for a diverse range of species to support a robust and resilient ecosystem. This method fostered resilience against diseases and environmental changes, ensuring the continued health of the entire system.

The Luminese's respect for the ocean extended beyond their immediate environment. They had developed sophisticated methods for monitoring the health of the surrounding oceans, employing a network of bio-sensors embedded within the coral reefs and other marine habitats.

These sensors monitored water quality, temperature, salinity, and the abundance of various marine species. Any significant deviations from the norm triggered an immediate response from the Luminese, who would swiftly implement measures to restore balance.

This proactive approach, rather than reacting to environmental damage, was a critical element in their long-term success. They viewed their environment as a patient requiring constant monitoring and care rather than an inexhaustible resource to be exploited.

The lessons learned from the Luminese were not merely scientific; they were philosophical. Their society operated on a principle of symbiotic coexistence, where the needs of the environment were not separate from the needs of its inhabitants.

This stood in sharp contrast to our often exploitative relationship with nature, where short-term gains frequently overshadowed longterm sustainability. Their methods highlighted the critical interconnectedness of all living things and the importance of respecting the delicate balance of the ecosystem.

The immediate implications of this knowledge were profound. Back on Earth, the environmental crisis had reached a critical point.

Climate change was accelerating, oceans were polluted, and biodiversity was rapidly declining. The Luminese's approach offered a beacon of hope, a viable alternative to our unsustainable practices.

Dr. Thorne's team, working with the remaining survivors, began to translate these environmental protection measures into a practical plan for Earth. It wasn't merely about adopting specific technologies; it was about shifting our entire mindset. We needed to transition from a linear, extractive economic model to a circular economy that minimized waste and maximized resource efficiency.

The plan involved several key strategies. First, a global transition to sustainable energy sources, emulating the Luminese's bio-electric systems, was prioritized. Massive research efforts focused on developing similar bio-energy technologies, exploring both bioluminescent organisms and other potential sources of renewable energy.

This involved not only technological advancements but also a restructuring of our energy infrastructure, moving away from centralized power generation toward decentralized, localized systems.

Next, a radical overhaul of our waste management systems was required. This included investing in advanced recycling technologies that mimicked the Luminese's methods of transforming waste into usable resources. Simultaneously, a global effort to reduce waste generation itself was launched, encouraging the adoption of reusable materials, minimal packaging, and sustainable consumption patterns.

Protecting existing ecosystems and restoring damaged ones became equally critical. This meant implementing stricter environmental regulations, creating protected areas, and investing in ecosystem restoration projects. The Luminese's approach to ecosystem management, emphasizing biodiversity and integrated agriculture, served as a model for developing more resilient and productive ecosystems.

It also involved promoting sustainable agricultural practices that minimized chemical inputs and maximized biodiversity, reducing the environmental footprint of food production.

Furthermore, implementing a global monitoring system, similar to the Luminese's network of bio-sensors, was deemed crucial. This would involve deploying advanced sensors to monitor the health of various ecosystems, enabling early detection of environmental problems and swift intervention.

This monitoring network would provide real-time data on water quality, pollution levels, and biodiversity, allowing for more informed decision-making and proactive management of environmental resources. It also necessitated the development of sophisticated predictive models to anticipate potential environmental challenges.

The integration of these measures would require a fundamental shift in global governance and international cooperation. Sharing the knowledge gained from the Luminese's society became paramount. International collaborations were established to share research findings, technological advancements, and best practices, fostering a global movement toward sustainable living.

Education played a crucial role, promoting public awareness about the importance of environmental stewardship and the interconnectedness of all living things.

The task was enormous—a global undertaking of unprecedented scale and complexity. But the legacy of the Whispers, the lessons learned in the depths of the underwater world, offered a glimmer of hope. The Luminese's example provided a roadmap, a blueprint for a future where humanity coexists harmoniously with nature, where technology serves to enhance sustainability rather than deplete resources.

The path ahead was challenging, requiring a profound change in our collective mindset and behavior. But as we gazed upon the bioluminescent wonders of the underwater world, we knew that the journey, though arduous, was one worth undertaking. The fate of two worlds now rested on our ability to learn from the past and shape a sustainable future.

The Whispers' legacy was not just a testament to a lost civilization; it was a call to action—a reminder of our interconnectedness and our responsibility to protect the delicate balance of life on Earth. The survival of our world depended on it.

CHAPTER 10

The humid air hung heavy, a stark contrast to the crisp, cool depths I'd spent months immersed in. My return to the surface world felt surreal—a jarring shift from the vibrant bioluminescence of the Luminese city to the muted grays of a world still reeling from the near-apocalyptic events of the past year.

Looking back, the crash of Flight 427 into the Bermuda Triangle—initially dismissed as another maritime mystery—now felt like a pivotal moment in human history, a cosmic nudge toward a greater understanding of our place in the universe and the delicate balance of all life within it.

The initial shock of discovering the Luminese civilization—a society so advanced yet deeply connected to its environment—had been profound. Their ability to harness bioluminescence as a primary energy source, their architectural marvels sculpted from living coral, their harmonious relationship with diverse marine life—it was a breathtaking revelation, a utopian vision juxtaposed against the ecological devastation we had inflicted upon our own planet. It forced a stark self-reflection: Were we, humanity, doomed to repeat the mistakes of the past, or could we learn from this other world's success?

Dr. Thorne, with his unwavering commitment to scientific accuracy and his quiet brilliance, had been instrumental in bridging the gap between our two worlds. His meticulous observations, his painstaking analysis of Luminese technology, and his deep respect for their culture were crucial in establishing the trust necessary for collaboration.

Captain Rostova, with her sharp tactical mind and unwavering determination, had been the backbone of our survival, her leadership guiding us through perilous encounters with the Abyssals and the ruthless Cetea.

The Abyssals, enigmatic creatures of the deepest trenches, initially appeared as a threat, their motives shrouded in mystery. Yet, as we learned more, we discovered their own struggle for survival—their silent protest against the destruction caused by the

Cetea's relentless pursuit of power.

The Cetea, on the other hand, were a stark reminder of humanity's darker impulses, their relentless exploitation of the "Whispers"—that ancient, powerful energy source—a mirror of our own history of resource depletion and environmental disregard.

Sarah Chen's unique connection to the Whispers proved to be a double-edged sword. Her ability to perceive and interpret their subtle energies provided vital insights, allowing us to understand their power and potential. But it also made her a target, a beacon in the turbulent waters of this underwater world. Her journey was one of remarkable growth and sacrifice, a testament to the human spirit's capacity for courage and resilience.

Jian's selfless act—his sacrifice to save others—was a moment etched forever in my memory. His bravery, his unwavering loyalty, his quiet heroism—all served as a powerful reminder of the values we often overlook in our relentless pursuit of progress. The Luminese response to his sacrifice underscored their own deep sense of community and respect for life, further cementing our determination to protect their world.

The battle for control of the Whispers had been a cataclysmic event—a clash of ideologies and ambitions that left its mark on both the underwater and surface worlds. The environmental consequences were significant, forcing us to confront the fragility of ecosystems and the long-term effects of conflict. The recovery process was long and arduous, demanding cooperation and a willingness to overcome ingrained prejudices.

Yet, amidst the devastation, there was hope. The alliances forged during the conflict, the shared understanding of our interconnectedness, the willingness to learn from each other—these were the seeds of a new beginning.

The lessons learned from the underwater world were profound, a potent reminder of the responsibility we bear toward our planet and all its inhabitants. The scientific breakthroughs inspired by Luminese technology offered a glimmer of hope for a more sustainable future.

The Whispers' legacy extended beyond the immediate conflict. Their influence subtly reshaped both worlds, inspiring a deeper understanding of the universe's intricate mechanisms and the interconnectedness of life. The Luminese society evolved, embracing new technologies while maintaining their deep respect for their environment. Sarah Chen, now a respected figure in both worlds, continued her work bridging the cultural and technological divides.

The lasting impact on humanity was undeniable. Our understanding of oceanography, marine biology, and environmental science was revolutionized. The insights gained from the Luminese's sustainable practices spurred global initiatives toward renewable energy and ecological restoration.

The narrative of Flight 427, once a tragic mystery, was transformed into a story of hope—a testament to human resilience and the power of interspecies cooperation.

As I reflect on the events, I find myself grappling with the implications of the Whispers and their potential. The knowledge we acquired was immense, carrying with it a tremendous responsibility. The power to harness such an energy source—so intimately connected to the very fabric of existence—demanded careful consideration and a profound commitment to ethical practices.

This narrative is far from over. The seeds of change have been sown, but the journey toward a truly sustainable future for both worlds remains long and challenging. The future of the underwater world, with its diverse inhabitants and breathtaking beauty, hangs in the balance.

The Luminese, having emerged stronger from the conflict, face the daunting task of rebuilding and maintaining their delicate ecosystem. They must learn to coexist not just with their ocean neighbors but with an evolving relationship to surface humanity.

The lasting impact on humanity will unfold over generations. Will we learn from our mistakes, from the environmental devastation we've witnessed? Will we embrace the lessons learned from the Luminese civilization and strive for a more harmonious relationship with our planet?

These questions remain, a haunting echo in the silence that follows the storm. The Whispers themselves—their very nature still partially unknown—continue to hum in the background, an everpresent reminder of the vast unknown that lies both beneath the waves and within our own souls.

The closing of this chapter is not an ending, but rather a transition—a bridge between the past and a future yet unwritten. The Whispers continue, hinting at the mysteries yet to be unveiled, the challenges yet to be faced, and the possibilities yet to be explored in the next installment of this story.

The fate of both worlds rests not only on the shoulders of the survivors, but on the collective actions of humanity—humanity irrevocably changed by its encounter with a world beneath the waves. The journey continues...

The whispers, once faint echoes in the depths, now resonated with newfound urgency. The underwater world, once a sanctuary of vibrant life and advanced technology, stood at a precipice. The events of the past year—the crash, the discovery of the Luminese, the conflict with the Abyssals and the Cetea—had irrevocably altered the delicate balance of this hidden ecosystem. The future, however, was not predetermined. It was a tapestry woven from the choices of its inhabitants, both Luminese and human.

The Luminese, initially hesitant to engage with the surface world, had begun to understand the shared threat posed by unchecked exploitation and the potential for mutual benefit. Their advanced technology, once cloaked in secrecy, was slowly being shared—albeit cautiously.

Dr. Thorne, instrumental in bridging this communication gap, had established a research collaboration focused on sustainable energy solutions derived from the unique bioluminescent properties of the Luminese reefs. This collaboration proved to be a watershed moment, not only fostering scientific advancement but also cultivating a sense of mutual respect and understanding.

Imagine harvesting light, not electricity, for power. A revolutionary leap—and one of the many fruits of this unprecedented collaboration.

However, the road ahead was fraught with challenges. The Abyssals, enigmatic and reclusive, remained a wildcard. While their motives were unclear, their advanced understanding of the "Whispers" suggested a crucial role in the future of both worlds.

Understanding their cryptic communications and uncovering their intentions became paramount. The Luminese, with their advanced sonar technology and a symbiotic relationship with certain deep-sea creatures, were leading the investigation, hoping to forge a dialogue, not an adversarial relationship.

The knowledge shared by Sarah Chen, her intuitive understanding of the "Whispers," proved invaluable in this endeavor. Through her visions and interpretations, they began piecing together a deeper understanding of the Abyssals' ancient language, finding hints of a shared history—a common ancestor, if you will—lost to time and the shifting tectonic plates.

The Cetea, on the other hand, posed a more immediate threat. Their ruthless pursuit of power, fueled by the desire to control the "Whispers" for their own nefarious purposes, remained a constant shadow hanging over the underwater world. Their exploitation of the deep-sea vents for weaponry, harnessing geothermal energy for devastating military applications, created an environmental catastrophe of unprecedented scale.

Their careless disregard for the delicate balance of the deep-sea ecosystem threatened to unravel the entire underwater world—including the bioluminescent forests that sustained the Luminese and the rich biodiversity of the abyssal plains. The fight against them, therefore, was not just a political or territorial conflict; it was a battle for the very survival of this hidden world.

The human survivors, scattered across the globe after their return from the underwater world, were crucial in this struggle. Captain

Armstrong, driven by a deep sense of responsibility, led the effort to establish international protocols for the responsible exploration and protection of the underwater world.

This involved delicate negotiations with world governments, still reeling from the ecological damage inflicted by decades of unchecked industrialization and the lingering effects of the nearapocalyptic events of the past year. He faced strong resistance, primarily from those who viewed the underwater world as another resource to be exploited, oblivious to the consequences of such actions.

The scientific community, however, rallied around the shared understanding gained through Dr. Thorne's research. The revelations about the advanced technology of the Luminese, the potential for sustainable energy solutions, and the profound interconnectedness of all life—from the microscopic organisms in the deep-sea vents to the colossal whales of the surface—shifted the global narrative.

A new era of scientific exploration and international cooperation dawned, propelled by a shared desire to understand and protect the underwater world—and the planet as a whole.

But even with this global shift, the challenges remained formidable. The "Whispers," though providing vital insights, also posed a significant threat. Their power, capable of shaping realities and influencing the very fabric of existence, required careful handling and a deep understanding of their implications.

Sarah Chen, though gifted with an intuitive connection, struggled to master this power. Her visions became increasingly intense and difficult to interpret. The future depended on her ability to manage this extraordinary gift—to channel its power for the greater good and to avoid unleashing its destructive potential.

The impact of the "Whispers" extended beyond the underwater world. The surface world, too, experienced subtle shifts—unusual weather patterns, seismic activity in unexpected locations, and even changes in global consciousness.

The interconnectedness, once a theoretical concept, became a tangible reality. The very fabric of reality seemed to shift and tremble in response to the changes in the underwater kingdom.

The coming decades witnessed a profound transformation in human society. Driven by the shared experience and the discoveries made in the underwater world, there was a global shift towards sustainability, ecological responsibility, and international cooperation.

The old paradigm of relentless growth and exploitation was replaced by a new ethic, one that prioritized harmony with nature and the interconnectedness of all life. Technological advancements, inspired by the Luminese, propelled a wave of innovation in renewable energy, sustainable agriculture, and advanced materials.

The world, once on the brink of ecological collapse, started on a path toward regeneration—healing from the wounds of the past.

However, the story of the underwater world and its inhabitants was far from over. The "Whispers" continued their cryptic pronouncements, hinting at future challenges and the potential for both immense progress and catastrophic failure. The delicate balance between the Luminese, the Abyssals, and the remnants of the Cetea remained precarious.

The survival of this hidden world—and perhaps the entire planet—hung in the balance, a constant reminder of the interconnectedness of life and the profound responsibility we carry as inhabitants of this fragile planet—and the even more fragile otherworldly home beneath the waves.

The journey, once a daring expedition into the unknown, had become a shared stewardship—a collective responsibility to protect a world that held both unimaginable beauty and terrifying power. The future, therefore, remained unwritten, a thrilling adventure that still unfolds—a testament to the resilient human spirit and the enduring mystery of the deep.

The whispers persisted, a constant reminder that the greatest mysteries often lie in the deepest depths, waiting to be discovered, understood, and, most importantly, protected.

The return of the survivors to the surface world was not a triumphant homecoming but a hushed re-entry into a world irrevocably altered by their absence. The year they spent in the underwater realm had been a year of upheaval above the waves.

News reports, initially dismissed as sensationalist fiction, gradually revealed the truth—a global ecological shift of unprecedented scale. Ocean currents had changed, marine life populations had fluctuated wildly, and weather patterns had become erratic and unpredictable.

The absence of any explanation fueled rampant speculation, with conspiracy theories swirling around the Bermuda Triangle incident, ranging from extraterrestrial intervention to government cover-ups. The survivors' account, initially met with skepticism and ridicule, was slowly gaining traction, propelled by the undeniable evidence of the technologies they brought back.

The Luminese's advanced understanding of oceanic ecosystems, their mastery of sustainable energy sources, and their profound respect for the interconnectedness of life offered humanity a path forward—a lifeline in a world teetering on the brink of ecological collapse.

Dr. Thorne's meticulous research on the Luminese's bioregenerative techniques, coupled with Sarah Chen's unique insights into the "Whispers," provided the scientific groundwork for a global initiative aimed at repairing the damaged environment.

The world watched, captivated and apprehensive, as the survivors—now hailed as unlikely saviors—unveiled their findings, demonstrating the power of symbiosis and the urgent need for global cooperation.

The initial resistance to their claims slowly eroded as evidence mounted. The technologies they had managed to salvage from the underwater world—efficient energy systems based on bioluminescence, innovative water purification methods, and advanced agricultural techniques—became the pillars of a global rebuilding effort.

The world witnessed a surge in scientific collaboration, driven by the shared desire to learn from the Luminese's wisdom and overcome the ecological crisis. The profound implications of the underwater world's advanced civilization sent ripples through various sectors, initiating paradigm shifts in multiple fields.

The most significant change was witnessed in the realm of environmental science. The Luminese's philosophy of environmental harmony, far removed from anthropocentric views, became the guiding principle of global conservation efforts.

Educational curricula worldwide incorporated the principles of symbiosis and sustainable living, while governmental policies shifted toward fostering cooperation and resource management. International treaties, driven by the shared threat of ecological collapse, sought to create a global framework for environmental stewardship.

The era of unchecked exploitation of natural resources ended, replaced by an era of meticulous conservation and ecological restoration.

The economic landscape also underwent a dramatic

transformation. The Luminese's advanced technologies, initially intended for environmental restoration, quickly found application in other sectors. New industries bloomed around sustainable energy, bio-regenerative agriculture, and advanced materials developed from bioluminescent organisms.

This shift toward a green economy created new employment opportunities, stimulating global economic growth while simultaneously addressing the ecological crisis. The era of environmentally unsustainable practices became a thing of the past, making way for a new economic model based on environmental responsibility and sustainability.

The social and political changes were equally profound. The events surrounding the underwater world and the survivors' experience fostered a new sense of global unity, replacing the previous divisions and conflicts. The shared threat of ecological collapse forced nations to work together, transcending national interests to address a common challenge.

International cooperation flourished, with joint projects focused on ecological restoration and the development of sustainable technologies. The shared experience fostered a new level of understanding and empathy, promoting a more collaborative and inclusive global community.

However, the journey wasn't without its challenges. The initial wave of optimism and collaboration gradually encountered resistance from various factions—both from powerful corporations resistant to the new paradigm and from extremist groups seeking to exploit the new technologies for their own ends.

The advanced technologies, while offering immense benefits, also posed a potential threat. The ethical implications of manipulating nature's intricate balance, particularly through gene editing inspired by Luminese technology, fueled heated debates and ethical dilemmas. Strict regulations and guidelines were introduced to manage this potentially disruptive technology and prevent its misuse.

The "Whispers," once a cryptic enigma, began to reveal deeper layers of meaning. Sarah Chen, continuing her research, discovered that these enigmatic pronouncements contained prophecies not just about the underwater world but about humanity's future as well.

The prophecies warned about the potential for both immense progress and catastrophic failure, depending on humanity's choices. They hinted at a coming convergence—a merging of technologies and understanding that would shape the course of civilization.

The legacy of the underwater world extended far beyond environmental science and technology. It sparked a philosophical renaissance, redefining humanity's relationship with nature and prompting a critical examination of our place in the universe. The

Luminese's concept of interconnectedness became the new philosophical cornerstone of global thought.

This shift in understanding fostered a sense of shared responsibility, emphasizing the importance of respecting both the environment and other cultures. The narrative shifted from anthropocentrism to a holistic perspective that embraced the interconnectedness of all life.

The long-term impact of this discovery and the subsequent collaboration with the Luminese civilization, along with the warnings embedded within the "Whispers," continued to shape humanity's trajectory. The story of the underwater world became a cautionary tale—a testament to the potential for both destruction and creation—urging humanity to tread carefully on the path toward a future dictated not by exploitation, but by collaboration and respect for the fragile balance of life. The survivors' tale served as a living example of how one daring expedition could transform the course of human history and the planet's future.

The "Whispers," always present, served as a constant reminder that the journey was far from over. The deep mysteries of the ocean, and of existence itself, continued to unfold, providing an endless source of learning, challenges, and opportunities for humanity.

The delicate balance achieved through collaboration with the underwater world needed constant nurturing—a testament to the intricate dance between technological advancement and environmental stewardship. The future remained uncertain, yet infused with a newfound sense of hope, driven by the realization that the path forward lies in embracing interconnectedness, sustainability, and a profound respect for the delicate beauty of the planet and its hidden wonders.

The echoes of the "Whispers" served as a reminder that the greatest advancements often arise from the most unexpected encounters and that the responsibility for shaping a harmonious future rests collectively on the shoulders of all humanity.

The story of Captain Rostova, Dr. Thorne, and Sarah Chen became a legend—a powerful narrative illustrating the triumph of human ingenuity and cooperation in the face of overwhelming challenges. Their journey served as a beacon, a symbol of hope for a future where humanity and nature could coexist in harmony, not as adversaries, but as partners in a shared destiny.

Their discovery wasn't just an exploration of a hidden world; it was a journey of self-discovery, a profound lesson in the interconnectedness of all life, and a testament to the enduring power of the human spirit to adapt, innovate, and strive for a better world. The whispers, faint yet persistent, continued to weave their cryptic narrative, reminding humanity that the exploration had just begun— an exploration into the depths of our planet, and into the depths of our own potential.

The legacy of the submerged world extended far beyond the realms of science and technology, touching every aspect of human civilization and shaping a future defined by interconnectedness, responsibility, and the unwavering pursuit of a harmonious coexistence with the planet.

The echoes of the Luminese civilization reverberated far beyond the shimmering walls of their underwater city. The technologies they shared, initially met with apprehension and suspicion, gradually became the cornerstone of a global ecological renaissance.

The Luminese's mastery of bio-regenerative processes, their understanding of symbiotic relationships within complex ecosystems, and their remarkably efficient energy systems provided humanity with the tools to begin repairing the damage inflicted upon the planet. Ocean acidification, a looming threat that had cast a long shadow over the future of marine life, began to reverse itself.

The Luminese's advanced filtration systems, capable of removing pollutants with unparalleled efficiency, were deployed globally, revitalizing once-dead zones in the oceans. Coral reefs, ravaged by warming waters and pollution, showed signs of recovery, their vibrant colors returning as the delicate balance of their ecosystems was restored.

The whispers, those enigmatic signals that had guided Sarah Chen and played such a pivotal role in the underwater world, continued to intrigue scientists. Their complex waveforms, initially deciphered only partially, began to yield secrets about the planet's deep history, revealing cyclical patterns of ecological upheaval and recovery.

This newfound knowledge provided a deeper understanding of the Earth's delicate systems and equipped scientists to better predict and mitigate future environmental crises. The data helped unravel the intricate relationships between oceanic currents, atmospheric conditions, and terrestrial ecosystems, allowing for more effective climate modeling and prediction.

A global collaborative effort, fueled by the legacy of the Luminese, emerged, uniting scientists, engineers, and policymakers in a common pursuit of sustainability. The Luminese's societal structure, based on cooperation and a deep respect for the environment, offered a compelling alternative to humanity's oftendestructive patterns of consumption and exploitation. Their approach to resource management, emphasizing sustainability and mindful utilization, inspired a paradigm shift in human societies.

Global consumption patterns began to change; renewable energy sources quickly surpassed fossil fuels, leading to a significant reduction in greenhouse gas emissions. Sustainable agricultural practices, inspired by the Luminese's methods, enhanced food production while minimizing environmental impact. The concept of interconnectedness, once a philosophical abstraction, became the foundation of a new global ethic, fostering collaboration and responsible stewardship of the planet's resources.

The tale of Captain Rostova, Dr. Thorne, and Sarah Chen, initially met with skepticism, evolved into a global phenomenon. Their journey became a powerful symbol of human resilience and the potential for transformative change. Educational programs incorporating the Luminese's wisdom were integrated into school curricula worldwide, emphasizing the interconnectedness of life and the importance of responsible environmental stewardship. The story of Jian's selfless act, the ultimate sacrifice for the greater good, served as a powerful reminder of the human capacity for altruism and courage. His heroism inspired countless acts of service and environmental activism, fostering a growing movement dedicated to preserving the planet's biodiversity and ecological balance.

The technological advancements brought back from the underwater realm were not simply tools; they were catalysts for a fundamental shift in humanity's relationship with technology itself. The Luminese's commitment to technological advancement that enhanced, rather than destroyed, the environment served as a beacon for human ingenuity. Scientists embarked on ambitious projects aimed at harnessing the power of the ocean's currents and harnessing renewable energy resources at unprecedented scales. The advanced bio-materials developed by the Luminese revolutionized industries, leading to the development of sustainable building materials, efficient transportation systems, and more effective methods of waste management. The once-ominous specter of resource depletion began to fade as humanity embraced innovation guided by ecological principles.

However, the path toward a sustainable future was not without its challenges. The initial euphoria gave way to a sobering realization of the magnitude of the task. The ecological damage caused by centuries of human activity was not easily reversed. Political and economic hurdles remained, particularly in regions resistant to change and clinging to outdated systems of resource exploitation. Conflicts arose regarding the equitable distribution of the new technologies and resources, highlighting the ongoing need for global cooperation and responsible governance. Yet, the seeds of change had been sown; a new generation, inspired by the story of the underwater world, emerged, determined to build a more sustainable and harmonious future.

The whispers continued, faint but persistent, guiding humanity on its journey toward a new equilibrium. Their cryptic messages, once enigmatic, began to yield a deeper understanding of the planet's complex cycles and its intricate relationship with life itself. The narrative woven by the whispers encouraged humanity to view the Earth not as a resource to be exploited, but as a living entity worthy of reverence and protection. The whispers served as a reminder that the journey toward sustainability was not a destination, but an ongoing process requiring constant vigilance and commitment.

The transformation was not merely technological or environmental. It encompassed a shift in human consciousness, a profound change in how humanity viewed its place within the intricate web of life. The old paradigms of dominance and exploitation were gradually replaced by a worldview based on mutual respect, collaboration, and shared responsibility. This new consciousness found expression in diverse spheres of human activity, from art and literature to politics and economics. Stories of interconnectedness and ecological harmony became dominant themes in popular culture, shaping societal values and inspiring a new generation of environmental stewards.

The discovery of the Luminese civilization and the exploration of their underwater world led to a wave of scientific breakthroughs in diverse fields. Marine biology flourished, uncovering new species and ecosystems, while advancements in materials science, bioengineering, and renewable energy technologies revolutionized various sectors. The lessons learned from the Luminese's mastery of bio-regenerative systems transformed agriculture, leading to the development of highly efficient and environmentally sustainable farming practices. This resulted in a global food security system that ensured adequate food supplies for a growing population while minimizing the environmental footprint of food production.

The integration of Luminese technologies into the global infrastructure also spurred remarkable progress in healthcare. Advanced bio-medical techniques, inspired by the Luminese's understanding of biological processes, were successfully applied in various medical fields, improving diagnostics and treatments and expanding the lifespan and well-being of people worldwide. The collective knowledge gained from the underwater world brought unprecedented advancements in the understanding and management of human health, fostering a global health landscape characterized by accessibility and sustainability.

The legacy of the Luminese extended beyond practical applications, profoundly shaping human consciousness and the way humanity perceived its place within the larger cosmos. The onceisolated human experience was transformed into a broader vision encompassing the interconnectedness of all living beings and their interdependence with the planet. This expanded worldview fostered a new sense of shared responsibility and a profound respect for the delicate balance of nature. The echoes of the whispers, the remnants of a lost civilization's wisdom, continued to guide humanity toward a more sustainable and harmonious future, emphasizing the vital interdependence of all life forms. The journey had just begun, with the lessons learned paving the way for an era defined by cooperation, innovation, and a renewed commitment to preserving the planet for generations to come.

The world above the waves, once fractured by conflict and environmental degradation, had begun to heal, mirroring the harmonious underwater realm that had once seemed so far removed from human experience. The whispers, a testament to the enduring power of knowledge, continued to weave their subtle influence, shaping a world where human ingenuity and ecological harmony finally coalesced. The future, once uncertain, began to shimmer with a new and hopeful promise.

The shimmering, bioluminescent city of the Luminese faded behind us, a memory as vivid and unreal as a dream. The submersible, christened *The Siren's Call* – a fitting name considering our journey – ascended, the pressure slowly releasing its grip. As we broke the surface, the world above was a stark contrast to the vibrant underwater metropolis we'd left behind. The sky, once choked with smog and pollution, was a clearer, brighter blue. The air, once heavy and acrid, was crisp and clean, carrying the scent of salt and a hint of unfamiliar, sweet floral notes – a testament to the Luminese's ecological intervention.

The transition wasn't seamless. The world above was still grappling with the aftermath of our disappearance, the initial chaos and fear gradually giving way to cautious optimism fueled by the technology and knowledge we'd brought back. The initial wave of skepticism regarding the existence of the Luminese civilization and the underwater world had subsided, replaced by a grudging acceptance and a burgeoning scientific curiosity. Governments, once locked in conflict, were forced to collaborate, united by the sheer magnitude of the technological advancements and the urgent need to implement them. The whispers – those enigmatic, almost ethereal messages – continued to guide humanity's efforts toward a sustainable future, subtly shaping policy and scientific endeavors.

Captain Armstrong, his face etched with the wisdom of our shared ordeal, stood at the helm of the *Siren's Call*, his eyes scanning the horizon. Dr. Thorne, ever the scientist, meticulously analyzed the data streaming in from the various sensors, her brow furrowed in concentration. Sarah Chen, her connection to the Whispers more profound than ever, sat quietly, her gaze distant, almost prophetic.

The atmosphere on board was charged with a mixture of relief, exhaustion, and an underlying sense of unease. While we had brought back hope, we'd also brought back warnings—warnings woven into the very fabric of the Luminese's history.

The Abyssals, the shadowy figures that lurked in the deepest trenches of the ocean, remained an enigma, their motivations shrouded in mystery. Their connection to the Whispers, however, suggested a power far exceeding our understanding.

The Cetea, with their ruthless ambition and their mastery of destructive technologies, presented an even more immediate threat. Their emergence from the depths, fueled by a hunger for domination, signaled a conflict far grander in scale than anything humanity had ever faced.

The Luminese, despite their advanced technology and peaceful nature, were not invincible. Their ability to withstand the threats posed by the Abyssals and the Cetea was tenuous at best. Their society, while seemingly utopian, had its vulnerabilities—a reliance on a delicate balance of nature, a pacifistic stance that could be interpreted as weakness.

The Whispers hinted at a coming cataclysm, a seismic shift in the balance of power beneath the waves, a struggle that could ripple outward, engulfing the surface world.

The final message from the Luminese elders resonated deeply, a chilling prophecy whispered across the vast expanse of the ocean:

"The tide will turn. The Whispers will grow silent. Only then will the true nature of the abyss be revealed."

This unsettling prophecy cast a long shadow over our celebration. The surface world, though healing, was still fragile. The technologies shared by the Luminese were powerful tools, capable of transforming our world, but they were insufficient to completely counter the threats posed by the Abyssals and the Cetea.

The healing of the planet was far from complete; it was a process that would require generations of careful stewardship. The ecological renaissance, a glimmer of hope in the face of impending doom, had barely begun.

Our return was met with a mixture of elation and concern. The news of our survival and the Luminese civilization spread like wildfire. The world, unified by a common purpose, poured its resources into understanding and implementing the Luminese technologies. But the deep-seated anxieties remained.

The Abyssals were a constant reminder of the unseen, the unknown forces that lurked beneath the surface. The Cetea, with their relentless pursuit of power, represented the dark side of ambition, a mirror reflecting humanity's own past mistakes.

Our journey had just begun. The ecological restoration, the technological advancements, were but the first steps in a much larger, more complex undertaking. The prophecies, the warnings, were not mere fables. They were a stark reminder of the delicate balance of nature and the perilous path humanity had walked.

The Whispers were a call to action, a summons to face the challenges that lay ahead, and the preparation for an inevitable confrontation. The future, once a shimmering promise, was now cast in a new light, a mixture of hope and apprehension. The darkness stirred in the depths, a testament to the unknown forces that sought to dominate, not just the underwater world, but the very fate of humanity itself.

We had glimpsed the wonders of the underwater realm, the harmony and technological prowess of the Luminese, but we had also witnessed the shadows that lurked beneath. The Whispers, initially a source of guidance and wisdom, had become a cryptic warning, foreshadowing a conflict of epic proportions.

The struggle for control of the Whispers, the ancient secrets of the underwater world, the balance of power between the Luminese, the Abyssals, and the Cetea, all converged into a perfect storm—a maelstrom of conflict that threatened to engulf both worlds.

The cliffhanger was not just a narrative device; it was a reflection of our own uncertainty, a stark realization that the battle for the future was far from won. The Luminese's technology offered a lifeline, a chance to heal the wounds of the past, but it was only a beginning.

The real struggle lay ahead—a struggle against the forces of darkness, against the implacable drive for power, against the very essence of chaos. We had returned, bringing with us the promise of a new era, but also the weight of a looming crisis. The echoes of the Whispers, once comforting, now carried a note of urgency, a chilling reminder that the true test was yet to come.

The final image burned into my memory: a vast, impenetrable darkness, punctuated by the sudden, blinding flash of a colossal Cetea warship, its menacing silhouette outlined against the ethereal glow of the Luminese city as it retreated deeper into the abyss.

The silence that followed, the void of unanswered questions, was more terrifying than any sound. The fight for the future of both worlds, the surface and the underwater, lay before us—a battle for survival, for dominance, for the control of the very essence of life itself.

The echoes of the Whispers faded, leaving a haunting silence in their wake—a silence pregnant with the promise of conflict, of struggle, of a future yet unwritten, a future hanging precariously in the balance. Our journey, far from over, had only just begun its perilous descent into the unknown.

The seeds of a new conflict had been sown, and the future, once filled with hope, now felt like a stormy sea—a vast expanse of uncertainty, ready to engulf us all.

The last transmission from Sarah Chen, barely audible above the static, hinted at a greater threat—a power that predated the Luminese, the Abyssals, and the Cetea. It seemed we had only scratched the surface of this underwater world, barely glimpsed the true depths of its mysteries and the power that controlled it all.

The Whispers were not just prophecies; they were warnings, desperate pleas from a long-forgotten age. The technological marvels we'd acquired were not just tools for progress; they were weapons in a war yet to be fought. The surface world, healed in some respects, was still profoundly vulnerable.

A false sense of security lay draped over the fragile peace. The very foundation of our newfound hope was built upon an abyss of unanswered questions, upon the fragile truce between the surface and the hidden realm beneath the waves. This underwater world was not a paradise; it was a battleground, a crucible where ancient conflicts and future wars would be decided.

The *Siren's Call*, a symbol of our triumph and our potential doom, cut through the waves, leaving behind the shimmering reflection of the underwater city and entering the vast uncertainty of the future. We were heading toward the unknown, guided only by the cryptic Whispers of the deep, our knowledge dwarfed by the vast mysteries that lay ahead.

The next installment in this saga wasn't simply a chapter; it was the prelude to a confrontation of unimaginable scale. The true battle was only just beginning. The Whispers of the deep, once a comforting guide, now echoed like a death knell—a chilling reminder of the titanic struggle that lay ahead.

The future of humanity, and the destiny of the underwater world, hung precariously in the balance, a testament to the complex interweaving of our fate with the wonders and the terrors of the deep.

BACKSTORY

This book wouldn't exist without the tireless support and encouragement of many individuals. First and foremost, my deepest gratitude goes to my family and friends for their unwavering support and understanding during the long writing process. Their patience and encouragement were essential in bringing this project to fruition.

This appendix contains supplementary information related to the fictional world presented in *Whispers of the Deep*.

APPENDIX

This appendix contains supplementary information related to the fictional world presented in *Whispers of the Deep*.

A.1 Map of the Underwater Realm

A.2 Luminese Language Glossary

Aquatica: The Luminese name for their underwater world.

Avani: The name of the specific Luminese city where the survivors find refuge.

Abyssals: The enigmatic beings dwelling in the deep trenches.

Cetea: The hostile, technologically advanced faction.

Whispers: The mysterious phenomenon, a kind of oceanic consciousness.

Xylos: The ancient, ruined city where the origins of the Whispers are found.

Triton's Kiss: The name the survivors give to the Luminese submersible.

Heart of Aquatica: The ancient artifact rumored to hold the key to controlling the Whispers.

Lumina: The name of the underwater city in the first-person POV version of the story (from document 2).

Luminians: The name the survivors give to the inhabitants of Lumina in the first-person POV version (from document 2).

K'tharr: A bioluminescent jellyfish-like creature used for transportation in the first-person POV version (from document 2).

The Great Sundering: A cataclysmic event in the Luminians past that reshaped their world (from document 2).

A.3 Technical Specifications of Luminese Technology

1. Bioluminescent Energy Sources

Concept: The Luminese harness bioluminescence—the natural light produced by living organisms—as their primary energy source. This is similar to how solar panels convert sunlight into electricity, but the Luminese use bioluminescent organisms like algae and coral to generate energy.

Mechanism: They cultivate vast fields of bioluminescent organisms, channeling the light they produce into a network of organic conduits. These conduits, similar to fiber optic cables, transmit the light energy throughout their cities.

Applications: Powers their homes, transportation systems, and communication devices.

2. Communication Systems

Concept: The Luminese communicate through a combination of bioluminescent displays and subtle sonic frequencies. This is analogous to how humans use both visual cues (body language) and auditory cues (speech) to communicate.

Mechanism: Their bodies can produce intricate patterns of light, and they also emit clicks and whistles that convey meaning. Dr. Thorne speculates that they might even have a form of telepathic communication.

Applications: Allows for complex and nuanced communication, conveying not just information but also emotions and intentions.

3. Symbiotic Technology

Concept: Luminese technology is deeply integrated with the natural environment, often using living organisms as components in their devices. This is similar to biomimicry, where humans design technology inspired by nature, but the Luminese take it a step further by incorporating living organisms into their technology.

Mechanism: They cultivate bioluminescent organisms within their buildings, providing both light and energy. Their submersibles are designed to blend seamlessly with the marine environment.

Applications: Creates a sustainable and harmonious relationship with their surroundings, minimizing environmental impact. **4. "Whispers" Technology**

Concept: The Luminese have a deep understanding of the "Whispers," a kind of oceanic consciousness. They can sense and interpret the subtle shifts in energy and currents that the Whispers produce. This is similar to how scientists use sensors to detect and analyze natural phenomena, but the Luminese have a more intuitive and direct connection to the Whispers.

Mechanism: They have developed devices that can amplify and interpret the Whispers, allowing them to glean information about the past, present, and future.

Applications: Used for guidance, prophecy, and maintaining the balance of their underwater world.

A.4 The Entities

Abyssals: A mysterious and reclusive underwater civilization inhabiting the deepest trenches of the ocean. Their motives and intentions remain largely unknown.

Cetea: A technologically advanced and aggressive faction in the underwater world, known for their ruthlessness and ambition to control the Whispers.

Luminese: A technologically advanced and peaceful underwater civilization characterized by their bioluminescent city and unique understanding of the Whispers.

The Whispers: A mysterious phenomenon, possibly an energy source or ancient technology, that holds significant power and is at the center of conflict among the various factions in the underwater world.

Note

While this world is entirely fictional, many elements are inspired by real-world scientific concepts and discoveries. For further reading on topics related to deep-sea exploration, bioluminescence, and environmental concerns, please consult the following resources:

Scientific Journals

Deep-Sea Research, Part I: Oceanographic Research Papers – Covers deep-sea biology, chemistry, geology, and physics.

Deep-Sea Research, Part II: Topical Studies in Oceanography – Provides in-depth analyses of specific regions or phenomena.

Marine Biology – Publishes research on all aspects of marine life, including deep-sea organisms and their ecosystems.

Journal of Geophysical Research: Oceans – A key journal for physical oceanography, including studies of currents, water masses, and deep-sea climate impact.

Nature – Features groundbreaking research in marine biology, oceanography, and deep-sea discoveries.

Science – Similar to *Nature*, publishing high-impact research on ocean-related topics.

Books

The World Beneath: The Story of Ocean Exploration by Dr. Richard Ellis

Deep: The Extraordinary Creatures of the Abyss by Claire Nouvian

Bioluminescence in the Sea, edited by Peter J. Herring

The Silent Deep: The Discovery, Ecology, and Conservation of the Deep Sea by Richard L. Haedrich and George T. Rowe

Oceanography: An Invitation to Marine Science by Tom Garrison

The Sea Around Us by Rachel Carson

Song for the Blue Ocean by Carl Safina

Organizations and Websites

NOAA (National Oceanic and Atmospheric

Administration) – Provides information on ocean exploration, research, and conservation.

Woods Hole Oceanographic Institution (WHOI) – A leading research institution in oceanography.

Scripps Institution of Oceanography – Major research institute in marine sciences.

Monterey Bay Aquarium Research Institute (MBARI) – Focuses on deep-sea research and technology development.

Ocean Exploration Trust (E/V Nautilus) – Live streams deep-sea explorations and provides educational resources.

Environmental Concerns

Intergovernmental Panel on Climate Change (IPCC) Reports – Assess climate change and its impact on the oceans.

World Wildlife Fund (WWF) – Works on ocean conservation.

Greenpeace – Campaigns on ocean protection and conservation efforts.

ABOUT THE AUTHOR

Diane Kann is an author with a lifelong fascination with the ocean and its mysteries.

This passion fueled her storytelling, leading to the creation of the vibrant and immersive world of *Whispers of the Deep*. Her work combines scientific accuracy with imaginative storytelling, creating narratives that both entertain and educate. She currently resides in central Florida and is working on the next installment in the *Whispers of the Deep* series.